DEAD
SOUTH

The Zombie Apocalypse in London

David Brinson

Copyright © 2015 by David Brinson. All rights reserved worldwide. No part of this publication may be replicated, redistributed, or given away in any form without the prior written consent of the author/publisher or the terms relayed to you herein.
First printing 2015.

davidbrinson.blogspot.co.uk

ISBN: 1507648294
ISBN: 978-1507648292

For the three most amazing people in my life. My wife, my mum and my sister.

ACKNOWLEDGMENTS

I would like to start by thanking my wife, Leyla, she has had to listen to me go on about this story for 2 years! She has read and listened to every word at least 3 times and her honesty and insight have benefited it greatly. Her encouragement got me through the tough times and she made me get the laptop out and start writing even when I didn't feel like it.

I want to thank my sister, Layla, she got an email from me each time that I finished a chapter and she painstakingly read them and always told me her honest opinion. There was nothing better than getting an email back from her telling me that she thought it was good.

David Brinson

My editor, Gary Smailes and the rest of the team at Bubblecow, have been brilliant. Gary has added so much value and helped my story become a novel.

I'd like to thank the following people for their feedback - Andy, Gary, Uncle Mike, Ben, Paddy, Kristina, Kamal, Kelly and Sam.

I would also like to say thank you to James from GoOnWrite.com for the cover design. It is superb.

And finally, none of this would have been possible if it wasn't for my Mum. Mum you are the best. Thank you for everything.

DEAD SOUTH

The Zombie Apocalypse in London

CHAPTER ONE

My day started with a jolt when Troy, my fawn greyhound, licked me awake. It was seven am and he wanted his breakfast. I'd had a bad night's sleep and was still pretty tired, but thanks to his prompting I managed to extract myself from my warm bed and lumber into the kitchen. He waited impatiently by his bowl as I prepared his food, and then he forgot all about me as he set about devouring it. My hot shower livened me up a little, which was lucky, as Troy was back on my case the second that I was dressed. It was seven-thirty am and he wanted his walk.

We walked down the two flights of stairs to the block's entry hall, where I was confronted by a God-awful smell. Now one of the problems with living in a block of flats is that you can have some seriously strange people as your neighbours. My block was no different and our resident crackpot was a middle-aged gentleman called Mr Trotter, and God-awful smells emanating from his flat were, sadly for us, nothing new. So I didn't really pay it much attention as I left the block.

It was a beautiful November morning. It was crisp and fresh and there was not a hint of moisture in the air. Thinking about it now, it may not have been that fresh but anything would have been bliss compared to the stench that was coming from Mr Trotter's.

When we got back to the block's front door I held my breath as I ran past Mr Trotter's and up to our own flat on the second floor. As we entered the flat my wife, Sarah, was emerging from the bedroom. Sarah is quite simply stunning; I love her long brown hair and her beautiful brown eyes. Troy walked over to her and licked her hand to say hello. She rubbed his face for a few seconds before he forgot about us both, went to his bed in the living room and passed out.

"Worn him out again, have you?" she said to me with a smile.

I just nodded and shrugged my shoulders. "You know what he is like, anything more than a five minute stroll and he is exhausted!"

I approached to give her a kiss and a cuddle good-bye, she sniffed the air. "What is that?"

"Trotter."

"That explains it," she said, laughing. She gave me a huge hug, kissed me on the lips and I left for work.

As I was getting into my car I saw one of my neighbours from the other block, Mrs Johnson, coming out of her garage. Mrs Johnson is in her forties and is usually dressed immaculately, however, this morning she looked dishevelled as she stumbled out towards me. I thought it was best to leave her be, so I just waved as I drove out of the large communal car park.

My drive to work is a short one really; it only takes about fifteen minutes to get to Lewisham. I put my car radio on and tuned into The Breakfast Show on Talk Sport. Now the show is usually full of high jinks, and concentrates on the previous day's sporting headlines. But today was very different; instead they were talking about a killing spree that was carried out on the Kent coast in Margate. Scores of men, women and children had been found dead in a part of the town that had a high proportion of Eastern European immigrants and the attack was thought to be race-related.

I listened intently, sickened by the grim nature of the crime. I even stayed in my car when I got to work because I wanted to hear more. In fact it was only the high pitched whine of my mobile phone that made me turn it off.

I checked the screen and saw it was my brother.

"Morning, Steve, is everything alright?" I asked.

"It's all good, thanks. Just wondering whether you'd heard the news about Margate?"

"I'm just listening to it. Unbelievable."

"To think Mum used to take us down there every summer."

"I know. What's the world coming to?"

"Well it's a bloody cesspit, isn't it? Let's just hope they catch whoever did it soon."

"I'm sure they will. You can't get away with that sort of thing in this day and age."

I ended the call as I got out of the car. My short walk to the office was interrupted by my friend Phil skipping towards me clutching a pink piece of paper. "Top of the morning to you, Dean."

"I see your Irish accent becomes more prominent when you're in a good mood."

"And I still see that you're trying to hang on to your youth by driving a ten-year-old red sports car."

"Tut, tut, Phil. You know better than to try and knock the Celica. And anyway I hardly think that thirty-two is old."

He dusted some imaginary lint from the shoulder of his black jacket and fixed me with a cheesy grin. "I wasn't knocking the Celica!"

I laughed as I looked him up and down. His grey quiff was looking particularly perky. "That's rich, considering you've got to be about twenty years older than me!"

"Age is just a number. You're only as old as you feel."

I pointed at the piece of paper in his hand and slowly started to nod. "Anyway, your happiness to cockiness ratio can only mean one thing. You had a winner last night, didn't you?"

"I might have. Maybe a rather large accumulator came in. Let's just say that Arsenal, West Brom and Nottingham Forest all winning went down particularly well for me."

"Good for you, mate. How much did you win?"

He theatrically looked over both of his shoulders and took a step closer to me. "About three grand."

My eyes nearly burst out of their sockets. "Three grand!"

"Carla practically wet herself when I told her!"

"Wow! That's—"

"What are you two whispering about?" I heard a familiar voice say.

I turned to see Colin Bishop, the Council's Health and Safety Manager, walking towards us.

"Nothing much," I said.

Colin was a nice guy whose heart was in the right place, but he was a serious pedant with probably the most monotonous voice you could ever hear. "Why aren't you two wearing your high-visibility vests?"

Phil winked at me. "Well you know, Colin; we were just looking for you. We seem to have misplaced them. Any chance that we could borrow one of yours?"

I suppressed a grin as Colin tugged the bottom of his high-vis vest. It was his most cherished possession. He was so attached to it that he would even wear it down the pub after work. He ran his fingers over his bald head and took a deep breath. "That's very—"

His sentence was interrupted by a loud crash.

Colin nearly jumped out of his skin. "Blimey! What was that?"

A group of about six dustmen ran through the car park and charged past us. They were a blur of blue uniforms and yellow high-visibility vests. I don't know what came over the three of us, but we followed them. We ran along the concrete path and headed towards the front gate. A crowd of dustman had already gathered outside the depot. I couldn't see what was going on, so I worked my way through the bodies.

Phil got to the front before me. "Holy Mary Mother of God!"

Even now I still can't believe what I saw. One of the big blue twenty-six tonne dustcarts had ploughed into a house on the road outside of the depot. A girl in a McDonald's uniform was crushed between the truck and the house.

"Call 999!" I screamed.

I ran towards the trapped girl. Before I could get there the truck door flew open and the driver jumped out of the vehicle and in front of me.

"Don't go anywhere near her!" he shrieked in a Jamaican accent.

"What the fuck are you saying? You've probably killed her!" I shouted.

"Man, she crazy. She try to get in the cab and eat Jermaine!"

Another two dustman, one of whom I assumed was Jermaine, got out of the cab and shouted in a heavy south London accent, "It's fucking true. The crazy bitch scratched my face and then tried to bite me up. I'd be dead if Lionel hadn't run the slag down!" He looked at the final member of his crew. "Tell him, Sid. Tell him!"

Before Sid could say a word, a man in a McDonald's uniform with five stars on his badge came up behind Jermaine. He lunged at Jermaine's back and pushed him to the ground. Within the blink of an eye, Five Star bit into the back of his neck. Time seemed to stand still as Jermaine howled with pain.

Sid bent down and tried to pull Five Star off him. He was a big strong lad, but he couldn't shift him. Lionel pulled a fire extinguisher out of the dustcart and started beating it against Five Star's body. The body blows got Five Star's attention and he turned to Lionel. Five Star leapt at him, but before he could reach him, Sid clubbed his head with a stray brick that had come loose from the house. Five Star did not have a chance to react. I will never forget the truly horrific sound that the brick made against his head. His skull collapsed before my eyes and he dropped to the ground.

I'm ashamed to say it; but seeing Jermaine's blood trickle out of Five Star's mouth paralysed me with fear. Before you judge me and say that I should have helped stop Five Star, let me explain something to you. In my old life I had always seen myself as a lover not a fighter. I had never been in a fight and the closest I ever came to one was when a couple of my school friends got into a punch-up behind the school bike sheds. And let me tell you, that is no preparation for seeing one man try and eat another.

God knows how much time had passed, but I finally pulled myself together when I saw that Jermaine was still breathing. I threw my bag to the ground, turned around and looked at the stunned crowd. I fixed my gaze upon Colin Bishop.

"Take off your vest."

"What?"

"Colin, give me your high-vis vest!"

He looked at me blankly, but the force of my stare compelled him to take it off and give it to me. I rolled it up into a ball and stuffed it at the back of Jermaine's neck. More garments were thrown at me and I managed to reduce the bleeding to a trickle. I stayed with him until the paramedics arrived and then I just sat on the floor covered in his blood. Whilst the paramedics attempted to save his life, I chastised myself for not helping sooner. I made a promise to myself that I would never freeze again.

⋙⋘

Thirty minutes or so later I stared at myself in the large mirror that dominated the Gents toilets. The harsh fluorescent lighting did me absolutely no favours. My thick brown hair was all over the place and Jermaine's blood had dried all over my face. I looked a mess.

Phil put his hand on my shoulder. "You'd better clean yourself up."

I nodded.

My coat was okay, but my shirt was ruined. Trust me to wear a white shirt on the day that I was going to try and stop somebody from bleeding to death. I took it off and reluctantly dumped it in the bin.

"Don't worry about the shirt. Sanjay's going to bring you something to hide your modesty."

"Thanks."

I scrubbed Jermaine's blood off my face, hands and forearms. Red water splashed all over the mirror and a red film covered the white porcelain sink. I used my hands to try and wipe it off, but I just made it worse.

"Don't worry, Dean. That's not your job."

Sanjay appeared in the doorway and handed me a blue t-shirt. "Cover yourself up, mate."

I smiled weakly at him. "Thanks."

"You're welcome," he said, stroking his beard.

"Do you know if Jermaine is going to be okay?"

Sanjay's eyes darted between Phil and me. "Well, the paramedics managed to stabilise him, but he did lose a lot of blood. It's touch and go."

I looked at the floor and pinched the bridge of my nose. "Yeah, I thought so."

"Dean," Phil said. "He would be dead already if you didn't act."

I nodded. "You know what, guys; I'm not really in the mood for work now. I think I'm just going to head home."

"Yeah, yeah of course. I will square it away with the boss."

"Thanks. Oh, and if you hear anything about Jermaine, can you let me know? If not, I'll see you tomorrow."

"No problem."

A large group of onlookers had gathered outside of the depot. People from the local community and officers of the Council gawked side by side at the crashed dustcart. It took me a good few minutes to try and manoeuvre the car around it all and when I did, I saw Sid and Lionel sitting on a wall about fifty metres away talking to a female PCSO, who was writing in her notebook.

I couldn't help myself, I had to pull over and find out what was going on.

Sid noticed me as I approached them. "He's the one who tried to save Jermaine. He saw it all too."

The PCSO turned to me and looked at her notes. She was tall and thin and must have been over six foot, because she towered over me. "You're Dean Baker."

"Yes I am."

Her skin was pale and her features were very severe. "Someone will be in touch with you for a formal statement over the next few days."

"Is that all?"

She ignored me and looked at Sid and Lionel. "Thank you for your time, gentleman. I hope your friend is okay."

She walked off in a hurry, leaving the three of us together.

"That was odd," I said.

Lionel started to fiddle with one of his dreadlocks. "Rather a quick five minutes, than have to go down to the police station."

"Five minutes!" I said. "She took both your statements down in five minutes?"

Sid put his giant hand on my shoulder. "As Lionel just said, better than having to go down to the station."

"Was she the only person that spoke to you about it?"

Sid nodded his large head.

"But she was only a PCSO. What's that all about?"

"I'm not a copper, son, how am I supposed to know?"

"And she didn't once mention going down to the station?"

"She said it was clearly self-defence."

I looked back at where the dustcart had crushed the woman against the house. Her body was no longer there, but the vehicle still was. "No offence, lads, but how was that self-defence?"

"Believe me, Dean. It was self-defence."

Lionel got up from the wall. "Look, Dean. Me thankful for what you did for Jermaine and all, but me no want to talk about it no more."

"Sorry, guys, it's not that I don't believe you or anything. I'm just a bit shocked really. Two people are dead and another person is in critical condition and the police don't seem too worried by it."

Lionel shrugged his large shoulders.

I shook my head. "Real police work isn't anything like they show on the telly, is it?"

I am a happy-go-lucky kind of guy and I rarely let life get me down, so I found it quite easy to put the strangeness of the morning to one side as I drove home with Green Day blaring out of the speakers. I actually started to feel pretty good about saving Jermaine's life by the time I got back to the block. Not even the smell emanating from Mr Trotter's flat could put me off. I held my breath as I ran up the stairs and opened my front door.

Troy raced up to me as soon as I stepped over the threshold. I could hear Sarah pottering around in the kitchen.

"I need to speak to Mr Trotter about the smell," I said. "I think it's getting worse."

"You're home early," she said as she walked towards me. "What the hell has happened to you?"

"It's a long story."

We moved into the living room and sat on our plush brown leather sofa. Troy lay by my feet on the thick dark rug. "I don't know where to start."

Sarah pushed a lock of her long brown hair behind her ear and smiled at me. "Why don't you try the beginning?"

I laughed. "Yeah, good idea. Well I was talking to Phil and Colin in the car park and we heard a loud crash. We ran to see what was going on and we saw a woman crushed between one of our dustcarts and a house."

"Oh my God! What did you do?"

"Well, I tried to help her, but the dustmen stopped me. And before I knew it another man was attacking this guy Jermaine, who was one of the dustmen that stopped me."

Sarah took a deep intake of breath and covered her mouth with her hand. "Why?"

"I have no idea. He just started biting him. He was like an animal. They tried to pull him off and they ended up killing him."

"They really killed him?"

"Yeah, right in front of my eyes."

"Then what happened?"

"Jermaine was bleeding really badly from his neck, so I tried to help him. I managed to stop the bleeding and then the paramedics took over."

"Oh my God! Oh my God! Are you okay?"

"I think so. I was a bit shaken by it, that's why I left work early. But I think I'm alright."

She hugged me. "Okay, good. I'm glad… What did the police say?"

"The police said it was self-defence. They said that I might need to make a statement at some point. But it looks like the case is closed."

"Really?"

I nodded.

"Well as long as you're okay, then that's all I care about."

"Yeah, I'll be fine. I just hope that Jermaine is okay. Phil said he'd call if he hears anything about him. But whatever happens, I'm sure I'll find out tomorrow."

Sarah got up from the sofa and gave me a kiss on the cheek. "I'm going to do a bit of lunch. Just try and relax."

I put my feet up on the sofa and put the TV on. Every channel had the Margate killing spree on as the lead story; I flicked through all of the stations and finally settled on the BBC as it had a breaking story.

"Sarah, come and see this."

She came into the room just as the seasoned newscaster came back on. He dominated the screen in his black suit and red tie, and his solid Home Counties accent radiated professionalism.

"The BBC has obtained footage from a local resident of this morning's events in Margate. Please be warned that the upcoming images are quite disturbing and they are not suitable for children or anyone of a sensitive disposition."

A grainy image of the inside of a window filled the screen. The picture was not steady and it was clear that the person recording it was shaking. The camera juddered across the street to a row of red brick terraced houses. The image suddenly blurred and refocused on a half-naked man in an apron running along the pavement. He jumped onto the back of another man in chef whites. The picture zoomed in on the half-naked man and I clearly saw him bite into the chef's neck.

I pointed at the screen. "That's just what happened to Jermaine!"

The chef fell to his knees and the half-naked man moved on to someone else. If I was engrossed by the radio, I was bloody well mesmerised by the TV and the images that were unfolding on it. It was like something out of a horror film. It didn't matter how bad the footage got, I just could not look away.

Eventually the clip ended and the screen was replaced by a very solemn-looking newscaster. "We can now go straight to Margate for a live press conference with Cyrus Green, the Chief Superintendent of Kent County Constabulary."

The newsman was replaced by a very serious looking police officer. He was dressed in full uniform and had short grey hair. He addressed the assorted press from a wooden podium.

He pointed into the audience and spoke in a crisp, clear voice. "Go ahead."

"Thank you, Chief Superintendent. Tom Sharp, Thanet Times. Can you assure the people of Margate that they are safe?"

The police officer fixed the room with a stern look. "Of course they are safe. This was a one-off crime that was perpetrated by a madman. Whom, I hasten to add, we have already apprehended."

"Do you know what caused him to do it?"

"I'm just a policeman, not a psychiatrist. It's not for me to speculate. What I can say is that drugs may have been involved. We have him in custody, and the only thing that is for certain is that he can't hurt anybody else."

"Niall Phillips, BBC. Judging by the footage that we have all now seen, it is clear that he was under the influence of something. Are the rumours of him perhaps taking a new amphetamine true?"

"It's too early to speculate."

"But, is it not true that you likened him to the Miami Face Eater in your team briefing earlier?"

The policeman's brow furrowed. "Where did you hear that?"

"You know I can't reveal a source."

The policeman sighed. "We are looking into that possibility. It could have been an extreme allergic reaction to a new amphetamine. The reaction causes a substantial increase in body temperature."

"Would this explain why the attacker was half-naked?"

"We believe so. The individual literally feels like they are burning from the inside and this can lead them to take off some of their clothes. The drug essentially combines all of the worst attributes of meth, cocaine, PCP and LSD."

"But why did he try to eat the other man?"

The chief superintendent looked like a rabbit in the headlights. He glanced at his unseen entourage, but nobody came to his aid.

"Chief Superintendent?"

"We have not worked that out yet. The man is now undertaking a psychiatric evaluation."

"Do you know where this drug has originated from?"

"We have located the drugs and they are no longer in circulation."

"But what about the other drugs that were sold—"

Finally a press officer in a blue and white pinstriped suit ran to the podium and whispered into the chief superintendent's ear. The chief superintendent rushed off the stage, leaving the press officer at the podium. "The chief superintendent has been called away to an urgent matter. I am afraid that we can take no further questions."

I looked at Sarah. "I'm telling you that was just what happened to Jermaine!"

"I can't believe that those drugs can make people eat each other."

"Well I suppose that adds a whole new meaning to having the munchies!"

Sarah shook her head and allowed herself a small giggle. "Dean, that is awful!"

CHAPTER TWO

After a restless night I got out of bed at around six am with a banging headache. I went into the kitchen and headed straight to the medicine drawer. I dry-swallowed a couple of painkillers and made myself a cup of tea. Troy seemed to be a bit confused when I barged into his bedroom (our living room) an hour earlier than he had anticipated. After a good ten minutes the tablets managed to take care of my headache.

I ate a little breakfast and passed out on the sofa next to Troy. I only woke up when Sarah came into the room two hours later.

"Are you okay?" she asked me.

"Yeah, I just didn't get much sleep. Yesterday must have got to me more than I thought."

"Don't go into work, if you're not up to it. I'm sure they will understand."

"No, I'll be fine."

I ran into the bathroom and literally got through the Three S's (Shit, Shave and Shower) in record time and was out the door in fifteen minutes flat. I flew down the stairs and exited the building. As soon as the door closed behind me I remembered that I wanted a word with Mr Trotter. So I went back inside, held my breath and gently tapped on his door. My gentle tap nudged his door open a crack.

I pushed the door with a little more force and it creaked as it opened. I took one step into the hall and gently called out, "Mr Trotter, it's Dean from upstairs. The door's unlocked, are you okay?"

I heard nothing, so I took a few more steps into the flat. All of the doors leading off from the hallway were closed. The place was filthy, the walls had marks all over them and the hallway was filled with items of old electrical equipment and bags of fetid potatoes (an odd combination, I know). Imagine the worst smell you have ever smelt and double it, no scrap that, triple it. It was as if someone had eaten a rancid doner kebab, thrown it up, taken a dump on it and then left it to stew in the sun for a year.

I stood outside the door for what I assumed was the master bedroom and listened. I couldn't hear anything. I lightly tapped on the door. There was no answer. I tapped again with a little bit more force. No answer again. I gently turned the knob and slowly opened the door. I took a single step in and looked around. The room was filled with dirty old clothes and had a filthy mattress tucked up against the wall. I couldn't believe the amount of clothing that he had in there and then I couldn't believe that he seemed to always wear the same things every day. I stepped out of the room and closed the door behind me.

I walked across the hallway, navigated a heavy look-ing VCR player and stopped outside the bathroom. I tapped on the door once, then twice. Nothing. I turned the knob, opened the door and looked in the room. There was just a dirty bathroom suite and about two hundred rolls of toilet paper. I suppose you can say what you want about Mr Trotter but at least he wiped his bum.

After coming up blank twice I didn't bother to knock on the living room door. I just turned the knob and pushed it open. The stench instantly cranked up a few more notches and I started to gag. The room was filled with junk. Stuff was piled so high, it was as if he had constructed a corridor within the room and within half a second I had seen several newspaper mountains, stacks of old cathode-ray TVs and piles of rusty old tin cans. But what was truly nasty, and what I thought was probably the cause of the foul smell, was that every empty bit of floor space and every miniscule surface was covered with half-eaten, decomposing fast food—pizza, KFC, McDonalds. Name a fast food chain and there was food from them in that room. Maggots were everywhere. I felt dirty just standing in the place. I ventured into the improvised corridor, took a couple of turns and then I saw him. Mr Trotter was standing in a small clearing beside a particularly tall stack of pizza boxes. He had his back to me but it looked like he was furiously eating something.

"Mr Trotter, sorry to bother you, it's Dean from upstairs. The door was ajar and—"

He turned around. He looked awful. His skin was grey and mottled and his nose and mouth were covered in blood. It looked like he'd gone a few rounds with Lennox Lewis. But as bad as he looked, he still had his favourite Thomas the Tank Engine baseball cap on at the exact same jaunty angle that it always was.

"Blimey! Mr Trotter, are you okay?"

He started to moan.

"Obviously not! Let me call you an ambulance."

I pulled out my mobile phone and he started shuffling towards me. "It's alright, Mr Trotter, they won't be long." I looked at my phone and started to dial '999'.

"Oh bugger. I don't have any reception. I will just go upstairs and make the call for you. Okay?"

I put my phone back in my pocket and casually looked up at him. He was now less than a metre away and coming dangerously close to entering my personal space. "I'll be quick, Mr Trotter. I promise."

He bared his teeth at me and took another step closer. It was then that I noticed that his eyes were completely black. There was something really wrong with him. "Back in a tick."

He didn't say anything; he just continued to moan, so I took a step backwards. He mirrored my step backwards with a step forward of his own. He was a small man and could easily navigate this junkyard maze. I'm not a particularly big man myself. I'm only five foot ten inches and weigh about twelve stone. But that was too big for me to turn around without entering the small clearing first and getting closer to him, and to be fair I wasn't going to do that. I didn't want to catch anything. So, if I wanted to go back through the corridor, I needed to shift my arse into reverse. I went to take another step back but my left foot had kind of stuck to a congealed Big Mac, which was itself stuck to the maggot-infested carpet.

"Ah that's disgusting."

He moaned this time even louder, stopping me in my tracks. I looked up and I saw his blood-stained mouth wide open and his outstretched arms trying to grab me. Now, it's not that I froze, it's more that it took my mind a second or two to process what was happening. He got hold of my jacket and tried to pull me towards him.

"What the fuck!" I shouted as he tried to bite into my neck.

I pushed him off me as I yanked my foot up off the Big Mac and I ended up stumbling into a newspaper tower. Mr Trotter wasn't deterred by my push and he came straight back at me. I regained my footing and kept my back against the wall; I moved crab-like along the makeshift corridor and stumbled back into the turn behind me. I looked over my shoulder and could see that I was nearly in the hall.

I was going to get out, I was home free, but then I slipped. I slipped on a fucking banana skin. What a cliché! It was probably the only bit of fruit this geezer had ever eaten. If I didn't think I was going to die, I might have laughed. He turned the corner and was now only a few feet away from me. I scooted backwards, dragging my backside on the floor. I felt rancid food go up my shirt and maggots fall down into my jeans. It felt like I was in Hell. My back bashed into the door, I turned onto my hands and knees and crawled out of the room.

He never stopped, he kept on coming.

I just wanted to get out of the flat, shut the door behind me and go upstairs as quickly as I could. As I said earlier, I'm a lover not a fighter.

I lost another second as I bumped into the wall trying to get back onto my feet. And he was now gaining on me. He was that close that I'm sure I could feel his putrid breath on the back of my neck. I lurched forward and just missed a stack of TVs. I eyed a seventeen-inch Panasonic one as I went past and I was suddenly overcome by some kind of primordial urge. The TV was at waist height and perfect for me to pick up. I stopped in my tracks, lifted it and turned around to face him. He didn't stop coming so I raised the TV as high as I could. As he took another step forward I smashed it over the crown of his head. But it didn't stop him and although he could no longer see me, he still tried to grab me.

I looked around the hall and noticed the stray VCR player from earlier. I quickly picked up the heavy machine and launched it right into his left knee. The impact must have shattered his kneecap into a thousand pieces as it gave way from under him and he clattered to the ground. As he hit the deck, the TV fell off his head, but his beloved baseball cap somehow stayed in place. Thick bloody goo started to ooze out of his neck, but it didn't stop him and he kept on crawling towards me. I was shaking, adrenaline surging through my body; I picked up the VCR player again and I smashed it into his skull. Two times, three times, again and again and again and finally his skull caved in. His body went limp.

I staggered out of the flat, I was covered in filth and I was still shaking. My head felt light and I vomited all over the communal entrance. I walked up the stairs and stood outside my flat. I couldn't steady my hand to put the key in the lock. I banged on the door and called for Sarah. A moment passed before the door opened. She looked at me. I was crying uncontrollably and tears were streaming down my cheeks.

Her face contorted as she said, "Dean, what's happened?"

I just stood in the hallway sobbing. Sarah dragged me inside the flat and Troy came trotting into the hall to investigate. I was covered in a foul combination of rotten food, maggots and blood. I must have stunk. I wanted so badly to explain what had happened but I couldn't get the words out. Sarah was panicking, but in fairness she managed to hold it together. She looked me in the eyes.

"Dean, are you hurt?"

I shook my head.

It might have taken a few seconds, but I slowly started to regain my composure. When I did I realised that I didn't know how to explain what had just happened. I mean, how do you tell your wife that you just killed your next door neighbour?

"I killed him," I finally managed to say.

"What?"

"But I don't think it was him."

"You're not making any sense."

"I went in his flat to talk to him about the smell. But he came after me."

"What?"

"I smashed his head in."

She gasped.

"I had to. It was either him or me."

She was stunned. Plain and simple. But as she stood there dumbfounded, it all started to make sense to me. "He was already dead."

"How can you kill someone who is already dead? He was either dead or he wasn't!"

"I think he was a zombie."

"What?"

"His eyes were black, his skin was grey and his face was covered in blood."

"Dean. You need to sit down. You're in shock."

"No I'm not… well, I might be. But I'm right. It all makes sense, especially after yesterday. The bloke from McDonald's biting Jermaine. Trotter just trying to eat me."

To Sarah's massive credit she didn't shout at me, she didn't slap me round the face and tell me to get a hold of myself, nor did she make an immediate call to the men in white coats to have me taken away. She just stood there staring at me. "Was it self-defence?"

"Of course it was. He tried to rip my neck out with his teeth!"

She nodded. "Okay, you need to call the police and explain exactly what has happened."

"They will never believe me."

"It doesn't matter if they believe he was a zombie or not, does it? They just need to believe that you were in danger and protecting yourself. Like the two dustman yesterday. Remember?"

"You're right," I said, walking into the living room to make the call.

"Stay there. I'll get the phone. You're not taking another step in here covered in that filth."

Sarah came back clutching the phone and as I took a step forward to meet her, I felt a clump of squashed maggots and congealed meat fall from my bum cheek and slide down my leg. My throat instantly filled with bile. With a concerted effort I managed to swallow it down as she handed the phone to me. I dialled '999' and waited. After three rings my call was answered. I was connected to a recorded message.

A lady's voice simply stated, "All operators are busy at present, please try again later."

"Holy shit!"

"What?"

"It's a recorded message. A bloody recorded message!"

"Try again. It must be a mistake or something."

I did as she asked and again the phone rang through to the recorded message. This time I held it to her ear. "Oh my God! What's going on?"

"Zombies, Sarah! It's got to be. Think about it. Think about what's just happened."

"I don't know. It all seems a little farfetched."

"I know it does."

"Anything could have happened. It could be a terrorist attack or something."

"If Mr Trotter hadn't just tried to eat me, I would probably agree. But I'm telling you that he did and I'm lucky to be alive."

She didn't respond, she just looked at me. I mean really looked at me. Did she think I was mad? Maybe I was. Eventually she nodded. "Okay, let's say it's zombies. What are we going to do?"

"We need to warn as many people as we can. Call your mum and dad and make sure they're okay. I'll call my side of the family."

I frantically tried to call my mum, but I couldn't get through to her. I also tried my brothers, Pete and Steve, and my sister, Emma. But I had no joy with any of them. I didn't give up and after a good ten minutes of trying I eventually got through to my mum.

"Dean, is that you?"

"Oh thank God. I've been trying to call you for ages. I think there's something wrong with the phones."

"It must be your one. I've got full reception."

"Well anyway, don't worry about that now. You've got to listen to me."

"You sound panicked, Dean. What's wrong?

"Mum, something really bad is happening." I paused a second. Would she believe me if I told her what I thought was really going on? "Look, I can't really explain it. But people are attacking each other for no reason and I don't want anything happening to you. Promise me that you won't go out today."

"Okay, no problem."

"That's great, Mum. Just sit tight."

"I'll just pop out to the Co-op to get a chicken for dinner and then I'll be right back."

"Mum, please! I need you to take this seriously. Bad stuff is happening out there. Someone I know just got attacked."

"Are they okay?"

"Just; but they nearly weren't. Please listen to me about this."

"Okay. Well I suppose Graeme can make do with pork chops."

"Good. Good. Tell Graeme to go and get Nan."

"You just said to not go outside."

"Mum, she only lives next door. Just tell him to be quick and not to speak to anyone."

"What about Emma and your brothers?"

"I've been trying to call them as well. They need to stay home too."

"They've probably all left for work already."

"Perhaps. But we still need to warn them. Can you try too? One of us should be able to get through to them. And anyway Pete and Steve are more likely to listen to you than they are to me."

"If you really think it's necessary. Of course I will. Now try and relax. I promise that we won't go anywhere."

I breathed a huge sigh of relief as I ended the call. Speaking to Mum had really put my mind at ease. I looked over at Sarah to see how she was getting on. "Have you got through to them yet?"

"No, it's still not connecting. What are we going to do?"

"It's okay. Just keep trying. Don't give up. I'm going to try Emma again. It will be okay."

I scrolled to my sister's number in my mobile phone and hit the call button. I impatiently tapped my right foot as I waited for it to connect. It took about twenty seconds but eventually the phone started to ring.

"Morning, Dean. This is early."

"Where are you? Are you and Jeff okay?"

"We're both at the bank, just waiting for a meeting to start. What's wrong? You don't sound yourself."

"I know this might sound a bit weird, but something strange is going on. How is everything where you are?"

"Everything's fine."

"Thank God."

"Although thinking about it, it is a little odd around here. There aren't that many people in yet and my meeting is running about twenty minutes behind schedule. This place is usually full of people by now and things do normally run like clockwork around here."

"Shit. It sounds like something's wrong where you are too."

"Dean, what do you mean?"

"Okay," I said, blowing out my cheeks. "I got attacked earlier."

"Oh my God! Are you okay?"

"I am. But I nearly wasn't."

"Do you know who did it?"

"Kind of… you know Mr Trotter, don't you?

"What, the smelly little man who lives downstairs to you?"

"Well it was him, but it wasn't him."

"What does that mean?"

"I know that this is going to sound crazy, but I think he was a zombie."

"Dean, is this some kind of a wind-up?"

"I promise you that I am telling the truth, okay. He tried to eat me, for God's sake."

"Like what happened to the people in Margate?"

"Yes exactly, it was just like that. I need you two to leave work as soon as you can. Come straight to mine. It isn't safe to be out."

After a few seconds she started to laugh. "You nearly had me. Very good. You know we can't leave work. It's not like working for the Council up here, you know."

"For fuck's sake, Emma, this isn't a joke! Just leave and get to me as quickly as you can. Don't go on the train, just jump in a black cab and come now. It will be quicker for you to come to me from London Bridge than it will be for you to go all the way home."

"Dean, are you being serious?"

"Of course I am. I've never been more serious in all my life. This isn't a wind-up and I'm not bull-shitting you. Please listen to me, okay?"

"Okay, okay. I believe you. We're leaving now."

"Thank you. Just be careful. Don't hang around, and get straight into a cab."

I got off the phone at the same time that Sarah finally managed to get through to her parents. Relief instantly cascaded all over her face, but it didn't take long for it to be replaced by dread. "Dean! Dean!"

"What's wrong?"

"Dad's just said that some strange people are trying to get into the house."

Without thinking I said, "Tell him to lock the doors and shut the windows. I'm on my way."

CHAPTER THREE

As the door shut behind me I sprinted full pelt down the communal stairs. I stopped when I got to the ground floor; I was standing directly outside of Mr Trotter's. I think the smell of Mr Trotter's flat combined with my vomit brought me back down to earth, and the full reality about what I was attempting to do finally hit me. Who did I think I was? Last time I checked I was Dean Baker, not Jack Bauer. I worked for the Council, I wasn't an action hero. I thought about turning round and running back upstairs, I'm sure Sarah would have understood. But I couldn't do it, I had to try and save them. Anything less and I wouldn't have been able to live with myself.

I opened the front door and stepped outside. The air was crisp and dry; it was another beautiful November morning. I tentatively walked down the path towards the communal car park. The car park is actually quite big. It is about half the size of a football pitch and all twelve flats have a garage and an allotted parking space. A thirty-metre-long driveway connects it to the road. I paused just before I got to the end of the pathway and looked around. I saw a few of my neighbours' cars parked in their allotted bays but I didn't see any people. Gravel crunched under my feet as I hurried to my car. I got in it and started the engine. My music started blaring out of the speakers. It was ridiculously loud. I instantly turned it off and I cursed myself. I went to pull away and then I saw them. Three zombies were shuffling from behind some bushes and coming towards my car. *Thanks a lot, Green Day.*

The zombies were still about forty metres away from where my car was parked, but they were walking up the driveway and were directly between me and the road. I sat in my seat and couldn't help but stare at them. One was male and the other two were female. They were all smartly dressed, but their clothes were quite tatty and stained with blood. The two females looked particularly bad as their faces were covered in abrasions. The male one looked like he was fighting against gravity just to stay upright as one of his legs looked badly damaged. But as broken as they all seemed, they still relentlessly closed in on my position. They weren't particularly quick, but they were quick enough.

There was only one thing to do. I shifted the car into first, revved the engine hard and slammed my foot onto the accelerator. The engine roared and the car took off in a flash. The zombies didn't seem to care that they were moments away from death. They held their line and carried on walking towards my speeding car. About five metres away from impact I veered left so that my car would only hit the male one. The poor bastard didn't have a chance as one and a half tonnes of precision Japanese engineering struck into his good leg. I heard the initial impact shatter the bone and then a sickening crunch as his head plunged into the bonnet. His lifeless body flew off of my car as I got on my way.

As I drove down Eltham Hill I saw an elderly couple go into the newsagents and a group of children horsing around as they walked to school. Every single one of them unaware as to what was happening. I was tempted to stop the car and warn them, but I knew they would never listen to me, so I pushed the thought out of my head and focused on the road. Sarah's parents lived less than ten minutes away from us in Lee, and going to theirs was pretty much like going half way to work.

I got to their street very quickly. The road itself was on quite a steep hill and their classic 1930s semi was about half way up it. Although all the houses kind of look the same in the area, Derek and Sheila's stood out because of a beautiful silver birch that stood proudly in their front garden. I scanned the horizon as I drove up the hill very slowly. When I was about fifty metres or so from their house I saw ten figures milling about on the lawn, all staring directly at the front door. From this distance they all still looked pretty normal; apart from the way that they carried themselves. I can only describe it as some kind of lumbering gait.

I pulled up about twenty metres away from their house, took in the surroundings and tried to formulate a plan. I picked up my mobile and dialled her parents' house. Unsurprisingly it didn't connect.

"Oh bollocks!" I cursed. "What am I supposed to bloody well do now?"

I nervously tapped the steering wheel as I tried to think of an idea. I needed to get Derek and Sheila's attention and I needed them to be ready to move, but there was no way that I could do that with the zombies right outside the house. I had to somehow lure them away from the front door. I thought about running up to them and using myself as some kind of live bait and then remembered how Jermaine had got jumped by Five Star. I was brave, but not that brave. Then it hit me. The answer was obvious. There was only one thing to do. I slammed my foot onto the accelerator and raced onto the driveway. The zombies noticed me and started ambling the ten metres or so to my car. I hoped that my car had made enough noise to alert Derek and Sheila to my presence.

I had one hand on the steering wheel and the other on the gear stick. I was staring at the house, revving my engine and hoping that they'd notice me. After about five seconds I still hadn't seen any sign that they had. The zombies were now very close to the front and driver side of my car, and I was running out of options. My next move was either out of extreme desperation or sheer stupidity. I couldn't honestly say either way. Thinking about it now, it was probably both.

As the first zombie clattered into my door, I honked the horn. I didn't just tap it; I smashed my palm into it for a good couple of seconds. In fairness to me it certainly did the trick. Derek put his face to the downstairs bay window and waved. I made some kind of hand signal and I hoped he knew that I wanted them to get ready.

I reversed off the drive and slowly drove down the hill. One by one the zombies followed me. They pushed and shoved each other as they jockeyed for position, and eventually the bigger ones took the lead. I was like the Pied Piper and I started to feel pretty chuffed with myself. When we were about eighty metres away I decided that I had taken them far enough away from the house. So I sped up a bit, drove onto a random driveway and reversed back out onto the road facing my entourage.

I used the width of the road to swerve past them and went back up the hill. In less than sixty seconds I was back on Derek and Sheila's drive. The zombies had turned around but it was going to take them a bit of time before they had got back up the hill. As soon as Derek saw my car he opened the front door and walked out towards me, motioning for me to get out. I left the engine running and met him by the bonnet. Although in his late sixties, he was still very fit and at six foot two he could still be quite imposing if he wanted to be. He had a full head of silver hair and always wore his purple 'Desert Rats' regimental tie. He loved to spin a yarn and took every opportunity to do so.

He looked at me and slapped me on the back. "Good work, Dean. This situation reminds me of a time in Oman."

I looked him in the eyes. "Glad you approve, Derek. Can we get going?" I said, hoping to hold off the story.

He walked back towards the front door and signalled for me to follow. I nervously looked down the hill and saw that the zombies were still quite a distance away; it seemed like their progress was being hampered by the incline. So I complied with Derek's request and walked to the door. When I got there I saw two bags waiting to be put in the car.

"How did you pack these so quickly?"

Sheila smiled at me. She was the same age as Derek, but at five foot three, she was nearly a foot shorter than him. She wore her dark hair in a bun and despite a hip replacement she was still very active. "I always have bags packed just in case we decide to go away."

Derek and I both picked up a bag and took them to the car. I opened the boot and we loaded them in. After Sheila had locked up the house I helped her climb into the back of my car. The Celica isn't really noted for backseat roominess and Sheila looked a bit put out that she was being rescued in it. I helped her buckle up and ran round to the driver's side as Derek got into the passenger seat.

I reversed out of the drive and went to go up the hill away from the chasing pack. It was at this moment that I no longer felt chuffed with myself. My earlier idea had worked far too well, not only had I alerted Derek and Sheila to my presence, I had also alerted every zombie on the street too. The honk had acted like a giant dinner bell and my stupidity had set us up as the main course.

Coming down the hill must have been about a hundred zombies. They literally filled the entire road; there was that many of them. They looked like the walking wounded returning from the front. As scary as that was, it was nothing compared to their moans. The pitch and volume of it literally chilled my blood. Derek and I looked at each other in disbelief.

"Dear Lord!" Derek exclaimed.

I put the car into reverse and glanced in my rear view mirror. I heard a massive thud as one of my earlier followers clambered onto the back of the car.

"Do something, Dean!" Sheila screamed.

Before I could react another one of them thudded into the back of the car and started banging on the rear window.

I fixed my gaze on the hundred or so zombies in front of us; they were now only about seventy metres away. Time was running out.

"Hold on!" I shouted as I crunched the gear stick into first and accelerated hard up the hill, abruptly throwing the two zombies that were on the back of the car to the floor. With only thirty metres between us and the oncoming horde I executed a less than perfect three point turn. After completion I had the hundred or so zombies about thirty metres behind me and the original ten standing a similar distance away to my front. I shifted the car into reverse and accelerated, only stopping when I was about ten metres from them.

"What the hell are you doing, man?" Derek shouted.

"Make sure your seat belt's on!"

I slammed my foot onto the accelerator. I was nearly up to thirty miles an hour when I ploughed into the middle of the smaller group.

There is a reason why successive governments invested millions of pounds into speed-calming measures and imposing twenty miles an hour speed limits outside of schools and in densely populated areas. That reason is that speeding cars and human bodies do not mix particularly well. I learnt this for myself the hard way as I headed for the centre of the group.

In total the car smashed into five of them. The initial impact caused the two that were struck either side of the car to fly off and land on either side of the pavement. The next two were hit full on and were scooped up onto the bonnet, their bodies pummelled head first into the windscreen, whereby they some-how back-flipped onto the roof, slid down the back of the car and fell in a crumpled heap on the road. The force that their heads had hit the windscreen with had caused two giant cracks to form in it.

The fifth and final zombie was struck a second or two after the others; the number plate was broken in two as the car slammed into his knees. The collision probably shattered his legs. Like the last two victims he was scooped up onto the bonnet and his head clattered into the windscreen. Unlike the last two, he didn't do a backflip over the roof and land on the road. Oh no. His face must have hit the weakest point of the dam-aged windscreen because it somehow managed to punch through the toughened glass and wedged itself into the middle of it. The rest of his body pounded feet first onto the roof and then it slammed back into the bonnet. His head was inside my car, whilst his body was lying on my bonnet. And what's more he wasn't even dead, and oh yeah, I still had my foot on the accelerator.

I was coming up to the bottom of the road and this bastard was looking directly at me. He looked like the epitome of evil as his black eyes locked in on me. He had the eyes of a killer; they were as cold and dead as a shark's. The glass had skinned his face and his cut veins and arteries were pissing blood all over my dashboard. He started to move his jaw up and down as if in a chewing motion, and I could see all of his face's internal workings as his muscles expanded and contracted. It was disgusting yet fascinating at the same time. It was like staring into the face of an evil anatomy dummy.

Sheila was screaming probably the loudest, highest pitched scream I had ever heard. It was deafening. In fairness to Derek he kept his cool and unbeknownst to me he had gone into my glove box and pulled out my CD sleeve. The sleeve held about one hundred discs but wasn't particularly weighty. He didn't seem to care and he just started hitting the zombie in the face with it. He didn't do him much damage but at least he was trying. I managed to concentrate on the road long enough to see the upcoming T-junction and I slammed on the brakes. I must have been doing about sixty as the car skidded to a halt on the main road. The resultant force of my emergency stop tore the zombie's head free from the windscreen and his body skidded along the ground into an oncoming Ford Transit van. For about the tenth time that day I heard a sickening crunch as the van drove directly over its body. The van never stopped.

Fortunately for us there were no cars in the lane that we were sitting in and thankfully Sheila had stopped screaming. None of us said a word as I started the drive back home; we all completely ignored the gaping hole in the windscreen. The wind was whistling through it, and it was blowing clumps of dead and bloodied skin into my and Derek's faces. Blood had also started trickling down from the dashboard and onto the steering column, and once there it started to pool in my lap. I really needed a shower.

Within five minutes I was back on my tree-lined road, cautiously heading to the entrance of my drive-way. I looked around and incredibly everything still looked normal. People were still getting in and out of their cars and the street's large detached homes looked as peaceful as ever. As I pulled into my drive I saw the dead body of the first zombie that I had run over, but I couldn't see anyone or anything else, so I parked in my usual space and all three of us got out of the car. I hurried to the boot and passed one bag to Derek and slung the other one over my shoulder. I still didn't feel very confident that we were safe so I took the only thing out of my boot that could be used as a weapon. None of us spoke as we started to walk up the pathway.

I was hurriedly leading the way and then about twenty metres from the communal door I saw another zombie. This wasn't some random nobody, it was Mrs Johnson and she was hungry. She was even more dishevelled than the day before and her mouth was covered in blood. Her sickly grey pallor made her black eyes stand out even more. It would be a massive understatement to say that she wasn't a pretty sight. She was heading directly for us and all I had for protection was my squash racquet. At that moment I really wished that I had taken up golf.

The pathway was actually like a long corridor. It was about four metres wide and had the two blocks of flats on one side and a tall brick wall on the other. Mrs Johnson was standing slap-bang in the middle of it, directly between us and the door. The three of us had stopped in our tracks, but she pressed on, slowly cutting the distance between us. We took a few steps back, but it didn't deter her and she kept on coming.

After a few more steps I'd had enough of retreating so I turned around and threw my keys to Derek. "You two get back in the car."

"Don't be ridiculous, Dean! We can't leave you."

"Derek, just go back to the car and protect your wife!"

There was no more arguing and I heard them get to the car pretty quickly. I knew they were safe when I heard the car door slam shut. It was now just me and Mrs Johnson.

I threw Derek's bag to the floor, took my racquet out of its case and gripped it in my right hand. I held my ground and stared into her eyes; they were as cold and dead as the others and she was now only fifteen metres away. I still hadn't moved, but I was on my toes waiting for my moment to strike. When she was ten metres away I sprang into action. I ran full pelt at her. I'm sure I could see excitement in her black eyes as she lunged at me. Her arms shot out in front of her as I checked left towards the building. She didn't expect my sudden change of direction and her hands were left clutching thin air. She turned her head to follow my movement and she couldn't have set herself up any better. Just as she got me in her sights I swung the racquet as hard as I could and the frame connected with her mouth. I wasn't a great squash player, but the one thing I did have in my locker was a booming forehand. That combined with the titanium and Kevlar composite literally smashed her jaw to smithereens.

A combination of teeth, blood and saliva exploded out of her mouth and landed on the block's brick wall. The force of the blow took her feet from under her and she started falling. Before she hit the ground, my back hand was in full motion. I had never hit anything so sweetly in all of my life, the frame clobbered into the back of her head and her face pounded into the concrete paving slab. But she wasn't dead, I could still hear sound coming out of her mouth. So, I raised my racquet and put every last ounce of strength into my next brutal stroke. The impact shattered the back of her skull. She was probably dead, but I couldn't stop. I kept on slamming the racquet into her head until it broke in two and my hands were covered in blood and brain matter.

Exhausted, I took a step back from her body and just stared at it. It was like I was in a trance. It was only the sound of Derek's voice that brought me out of it.

"Dean! Dean! Are you okay?"

I looked up at him and nodded. Sheila was standing beside him shaking. They were both terrified, I don't know how much they saw, but I just hoped that their terror wasn't caused by me. I stepped over Mrs Johnson's lifeless body and picked up Derek's bag. I then walked over to Derek and Sheila and was thankful that neither of them flinched at my presence. I hustled them past the body and we walked to the communal door.

I turned to them both as I opened it. "Hold your breath. It doesn't smell that nice in here."

"Why, what happened?" Sheila asked.

"It's a long story."

Derek and Sheila walked into the hallway and headed straight for the stairs. I didn't heed my own advice as I followed them inside and I couldn't help but gag at the smell.

"Dean—"

I interrupted Derek before he could say anything else. "I'm fine, Derek, I just need to get away from the smell."

"No, it's not that. You've stepped in something."

I looked down at my boot and saw that I'd stepped in my own pile of vomit. Typical. I just shrugged my shoulders and walked up the stairs.

Sarah opened the door as soon as we got to our landing. Her eyes were red and puffy and her mascara had run. She reached out to me and I took her in my arms. She started to sob into my neck. "Are you okay? Are you hurt?"

"I'm fine. I promise. What's wrong?"

"I saw what happened out the window."

I didn't know what to say. She just saw me kill our neighbour.

"I wanted to come and help you, but it was all over so quickly."

Relief flooded my system. She understood what was happening. "Try not to think about it. I'm fine. I really am."

When we let go of each other she had odd bits of blood, brain and skin on her clothes. But I knew that she still looked a billion times better than I did. She then simultaneously hugged her mum and dad, and it was at this point that Troy saw his opening and came to welcome me home.

"Put the kettle on, Sheila," Derek said as they walked into the flat, leaving Sarah, Troy and me on the landing.

"It was Mrs Johnson, wasn't it?"

I nodded.

"You saved their lives."

I nodded again.

"Thank you for bringing them here."

I held her and kissed her on the forehead. "I would do anything for my family."

Our embrace lasted for a few minutes until Sheila shouted from the kitchen, "Tea's ready."

I gingerly removed my soiled boots and followed Sarah and Troy back into the flat. I caught a glimpse of myself in the mirror and was shocked at what I saw. I was rotten. My face was smeared with blood and my clothes were ruined.

Derek joined me in the hall and handed me a cup of tea. "That was some damn fine improvisation outside. It reminded me of the time I was in hand to hand combat with a couple of rebels in Lebanon."

Classic Derek. "What did you see exactly?"

"I saw enough, Dean. I saw enough. You went above and beyond and for that I am grateful."

"Did Sheila see it all too?"

"Don't worry about her. She's as tough as old boots. Being an army wife will do that to you."

Sheila came out of the kitchen and placed her hand on my shoulder. It filled me with immense relief. I briefly filled them in on the events of the last day and told them my theory.

"That makes sense to me," Derek said.

"Really? I thought you'd think I was mad."

"I've been in combat more times that I can remember and I've never seen an enemy like that. Zombies or not, they aren't human."

"Derek, I think we should let Dean have a shower now," Sheila said, walking into the living room.

Sarah brought me a towel as Derek left me in the hall. "You can't stand here like that."

"I suppose not," I said, smiling. "Did you manage to call anyone else?"

"I managed to leave a voicemail for Phil, but I couldn't get through to your brothers or Sanjay though."

"That's something at least. We should keep on trying."

"I just tried the landline while you were speaking to Mum and Dad. The dialling tone's gone."

"Okay," I said, pulling my mobile phone from my pocket. "I'll see if this is any better."

I dialled Steve's number and waited.

"Anything?"

"The mobile network's down too. God, I hope Mum got through to Pete and Steve."

"We just need to be positive."

I started to pace the hall.

"Dean, please have a shower and clean yourself up. Emma and Jeff will be here soon and you won't want them to see you like this."

I finished my cup of tea and walked into the bathroom. It couldn't have been any later than eleven in the morning and I looked like a complete mess. I turned the temperature up as high as possible and I climbed into the shower. I couldn't bear the feeling of dried blood, crushed brain and flayed skin on me. I scrubbed my body until I was raw. The hot water scalded my skin, but I didn't mind, it felt amazing. I let it run over me for a good ten minutes even after I was clean. I stood there thinking about what I had done that morning. I had killed at least six zombies. I hoped that the hot water was able to cleanse my soul as well as my body. Just as I was getting out of the shower I heard a frantic banging on the front door. I tried not to make any noise as I tiptoed over to it.

As I peered into the spy-hole I heard a familiar voice, "Dean, we don't have any time to mess around. Open the fucking door!"

I opened the door to see my older brother Pete standing there in his favourite black leather trench coat. Pete had always been a very big lad. When he was younger he was in good shape and had even played rugby for Kent. But since he settled down, had a couple of kids and became a big-shot he had kind of let himself go. He's six foot tall, got short cropped hair (he says he likes his hair like that, but I know it is because he is going bald) and has a massive gut. When I say a massive gut, I mean a spectacular gut!

He looked me up and down. "Get dressed now. Emma and Jeff are in the shit."

CHAPTER FOUR

The wooden floor in the living room took a pounding from Pete as he paced around, waiting for me to get dressed. "I was at Mum's with Julie and the kids waiting for Steve to turn up when I got a panicked call from Jeff."

"Jesus! What's happened?" I called out.

"They left work as soon as you told them to, but they hit a problem. The black cab they were in got mobbed by a bunch of druggies on the Old Kent Road."

Fully clothed, I came back into the room. "Are they alright?"

"For now they are, but that was at least twenty minutes ago. They've managed to barricade themselves into the ASDA, but fuck knows how long they will be safe for. So we need to get there quick smart."

I swallowed hard and nodded. I looked at Sarah and could see the resignation in her eyes. Pete could see it there too. He looked at her. "I promise that I will bring my little brother back to you safe and sound."

She managed a weak smile.

"We've got to leave now."

I nodded at him and walked over to Sarah. I held her in my arms. "I love you."

She started to cry, and to be honest so did I. "I love you too."

I left Sarah with her mum and joined Pete in the hall. Troy followed me and looked up at me with his big brown eyes. "He doesn't want me to go too."

"Don't be an idiot, Dean," Pete said. "He's just a dog."

I ignored him and patted Troy's head. "I promise I'll be back as quick as I can, boy. Look after Sarah for me."

Troy licked my hand and wagged his tail. Sarah was in safe hands.

As Pete pulled open the front door, Derek called out to us from the kitchen. "Hold on!"

"What now?" Pete muttered.

Derek came over to us clutching two bread knives. He looked at us both. "Protection." He handed me one with a six-inch blade.

Pete raised his hand when Derek offered the other one to him. "Thanks a lot, Derek, but I've got something a little bit better." He then looked at us both and said in his best Australian accent, "You call that a knife? This is a knife!" As soon as he finished his sentence he pulled out a huge twenty-five-inch machete from the inside pocket of his leather trench.

My jaw dropped. "Where—"

"Don't ask."

Pete and I walked along the path and came across Mrs Johnson's maimed body. My discarded squash racquet sat in what was left of her pulped brain. Pete stopped and studied it. He looked at the mangled racquet and then at me. I instantly averted my eyes.

"What the fuck happened here?"

"I'll tell you on the way."

We carried on towards the car park and I looked longingly at my car. There were dents in the bonnet and the windscreen was ruined.

"What the fuck happened to that?"

"I'll tell you on the way."

Pete had a brand new metallic grey BMW X5. The X5 is a luxury 4x4 vehicle and must have set him back at least fifty grand. It was in mint condition and seeing it in all its glory made me feel even worse about my own car.

Pete couldn't help but stare at the twisted body of the zombie that I had run over on the way to Derek and Sheila's. Its broken limbs were contorted in the most unnatural of ways. I went to say something and Pete cut me off. "Let me guess. You'll tell me on the way."

—⊷⊶—

As we approached New Cross we came to a halt behind a black Mitsubishi Warrior truck. The police had set up a road block at the junction where Lewisham Way becomes New Cross Road. It wasn't anything too impressive, just a little white trailer on the side of the road, a couple of orange traffic cones and a flimsy piece of plastic with 'Stop' written on it. Police officers were on both sides of the road, checking vehicles. A short police sergeant with a clipboard was speaking to the truck driver.

"What the fuck's going on here then?" Pete said.

"God knows. Open your window so we can have a listen."

Pete buzzed his window.

"I've already told you that the road is closed. Please turn your vehicle around, sir," the policeman said.

All of a sudden a large finger appeared out of the truck's window and started poking the policeman in the chest. "What's your fuckin' problem, copper?"

The officer took a step back. "Officer Brooks, can you join me over here please?"

A policeman in full protective gear came out of the caravan and walked over to the truck window. "Jesus, Pete, he's got a machine gun!"

"Is there a problem, sir?"

Not anymore! The cab of the truck slowly reversed as both the policemen walked away from the window. It mounted the small kerb and the policemen then turned their attention to us.

"Pete, look, the one with a clipboard has got a gun too! Don't give him any cheek."

Pete smacked the steering wheel. "But they're going to send us back."

"It's okay. I know another way. Just be nice and don't get us arrested."

Pete put on his best smile and stuck his head out of the car window. "What appears to be the problem, officer?"

"Sorry, sir, the road ahead is—"

Like a flash the Mitsubishi accelerated straight at the barrier. It broke in half as the big truck powered through it.

The sergeant spun around. "Brooks, do something!"

"What, sir?"

"Shoot his bloody tyres out!"

I looked on aghast as Officer Brooks raised the machine gun. "Surely he's not going to shoot him!" I said.

Officer Brooks got the truck in his sights.

"Fuck me! I think he is," Pete replied.

"Brooksy, over here!" a voice from the other side of the road shouted.

Officer Brooks dropped his weapon and turned to the voice. "Hey?"

Pete and I both followed his gaze. Coming out from behind the 'Marquis of Granby' pub was a large group of zombies. I have no idea how many of them there were.

"Holy shit!" I cursed.

The sergeant and Officer Brooks quickly forgot about the Mitsubishi. Within seconds they had run to the other side of the road and opened fire. The zombies were torn to shreds as hot lead cut through their bodies. Limbs were being blown off and heads were exploding and yet they were still coming. It was turning into a massacre as scores of zombie bodies hit the ground.

Pete, mouth wide open, couldn't take his eyes off the scene. I punched him in the arm. "Just fucking drive!"

Pete snapped out of it, instantly flooring the pedal. The X5 crunched over the remains of the barrier and we sped up the road. I didn't dare look back as we resumed our journey towards the Old Kent Road.

"What the fuck was wrong with those people?" Pete asked.

"I've already told you. They're zombies."

"Wind your neck in, you soppy tart. The one thing I can tell you is that there are no such things as zombies."

I shook my head at my brother and didn't say anything. We were now less than two miles away.

The Old Kent Road is a main artery into town,
and as we drove up it we started coming across more
and more abandoned vehicles. Scores of zombies
were aimlessly walking around. Some were trying to
follow cars, but they were having little luck as the
cars were still able to easily drive past them. Cars
were still coming out of London, but their progress
was just about as slow as our own due to the sheer
volume of abandoned vehicles in the way. After
some nifty driving we found ourselves approaching
the ASDA. The giant white building glistened in the
afternoon sun, as a large group of zombies jostled
for position in front of the polished glass entrance.
It was not a pretty sight.

Pete pulled off the main road and drove down the
side of the building into what was the main car park.
Numerous unclaimed cars remained and we ended up
stopping the car about one hundred metres away from
another one of the building's entrances. We stared at
the building in disbelief. As the seconds ticked by more
zombies kept on joining the group and their numbers
were getting larger and larger.

Pete turned to me. "Any ideas?"

"It will be impossible to get through either of the
main entrances. Drive around to see if there is another
way in."

He drove slowly, careful not to alert the group of zombies to our presence, and the car crawled around to the far end of the superstore. We passed a few fire exits but zombies were hanging around them as well. He stopped the car when we saw the big black Mitsubishi Warrior idling in a parking bay about fifty metres away from the store's delivery entrance. There were only around ten or so zombies at this door, but that was still ten too many.

"Drive up to the truck," I said.

Pete looked at me like I was crazy, but he did as I instructed.

We pulled up side by side to the truck and I buzzed my window down. After a few seconds the truck driver lowered his window too. He had long greasy hair tied back into a ponytail, and a faded scar on his neck. He portrayed no emotion as he stared directly at us from behind a badly reset nose. He was obviously hard, but was more likely to be double hard. He was clearly not the kind of bloke you'd want to upset.

Before I said anything Pete gave me an elbow in the ribs and whispered, "Don't mug us off to this bloke."

I ignored him and put my head out of the window. "Alright?"

He said nothing. He just stared at me.

I pressed on. "Listen, we're probably here to do the same thing and judging by the fact that you are just sitting here, makes me think that you are having as much luck as we are at figuring out what to do. We have family trapped in there and we just want to get them out and get back home. In my opinion our best chance would be for us to work together. You seemed pretty motivated yourself back at the roadblock, and three heads have got to be better than one, right?"

He scowled at me. After about twenty seconds of solid glaring a wide grin appeared on his face and he started chuckling to himself. "Yeah, those coppers didn't have a fucking clue I was gonna do that," he said in a harsh cockney accent.

"Well, mate, we are grateful that you did because there would have been no chance that we would have been able to get here if it wasn't for you. There's no way my brother would have driven through the road block. He would have been too afraid to get a scratch on his motor!"

"Fucking pigs trying to stop us from coming up here to get our families, who do they think they are?"

Pete and I looked at each other.

"Oh sorry, lads, I didn't mean to go over the top. I'm just angry that they weren't doing nothing to help normal people and that they would just let my old mum get hurt by those junkie bastards."

The truck driver got out of his cab and motioned for Pete to unlock the doors so that he could get into the back of the X5. He was a very big lad. He was easily over six foot tall, probably closer to six foot four and had huge shoulders. He was wearing a red and black checked shirt, stonewash jeans and black work boots. The bloke looked like a lumberjack.

As he got into the car he stuck his hand through to us. "Frank Arnold."

We took turns shaking his hand. "I'm Dean and this is my brother Pete."

Frank sat back in his seat and pointed out the windscreen. "I think those filthy smack-heads will wear themselves out soon."

"I'm not so sure. I think we could be waiting a long time myself."

"Oh yeah. Why's that?"

Pete cut me off before I could say anything. "Druggies don't give up when they need a fix. Do they?"

"I suppose."

"So the sooner we get in there the better."

Frank nodded. "You two got any bright ideas then?"

"Well," I said. "How much do you like your truck?"

We all got out of Pete's BMW and went to the back of the Warrior. The zombies were still fixated on the delivery entrance and didn't pay us any attention as Frank pulled the tarpaulin back and revealed a multitude of tools stored in there. He had all sorts. I didn't even know what half of them were for. There was an array of saws, drills and hammers. He immediately picked up a decent sized axe and pulled the protective cover off the blade.

"Take what you need, lads."

Pete wasted no time as he went straight for a pretty impressive nail gun. Frank and Pete had clearly taken two good weapons and after some rummaging I managed to pick up a medium sized crowbar. I was actually pretty happy with my find, because let's face it; a crowbar is unquestionably a better weapon than a squash racquet.

The three of us got into Frank's truck. I was in the back of the cab whilst Pete and Frank were in the front. Frank put the key into the ignition and revved the engine hard. Pete turned his head to look back at me and we both simultaneously put our seatbelts on. Frank put the handbrake down and we shot off towards the loading bay. The acceleration pinned me into my seat as the engine roared. I was transfixed on the looming ten-foot-high roller shutters.

"I'm coming for you, Mum!" Frank screamed as the truck smashed through the shutters. The toughened steel shrieked as it was torn from the supporting brick work and crashed to the floor.

The good news was that the Warrior quite literally destroyed six of the zombies that were in its way. The bad news was that Frank didn't see the loading bay's giant breezeblock wall in time and the vehicle pounded into it. Thankfully we were all buckled up, but to this day I'm sure that I am still suffering from the whiplash from that collision.

The three of us jumped out of the truck into the brightly lit expanse with our weapons at the ready. I stepped in a puddle of oil as I tried to get my bearings.

I looked around and saw steps leading into the main building. "Pete, go that way!"

Pete ran into the supermarket, shouting out for Jeff, Emma and Mrs Arnold. I have no idea how Pete managed to convince us that the slowest and fattest one of us would be the best bet to run into a giant supermarket to find our people, but he did. And that basically left Frank and me to deal with the four remaining zombies.

Frank just charged the first one that he saw and swung his axe into the top of its head. The axe literally cut through three quarters of the zombie's skull, and its black eyes rolled into the back of its head as it collapsed on the floor. Before I could blink Frank swung the axe again at the next unfortunate zombie that was coming his way. He obviously knew how to wield an axe and for a split-second I thought that maybe he was a lumberjack after all. The side of the axe struck it in the head and it dropped to the ground. Frank raised the axe high and brought it down on the zombie's throat. It was like he was cutting firewood as the blade split the head from the body. Frank didn't seem to care as blood sprayed all over his jeans. He just set about acquiring his next target.

I heard a giant crash coming from the other side of the building.

"Jesus, Frank! I think they've broken through the front doors."

"Let's just worry about these two for now."

As I took a step towards them I heard a cacophony of screaming and footsteps as about twenty of the human inhabitants of the ASDA came streaming into the loading area.

"Run for your lives!" a man screamed.

I tried in vain to stop people from going anywhere near the zombies, but it was chaos. It was a stampede. I was lucky to get out of their way myself. Now the thing with these zombies is that most of the time they are not particularly fast. However, as soon as they are in striking distance of someone they really speed up.

As the group of people passed me, the two remaining zombies converged on them. As if linked, the pair of them both jumped on a young woman who couldn't have been any older than twenty-one. The people that didn't get jumped paid no attention to the fallen and they carried on out of the loading bay. Within seconds the zombies had killed their prey and they were on their knees tearing the body apart. I couldn't help but look on as her blood ran down their chins as they swallowed chunks of her flesh. Of course it was gruesome but it was also strangely fascinating. It was like watching a wildlife programme when the lions take down a gazelle.

Neither Frank nor I could allow it to go on. He charged the one on the left and I went for the one on the right. Frank's axe connected with the first zombie seconds before my crowbar cannoned into the second one. Frank made short work of his and I must say that I was pleasantly surprised at the damage that I managed to inflict upon mine. The tip of the crowbar went straight into the zombie's left eye as the rest of the bar struck it against the skull. It hit the concrete floor and it only took me two more swings before I was convinced that it was dead.

I breathed hard as I scanned the now empty room. For some reason my feet were warm. I looked down at my boots and saw that I was shin-deep in the woman's remains. Her blood had seeped through my jeans and I felt it start to touch my own flesh.

Frank ran past me towards the stairs. "No time to fuck around!"

I extracted myself from the mess and followed him into the store. No sooner had we taken our first steps in there than we saw the final group of people running towards us away from the pursuing, hungry mob. I felt instant relief as I saw Jeff and Emma running towards us from the middle of the group.

"Pete's car is out the back," I said, still running towards them.

"Okay," Jeff shouted as he ran past.

Frank looked at me. "What about me mum?"

"Pete will find her."

We both ran further into the store and were rewarded with the sight of a flustered Pete bringing up the rear of the group whilst giving an old lady in a grey mackintosh a fireman's carry.

A big smile spread across Frank's face. "Mum!"

As soon as we reached Pete, Frank took his mother, turned around and headed back for the loading bay. Despite my prompting, Pete just stood there panting. I have got to say that those ten seconds that I spent waiting with him felt like an eternity. He only managed to get going again when he heard the moans of the pursuing zombies behind him. We caught up with Frank and his mother in the loading bay and the four of us ran through the doors and into the car park. I saw Jeff and Emma sitting in the BMW.

As we approached the car Mrs Arnold started to groan. Well, that is what I thought at the time. Before any of us could process what was actually happening she twisted in his grip and plunged her teeth into the side of his back. His scream was laced with surprise as well as pain. But he kept on carrying her. He either couldn't work out or didn't want to believe that his mother was trying to eat him. After her second bite, he finally got the message and he threw her off him in a combination of rage and sorrow. Her body crashed into the ground and her pelvis broke on impact, she didn't scream, she just tried to crawl towards us.

Angry guilt-laced tears flowed from Frank's eyes as he stood there staring at her body. Blood was gushing from his wound and after a few seconds his feet went from under him and he started to fall. Pete and I managed to catch him before he hit the deck and we dragged his large frame the final few feet to the car. Jeff opened the door and helped lay him on his front across the backseat. Emma took off her cardigan and put it in Pete's hand. Pete immediately put it on the wound and motioned for Jeff to remove his shirt. My fresh-faced brother-in-law tore it off and passed it to him, luckily for him he had a white vest on underneath and wouldn't need to sit there topless. The engine was already running so I got in the driver seat and put the car in gear.

"Please don't leave my mother like that," Frank gasped.

I put my hand behind the seat and told Pete to hand me the nail gun. He placed it in my hand and I buzzed down the electric window. I drove over to Mrs Arnold and took aim with the gun. I pulled the nail gun's trigger twice and two six-inch nails flew into the crown of her head, but she didn't stop moving. Thankfully, my next shot did the trick. The nail exploded from the gun and went directly into her brain through her right eye. Her head slammed into the tarmac and I put my foot on the accelerator and drove away.

As I left the car park I looked in the rear view mirror and saw zombies pouring out of the loading bay doors. I zigzagged around the abandoned vehicles and saw some of the people who had escaped from the ASDA trying to flag down the passing cars.

Emma turned to me in the passenger seat. Concern was etched all over her tanned face, and sweat had caused strands of her usually immaculate shoulder-length brown hair to stick to her face. "Dean, should we stop for those people?"

I took her hand and squeezed it. "We can't. We don't have the space in here."

"I know we don't, but I just thought maybe we should try and do something."

"I wish we could."

After a few minutes Pete and Jeff had managed to stop the bleeding, but I couldn't shake the feeling of dread that was gnawing at the back of my head. Frank was on the verge of slipping into unconsciousness and Pete was trying to do his best to keep him awake, but to no avail and it wasn't much longer before he drifted off.

As soon as Jeff noticed Frank close his eyes he started to speak. "If all those people out there are zombies, why are we taking this bloke back with us?"

"What are you saying?" Pete shot back at him immediately.

Jeff ran his fingers through his short blond side-parting. "I'm just saying that in every zombie film I have ever seen, anybody who gets bitten by a zombie usually turns into one of them."

Pete rolled his eyes, took a deep breath and spoke to Jeff as if he was a child, "Number one, those things aren't zombies. Dean's just said that because he's a fucking idiot. Number two, this isn't a fucking film, and number three, if it wasn't for this bloke we wouldn't have been able to rescue you two. So that is why he is coming back with us!"

"I might be an idiot. But you need to consider the possibility," I said. "I know the police said that this was drug-related. But this blatantly isn't. There is no way those things are human and if it is drug-related, ask yourself how many seventy-year-old crack-heads have you seen?"

Jeff shook his head. "No, the real question here is how many seventy-year-old crack-heads have you seen try to eat their own child? Think about it, Pete. We are taking a massive chance bringing him back with us."

"Do you know how fucking stupid you two sound? Listen to yourselves. I know full well that something isn't right. But to say that they're all zombies is madness. We are bringing him back with us and that is final!"

We remained silent for the rest of the journey, even Frank's breathing seemed to be less laboured. The one bit of good news was that there were a lot fewer zombies the closer that we got to home. That's not to say that there weren't any around, but I felt a lot better seeing dozens rather than hundreds. Frank started to regain consciousness at about the same time that I pulled back into the car park. Everything in the car park was as it was before we left. The dead body was on the floor and all of the cars were still untouched.

Sweat beaded on Frank's brow as he lifted his neck. "Where am I?"

"It's alright, Frank. We're in Eltham. I've brought you back to mine."

He coughed and started to shiver. "I'm really cold."

"Don't worry. We'll get you sorted in no time."

Emma stayed in the car, whilst I stood guard as Pete and Jeff set upon the tough task of getting Frank out of the car. Jeff was a similar height and build to me, perhaps a little slimmer, and he had to use all of his strength to try and shift Frank. "Come on, Pete; put your back into it. You're twice my size."

"Just shut up and stop moaning."

They huffed and puffed but eventually they got him out of the car and propped him up between them. "You are a big fella, aren't you, Frank?" Pete said.

"Sorry, boys. I don't seem to have any strength."

"Don't worry about them, Frank," I said. "They're fine. We'll be upstairs soon."

I gave Emma the nail gun as she got out of the car, and the five of us slowly walked along the pathway to the block. Emma was the first one to notice Mrs Johnson's body. "Oh my God! What happened to her?"

"Dean did," my brother said.

"Thanks, Pete."

"Bloody hell!" Jeff said. "Is that the squash racquet we got you for Christmas?"

"Yeah, sorry about that."

Just before we got to the communal hallway I heard a loud bang. Before today I would have just thought that it was a car back-firing, but I knew that it was a gun shot. We quickly entered the building and started to climb the stairs. After a few steps Pete stopped. "Dean, I'm fucking knackered. I need you to take him for me."

I swapped with my brother, and Jeff and I took Frank up the remaining thirty steps. Pete stayed at the bottom trying to catch his breath. I couldn't believe how unfit he was. Emma knocked on the door and it didn't take long for Derek to open it up. "Emma, you look as beautiful as ever," he said, engulfing her petite body in a hug.

"Thanks, Derek," she replied.

Jeff started to laugh. "He's always had a soft spot for her. If he wasn't forty years older than me, I'd have some competition!"

Troy and Derek waited for us at the top of the stairs as we carried Frank up the final few steps. As soon as Troy saw Frank he started to bark.

"It's alright, Troy. This is Frank."

That didn't placate him and he continued to bark. Frank flinched. "I'm usually okay with dogs."

"Derek, can you take him inside please?"

Derek took Troy by his collar. "Come on, boy, come back inside."

Troy fought against him and continued to bark. Greyhounds might look skinny, but they are all muscle and Derek had to use all of his strength to drag him back into the flat. "He's a strong bugger."

Sarah came out to see what was happening. "Troy!"

He stopped barking and went back into the flat.

"Good boy," I said. "Don't worry about him, Frank. He's a teddy bear. He'll be fine when he gets to know you."

Jeff and I carried Frank through the hallway and into the spare room. "I'm so cold," he said shivering.

"It's alright, mate," I said. "We'll get you fixed up in no time."

Frank was able to lower himself onto the bed. He was sweating profusely and his checked shirt was drenched. Sheila came in with some wet wipes, a bandage and a bottle of antiseptic. "Where was he hurt?"

I turned him on to his side and lifted the bloodied part of the shirt to reveal a very sore-looking bite mark. No flesh was missing but the skin had been cut quite deeply. "My goodness! Did a person do this?"

"Yeah, after he'd helped us get Jeff and Emma. How bad is it?"

"It looks nasty and he's certainly lost some blood. I don't think it's life-threatening in itself, but it looks like it could be slightly infected. All I can do is clean it up and let him rest."

I left the room when I heard Pete finally come into the flat. "How's he doing?"

"Sheila thinks he'll be okay. But I'm not sure. I'm worried, Pete."

"How many times do I have to tell you? There are no such things as zombies!" he said as he walked into the spare room.

I was still standing in the hall, when Jeff came out of the spare room. "I don't like it, Dean."

"Neither do I, but Pete is adamant."

"I hope he's right."

I blew the air out of my cheeks. "So do I."

I went into the living room and saw two of my new neighbours sitting on the sofa watching the TV. Although Sarah had got to know them a little, I'd barely said more than a hello to them over the last few weeks. The only thing that Sarah had mentioned to me about them was that they were from Poland and that they could only speak a little English. Before I could say anything, Sarah came into the room with enough sandwiches to feed an army.

"Look what Pavel and Magda have helped prepare for us all."

I picked up a sandwich from the tray. "Thank you both. They look delicious."

I sat on the sofa and Troy left the room. Any other day he would have been at my feet begging to have a sandwich of his own, but not today. Today, he paid the food no attention at all. He just sat outside the spare room like a sentry on guard duty. God, I love that dog.

CHAPTER FIVE

Pete angrily slammed the telephone handset back into its cradle. "There's still no fucking dialling tone."

"They're fine, Pete," I said.

"How do you know that then?"

"You dropped them off at Mum's before you came here. They're safe there."

"That's easy for you to say, they're not your wife and kids."

"You're right, it is easy for me to say. I've only got my mum, my nan, my brother, my step-dad, my niece, my nephews and a couple of sister-in-laws there."

"No need to get cheeky, is there."

"Look, I'm not being cheeky with you. I just want you to see that you're not the only one of us who is worried about things, okay? We just need to try again in ten minutes."

"Yeah okay, you're probably right."

"I am right. Just try and relax. Watch the TV or something."

Pete picked up the remote control and turned the TV on. "The news is on every fucking channel."

Derek tutted. "Do you really have to swear so much, Pete?"

Pete turned to him. "Yes I fucking do, Derek."

Pete turned the volume up, cutting Derek off before he could reply. Everybody in the flat quietened down to watch the BBC News. The same newsman was still in the studio and it looked like he hadn't slept a wink. Reports were coming in from all over the country about crazed drug attacks, but he never once mentioned the 'z' word. It might sound strange but I got pretty bored, pretty quickly, as none of the grainy video clips they showed could touch what I had already taken part in.

I set aside my own frustration at not being able to contact my mum and walked over to the chair where Pete left his coat. I stealthily removed his machete and walked over to Jeff in the hallway. Nobody noticed as I passed it to him. I sat on the floor next to him and started stroking the dog. Troy usually loves a good stroke but he took absolutely no pleasure from it and this made me feel even worse about bringing Frank back with us.

I leant over to Jeff. "Good idea for coming out here. I will swap with you in an hour. Okay?"

He looked at me and nodded his agreement.

"If you hear anything strange coming from that room, get me straight away."

Before he could reply Sarah came out of the room and looked at us.

"What are you three doing out here sitting on the floor? And why are you whispering to each other?"

As soon as she said it, everybody in the living room suddenly became interested in what Jeff and I were talking about.

I winked at her. "Oh babe, it's a bit too crowded in there so we just came out here for a little bit of quiet."

She nodded at me and kissed my forehead. She knew the score.

I quickly got to my feet and pointed at Jeff's dirty white vest. "You couldn't help me find a shirt to fit Bruce Willis over here, could you?"

She laughed and followed me to our bedroom. The little act had worked; nobody was paying us any more attention.

"Why are you sitting in the hall staring at that bedroom door?"

"I'm not comfortable with Frank being here."

"Why?"

"He was bitten."

"What… you think he's going to turn into a zombie?"

"I can't be sure."

"Well if you think that then why'd you bring him up here?"

"Because he might not, and it wouldn't have been right just to leave him after he helped us save Jeff and Emma."

Her brow furrowed as she looked at me. "I see that Jeff agrees with you then. What does Pete think?"

"Pete thinks I'm being ridiculous. He thinks that these people are just druggies."

"You've seen these things first hand, Dean. If you think they're zombies then so do I. I don't want him in here."

"I can't chuck him out now. What if I'm wrong?"

She closed her eyes and pinched the bridge of her nose. "Fine. Make sure that you and Jeff keep an eye on him and don't let my mum go back in there."

"That's exactly what I was thinking. I'll take care of it."

It took me a few more minutes to decide on what shirt to give Jeff. I finally settled on a red England football shirt and passed it to him as we left the room. Just as he was slipping it on I heard more gunshots coming from the road. I ran into the living room, opened the balcony doors and went outside. After a few seconds I saw a policeman running for his life down Court Road. He was carrying a gun and every few feet he was turning around and firing it off.

I shouted out to him. He stopped dead in his tracks and looked around furiously. He noticed me waving my arms at him. I pointed to the block's entrance and he raced towards it. I ran out of the living room, picked up my crowbar and went to open the front door.

Jeff got up to join me. "Hold on, Dean, let me get a weapon."

"Don't worry. Just stay here and keep an eye on Frank."

I got to the bottom of the stairs at the same time that the policeman was outside of the block. I poked my head out of the door. "Over here."

He ran through the door, panting. His dark, handsome face was dripping with sweat and his uniform was saturated. "Oh my God! Thank you."

"This way."

I charged back up the stairs and ran back into the flat with the officer following closely behind me. I ran straight into the living room and looked out of the balcony. I saw a large group of zombies on the pathway making their way towards the block. I closed the balcony doors and drew the blinds.

"Everybody be quiet," I said.

Everybody complied and Derek turned the TV off.

"Fucking hell! I was watching that," Pete said.

"I said shut up!"

This time Pete didn't say anything.

Now I'm not a particularly religious man, but at that moment I closed my eyes and prayed for those zombies to go away. After a few minutes I peered through the blinds.

"Are they still out there?" the policeman asked, clearly on edge. It looked odd as he was a tall man, at least six foot with an athletic build.

"It looks like most of them have gone."

He visibly relaxed. "Thank God! And thank you! You just, you just saved my life."

I smiled. "I think you might be exaggerating a little bit, Officer. I just let you come up here."

"Trust me. You've just saved my life. I've been running around out there for hours and I'm spent. I've run out of bullets too. I don't know what I would have done if you hadn't seen me. It was just a matter of time."

"Well in that case, you're welcome. I'm Dean, by the way, and this is my family."

"Oh gosh! How rude of me. I'm PC Holding... Otis."

Everybody took it in turn to introduce themselves and Sheila made him feel instantly welcome by putting a cup of tea straight in his hands. "You look like you need this, dear."

"Thank you. You don't know the half of it. It's mental out there."

"I don't suppose you can elaborate?" I asked.

"Just count yourself lucky that you're all up here. You don't want to be down there."

Pete shook his head. "Come on, Officer, can you please tell us what the hell is going on out there?"

"I don't know what to say. I've been on duty for nearly twenty-four hours straight and I have seen some really sick stuff."

"Tell me about it," I snorted.

"No, seriously. It's been awful. There is no way that you would believe me."

"Try us," Jeff uttered from the hallway. I looked at him; he was paying attention to the spare room door and the living room at the same time. Who said that men couldn't multi-task?

Otis closed his eyes and rubbed his temple. "Yesterday morning all leave was cancelled and every officer in London was called in to try and help contain a potential riot. Obviously it seemed serious, but we didn't realise just how serious it was until the army were called in to shore up our numbers."

"Go on," Derek said.

"By the time that the army guys started arriving things had changed. There was a lot less talk of a riot and more talk of a new drug that was turning people into murderers. If that wasn't strange enough, the real shocker was that yesterday evening every police officer in the city was given a firearm and told that a shoot to

kill order had been authorised by the Prime Minister."
As he said that, he removed his gun from his holster.
Like most Englishmen I wouldn't have been able to tell
the difference between a Colt and a Sig-Sauer, but it
turned out that the Metropolitan Police armed their
officers with Glock 17s.

"I can't tell you how wrong it felt when they first
gave it to me. Now I am so grateful that they did because I would be dead if it wasn't for this gun."

After a brief pause he continued.

"At about one in the morning a team of us were re-
sponding to an emergency on Westmount Road. It was
a panicked 999 call from a little boy who said that his
mummy and daddy were fighting. We knew that there
had been some bad stuff going on, but we hadn't really
seen that much of it ourselves."

Otis's eyes started to cloud over.

"As soon as we got to the house I was overcome
with a feeling of dread. I remember taking a few
steps up the driveway and hearing a child scream.
Jumbo kicked the door open and we all went inside. If I live to be one hundred years old there is
no way that I will ever forget what I saw. A woman
was crouching over a little girl and she was literally
eating her. We got there too late to save the girl, but
I can't imagine the dread and horror that poor little
thing must have felt as she was being eaten alive by
her own mother."

Jeff, Pete and I looked at each other; it was clear that we were all thinking about the incident between Frank and his mother.

"We must have disturbed her because she turned around when we came in. Her eyes were black and there was blood all around her mouth. I'm not ashamed to say it, but it was probably the single scariest thing that I had ever seen. She then started to shuffle towards Sarge. He tried to talk to her, to calm her down, but what the hell was he thinking? Did he honestly think that he could reason with somebody that was in the middle of eating their own family?"

Otis started to shake his closely-shaved head. "At first she moved slowly, but there wasn't that much room in the hallway and she was soon within a couple of metres of Sarge. She was only a small woman, perhaps half the size of him, but within the blink of an eye she attacked. He managed to get his arm in the way to push her off, but she managed to bite his hand. As she fell to the ground I took my gun out and shot her three times in the chest. I didn't want to; I just didn't have any other options..."

He paused again, as if he was struggling for his words.

"The thing is... she wasn't dead. She picked herself up and started coming back towards us. I couldn't believe what I was seeing. So I raised my weapon again and shot her point blank in the head. Thankfully, that stopped her."

Otis shifted from one foot to another; it was clearly difficult for him.

"She didn't hurt Sarge that badly, it was just a scratch really, so the three of us searched the house. We found what was left of the little boy's body in the bathroom and the father's one in the kitchen. It was horrific; we didn't understand what the hell was going on."

"You did what you had to, son," Derek said. "She sounded like a lunatic. I had to put a few down myself in the Gulf."

"After the incident we went back to Eltham Police Station. Sarge went and saw the paramedics that were based there so that he could get his injury properly checked out. They said that he would be ready to get back on duty within the hour. So we went off to the canteen to have a cuppa and to try and process what we had just witnessed."

"Where are Sarge and Jumbo now?" I asked.

Otis looked at me and took a deep breath. "I was afraid you were going to ask me that. They're both dead."

Jeff looked over at me and raised his eyebrows. "How did they die?"

"After twenty minutes or so we got word that Sarge had taken a turn for the worse. One of the paramedics came up to ask us more questions about what had happened to him, as he had come down with some kind of fever. Anyway, just as we finished our break all hell broke loose. About six officers came running into the canteen and barricaded the doors with tables and chairs. They were hysterical."

I had a knot in the pit of my stomach.

"Listen, guys, I have to warn you, this is where it gets really messed up. I want you to know that some of the officers that came into the canteen had been on the force for years and they were experienced blokes. They don't scare easily nor do they talk rubbish. They said that Sarge had taken a chunk out of the paramedic that was treating him."

"Bloody hell!" Jeff said.

Pete got up from his seat and pointed at Otis. "What do you mean, he took a chunk out of the paramedic?"

Otis looked him in the eyes. "I mean that my sergeant bit the paramedic, tore some flesh from his body and then proceeded to eat it."

Jeff jumped up and came running into the living room directly at Pete. He's a few inches shorter than him and has barely half of his girth, but that didn't stop him from totally losing it with him. I mean he pretty much tore him a new arsehole. He finished every sentence by poking Pete in the chest. "You fucking idiot (poke). You've fucking endangered us all (poke). You made us bring that bloke up here (poke). He's a fucking zombie (poke). I can't believe I let you talk me into bringing him up here (poke). You're a prick Pete (poke)! You know that (poke)? You're a useless fucking prick (poke)!"

Pete didn't even try and defend himself. He just stood there and took it. I was angry with him too, but with Frank being in the spare room there was no time for me to get stuck into him as well.

"Jeff, I think he knows that he made a mistake."

"Made a mistake, that's an understatement. He fucked up. Big time!"

"Yeah okay, he fucked up big time. But the longer we stand here shouting about it the worse it will get. We need to calm down and think!"

Sarah rose from her chair. "Dean, you need to get rid of him."

"I know," I said. "Otis, how long did it take for Sarge to attack the paramedic?"

"Well, we were at the house for at least an hour after he got bitten and then around another hour at the station before it all kicked off. So I'd say about two hours or so."

Jeff, Pete and myself all instinctively looked at our watches. It took us about thirty minutes to get back home after he was bitten and we had been back for at least another forty-five. Pete looked the most relieved of us all as he made the same mental calculations.

"Otis, we need your help."

Otis's breath quickened. "Has one of you been bitten?"

I nodded. "He's in the spare room."

"Whatever you need."

Jeff, full of nervous energy, was pacing the room. "Dean, we really need to hurry up."

Before I could reply, a heated argument broke out between my neighbours Magda and Pavel. I couldn't understand a word of it as it was in Polish, but it was still quite a show.

They were an odd looking couple. Magda was quite attractive, but Pavel wasn't what you would call traditionally handsome. Neither of them were old, but his face had a certain lived-in quality to it. Pavel wasn't a big guy, only about five foot eight inches and no more than eleven stone, he was thin but I could tell that he was muscular, I think that wiry is the best way to describe him. Magda was petite and a good five inches shorter than him. She said every word with her whole body and each syllable made her long blonde hair cascade down her back. Pavel was giving as good as he got and he was equally as passionate. Then as quick as the argument started, it stopped. I can't be certain who won, but Magda didn't look too happy.

Pavel walked towards us. "I help."

I looked at Pete, he was clearly in shock. He was sitting on the sofa, still dazed by Otis's revelations. I decided to leave him. I looked at Otis, Jeff and Pavel. "Let's get this over with."

We hustled out of the room and shut the door behind us.

"How are we going to do this, then?" Jeff asked.

I shrugged my shoulder. "Let's just get him out of the flat."

"But what if he's changed?"

I picked up my crowbar. "Hope for the best, but prepare for the worst."

Otis got out his telescopic baton, Jeff picked up Pete's machete and I gave Pavel my bread knife. I went to the bedroom door and placed my ear to it. I couldn't hear a thing. I slowly opened it and peered in through the crack. Frank was lying on the bed. I opened the door all of the way. I could hear him taking slow, shallow breaths. I stepped into the room and he started to stir. I raised my crowbar ready to strike.

Frank raised his large head and I immediately looked at his eyes, he was crying. Tears were pouring down his face. "Don't kill me. Please don't kill me." I felt a massive surge of relief. The three of us lowered our weapons. "I know what's going to happen to me. I heard everything."

"Frank, I don't want to hurt you. I wish that I could do something to save you, but I can't. I need you to leave my home now. I can't afford for you to change in here. You have to understand that."

He nodded at me and he tried to get off the bed. He lifted his body up, but he didn't even have the strength to throw the covers off. He fell back down into the mattress. The four of us looked at each other, deflated.

"We're going to have to carry him," I said.

"But what if he changes?" Jeff said. "We don't even know how it happens. Look at him, he's bloody massive. It's going to take two of us to shift him."

I clicked my fingers. "I've got it!" And boy, did I have it. It was a cast iron, one hundred percent 'eureka' moment. A moment of absolute clarity. I will tell you this now, if civilisation ever returns, I will be dining out on it for the rest of my life.

I ran into the bedroom and came out with a pair of goalkeeper's gloves and a big pair of red football socks. I then went into the kitchen and took a role of gaffer tape out of a drawer. I walked back into the spare room and looked at Frank; thank God he was still human.

"Frank, we are going to have to help you out of here. But we need to make sure that you can't hurt us. You won't like what we are going to do. But we really don't have a choice. Okay?"

He nodded his assent. I gave a glove each to Jeff and Pavel and they immediately put them on Frank's hands, Otis then gaffer-taped them around his wrists so that they wouldn't slip off.

"Frank, that takes care of your hands, but this next thing will be uncomfortable." I knelt down and looked him in the eyes. "Thank you for helping us save Emma and Jeff. I wish that this never happened to you and that we were unable to save your mum. I'm sorry."

I raised his head and stuffed the big red football socks into his mouth. Again Otis did the gaffer-taping; he wasn't taking any risks as he pulled the tape around his head three times. Frank was resigned to his fate and he let us do this without putting up a struggle. I didn't think that he could hurt us now, but we still needed to move him.

"Pete, we need you," I shouted.

He came out of the living room like a flash and he put his head into the room and looked at Frank. "What have you done to him?"

"We've made him safe."

"Now do us a favour and help us lift him."

He went over to the bed and tried to pull Frank up by his arms. He huffed and he puffed and he eventually got him into a sitting position. "Fucking hell, is someone going to help me?"

Jeff snorted. "Not us, you already made me and Dean bring him up."

Otis stepped forwards. "It's okay, I'll do it."

They both got either side of him and managed to lift him off the bed. They put his arms over their shoulders and shuffled him towards the front door.

Pete stopped as I opened up the door. "What should we do with him?"

"Take him into Mr Trotter's."

"Jeff, can you bring the bedding for him, please? We should at least make him comfortable."

I led the way down the first flight of stairs with my crowbar at the ready. Pete and Otis carried Frank behind me and Jeff and Pavel were a few steps behind them. All was okay as we descended to the first floor. The smell from Trotter's flat was slowly creeping up the stairs and had already got up my nose. As I walked down the last flight of stairs I stopped short at the last couple of steps and peered round the wall so that I could see through the glass entry door. Two zombies were hovering right in front of it. I froze and the others followed suit.

The seconds turned into minutes as we waited on the stairs. Jeff dropped the bed linen in a pile so that he could help Otis and Pete with Frank, as they were both starting to tire. The zombies had their backs to the door, but I didn't want to take the chance that they would hear us. After five minutes I let out a huge sigh of relief as they started to wander off. I walked onto the landing and I signalled for the guys to follow.

I pushed open Trotter's door and turned to everybody. "Sorry about the smell."

Just as I finished my sentence Frank's eyes closed and his chest stopped moving.

"Lads, I don't want to alarm you, but I think that Frank just died…"

The three of them did the last thing that they should have done. They instinctively let go of his body and it crashed to the ground. I didn't appreciate it at the time, but in a sick way it was actually quite funny as his face fell into the pile of vomit that I left earlier in the day. Now the reason why I didn't appreciate it at the time, aside from the fact that it is very disrespectful to laugh at the dead, was that the two zombies that had just walked away decided to come back and investigate the noise. When they saw us through the glass they went absolutely berserk. They started banging the door trying to get inside, thank God that they had no idea how that particularly complicated bit of kit worked.

Now you might think that a big heavy door would provide sufficient protection from most intruders, but this was not exactly the case with our block's front door. The block itself was built in the 1960s when the world was a safer place, free from zombies and crime, blah, blah, blah. So when they actually built it they decided that a heavy wooden, glass-fronted door without any locks on it would be sufficient to have on the entryway.

I looked at the guys. "We have got to shut those bastards up."

They all nodded their agreement.

"Get his body out the way!"

I inadvertently took a step back towards the door as I got out of the way of Pete, Otis and Pavel moving Frank's body, and my closer proximity seemed to send the zombies into even more of a frenzy.

"Hurry up, lads, they're going mental," Jeff said.

The three of them managed to roll him over to the side of the room. Pete lingered over his body. "Now what are we going to do?"

I raised my crowbar. "Bash his head in, I suppose."

"Fuck me! You're serious."

"Well what else do you suggest?"

"I do it," Pavel said, pointing at Pete's machete. "Give me big knife."

Pete slowly handed him the knife. "Rather you than me."

"Hold on," I said.

Jeff looked at me like I was mad. "What for? He's going to turn into a zombie, for God's sake!"

"But we don't know how long it takes after death and that's the kind of stuff we need to know."

Otis nodded. "That's actually a really good idea."

I looked at Jeff and Pavel. "You two watch him and see how long it takes. As soon as he turns, just do what needs to be done." I then turned to Pete and Otis. "Us three will deal with them."

Pete and Otis went to the door and slightly pulled it open; just enough for one of the zombies to put their head through. The two zombies couldn't believe their luck as they both fought for position. I couldn't help but think that the one who managed to get into pole position looked a lot like Patrick Stewart. Just as his bald head came through the gap Otis and Pete slammed the door shut, trapping his neck between the door and the door frame. Being quite a big fan of 'Star Trek, The Next Generation', I must admit to a slight pang of guilt as I swung my crowbar into his head. I don't know about the real Patrick Stewart, but this one could really take a crowbar to the face, as it took me three swings to finish him off.

When I was satisfied that he was dead, Pete and Otis pulled the door open so that Patrick Stewart's body could slide to the floor. When the body hit the ground I tried to kick it out before the other zombie could get its head inside. Kicking a dead body out by its head was more difficult than I originally anticipated and I had to jump back mid-kick as the second zombie dived at me. Luckily, Pete and Otis were paying very close attention and they managed to trap it in the door too. As this one didn't look like any of my favourite actors I had no qualms about using the crowbar to smash its face into oblivion. When I was done the crowbar was covered with blood, matted hair and brain matter, and the door frame wasn't much better either. I turned my attention to Frank as Otis opened the door and Pete launched the two bodies outside onto the pathway.

"How long's it been?" I asked.

Jeff looked at his watch. "Around three minutes."

Pete stood next to me. "Nothing will happen, he's dead. I told you they weren't zombies."

Otis turned to him. "Trust me, it will happen."

And after another minute or so, it did.

Frank's body twitched and his eyelids opened to reveal two lifeless black pools. He was clearly no longer human. He raised his head and saw Jeff standing by his feet. He jerked his gloved right hand towards him.

Jeff didn't panic; he just took a small step backwards and checked his watch. "Five minutes."

Pavel had been fixated on the body for the entire time, waiting for this moment. On Jeff's cue he brought the machete down on Frank's throat. The first stroke cut through the trachea, and the second finished the job as the blade cut through the oesophagus and the back of the neck. As the blade struck the floor, Frank's head rolled away from the body and the blood flowed, pooling upon the already ruined carpet. It is one thing to execute a random zombie, but it is another thing altogether to have to kill one that you knew before they turned. It might sound overly sentimental as I had only known Frank for a few hours, but I will always be grateful to him for his help in saving Jeff and Emma.

CHAPTER SIX

Pete trudged up the stairs, leaving Jeff, Otis, Pavel and me in the hallway. The last thing that I wanted to do was to leave the body in the entryway, so we picked it up and put it into Trotter's flat. The smell was just as bad, but it didn't seem to bother me quite as much anymore.

"We need to barricade that door," Jeff said.

"No arguments from me," I replied.

We both looked at Otis for his agreement, but he didn't answer straight away. Eventually he spoke; "I think that it could be a mistake to totally block this door up."

"How so?" I asked.

"Well, I don't think that they can actually open doors."

"It doesn't mean that they couldn't eventually figure it out," Jeff said. "Anyway, it wouldn't take that many of them to push against it and open it up without realising it."

"I know what you mean, but what happens if one of the neighbours gets back here and ends up smashing the door down, just to get back inside? We will be in far worse shape then."

"I do see your point, but I don't think that it would be wise to just leave the door as is," I said. "But by the same token, we probably don't need to go to town on it and make it totally impregnable just yet."

Otis nodded. He was on board. We ended up making a rudimentary barrier out of some of Mr Trotter's furniture. Let's face it; he wouldn't need it anymore.

On the way back up we decided to check the other flats. The block had six flats in it and I knew that four of them (including my own) were safe. Mr Trotter used to live in Flat One, Pavel and Magda were from Flat Four and Flat Six (opposite my own) was empty and hadn't had anybody living in there for quite some time. Before you start thinking that I forgot about Mrs Johnson, she used to live in the block next door and at that moment I had no desire to check that place out.

As we were downstairs outside of Flat Two we started there. It might sound strange but neither Sarah nor I had ever met the people who lived there. I didn't know how many of them there were or what they did for a living. I just knew that they smoked and that whenever they opened their door they stank the whole hallway out.

Otis knocked on the door, like only a policeman can. "This is the police. Is anybody in there?" There was no reply. "This is the police. We just need to know that you are safe." Again there was no answer.

I knelt down, opened the letterbox and listened. I heard nothing, but the acrid smell of stale smoke wafted up into my nostrils. "It's empty, let's go upstairs and try Flat Three."

The residents from Flat Three were an elderly couple called Eddie and Iris. They kept themselves to themselves but they were genuinely nice people. As we approached the door we could hear the familiar sound of the TV. I took the lead and rang their doorbell. After a few seconds we heard feet shuffling.

"Who is it?" Iris's voice was muffled by the door.

"Hello, Iris, it's Dean from upstairs. I've just come down to check that you and Eddie were okay."

Iris slowly opened the door and craned her neck up to me. Her jaded eyes met mine and she gave me a toothy smile. "Hello, Dean. We are fine, dear. Why wouldn't we be?"

"Have you two been watching the news?"

She pushed a lock of her white hair behind her ear and laughed. "No, we are too old for all of that nonsense. Bad news is for young people. Although we do like the man who tells us about the weather."

I looked at my companions to see if they could give me a little help. They shrugged their shoulders and left it to me. Whilst I was pondering on how to explain the events of the past two days, Eddie joined us at the door and looked at me. I still didn't know what to say.

Eddie removed his spectacles and squinted at me. "What's all the commotion about, Dean?"

"Ah, well. I don't really know how to explain this."

He straightened his moth-eaten cardigan. "Well, try then, son."

"It isn't safe outside."

"What do you mean, it isn't safe outside?"

"Exactly that. I've been attacked a couple of times over the last two days and I'm lucky to be alive."

"Blimey! Are you okay?"

"Yeah, just about."

Iris took a step towards me. "What happened, dear?"

I cleared my throat. "Look, I know that this is going to sound ridiculous, but have you ever heard of a zombie?"

Eddie screwed up his face. "A what?"

I shook my head. "It doesn't matter. Something terrible has happened. I don't know what it is, but what I do know is that people are running around all over the country trying to eat each other. It's like people are turning into cannibals and it's not safe outside. The three of us have just barricaded downstairs so nothing can get in. I think that we will all be safe in here."

Iris looked at Eddie. "Eddie love, did he just say that people are eating each other?"

Eddie nodded at her. "Yes, love, and he also said that he has barricaded the door downstairs."

"That's what I thought he said. I just wanted to make sure."

Eddie turned his gaze back to me. "Did you take a hit on your head when you got attacked earlier, son?"

"I'm being serious. It's mayhem out there."

Eddie smiled at me. "That is all very interesting, Dean. You know that it is nearly as good as the episode of Quincy that we were just watching. Now come along, Iris, let's let these youngsters get back to their 'Caribbean cigarettes', so that we can get back to our afternoon."

I stood in the hallway dumbfounded. Of course it sounded like I had been smoking drugs. My exhaustion probably gave me the look of a stoner too. But I was telling the truth and I just wanted them to understand the gravity of the situation. For the second time I looked at my companions for some help. This time

Otis removed his warrant card from his wallet and handed it to Eddie.

"I know that it sounds ridiculous and if I was in your position I would probably think that we were having you on too. But we are not. I know that I look quite dishevelled, but this is a police uniform and I am a police officer. Everything that Dean has just told you is true. We just wanted to check that you were okay, which you are, so we will leave you alone. But I strongly suggest that you pause that episode of Quincy for a little while longer and watch the news. When you have seen it I am sure that you might give what Dean has said more thought."

When Otis had finished speaking, Eddie looked at the three of us and slowly started to shut the door.

Jeff shook his head. "Silly old sods didn't believe a word."

I sighed. "Would you if you were in their position?"

"I don't know. Probably not, I suppose."

"They'll see soon enough. Anyway at least we don't have to worry about any zombies being in the building now."

We walked back up the stairs in silence, each of us lost in our own thoughts. I pushed open the front door and trudged in. Troy instantly came up and greeted me, and Sarah followed behind him.

She put her arms around me. "Are you okay?"

I nodded at her. But before I could elaborate, Derek came out of the living room and made a beeline for me. "What happened out there? What did you have to do? Where is that man now? What's wrong with Pete?"

"Whoa, Derek, whoa. One at a time."

"I'm not a horse, Dean!"

"Derek, you know that's not what I meant. Let's all just try and calm down, shall we? Everything's okay. We don't need to worry about Frank. And well... Pete's just a little upset about the whole situation."

As Troy was probably the only one who wasn't going to try and engage me in conversation I followed him into the living room and sat down with him on his bed. Now that Frank was out of the flat, Troy was back to normal and was enjoying all of the attention that I lavished upon him. I scanned the room and looked at all of my houseguests. Everybody seemed to be quite calm. Considering that this was the beginning of a zombie apocalypse everybody was taking things remarkably well. Apart from Pete, that was.

I looked at Sarah. She pointed to the spare room. "He's in there."

I decided that he just needed some time to get his head straight so I left him in there and continued stroking Troy. Within two minutes of me sitting down Sheila had brought me a cup of tea, and halfway through my cup I was actually feeling pretty okay.

My tea was ruined by Pete storming back into the room. "I'm going back to Mum's now! I need to be with Julie and the kids."

I got up from Troy's bed and walked over to him. Everybody stopped what they were doing and looked at me. I tried to put on my most sympathetic voice. "Pete, I understand that you want to go. If I was in your position I'd want to do the same thing. But I can't let you."

"You can't let me. Are you taking the piss? I'm a forty-one -year-old man; I can do what the fuck I like!"

"Pete, you're right. Of course I can't stop you from doing anything. But you need to think straight. Have a look outside. Look at how dark it is. It's only going to get darker and do you really want to put your life in the hands of badly maintained Greenwich Council street lighting? You won't be able to see a thing out there, and those things could be anywhere."

Pete looked out of the window. "All I have to do is get to my car and I'll be home free."

Emma shook her head and went up to him. "No, Pete. Listen to him. It is too dangerous out there. Julie would be devastated if anything happened to you."

"What, and I wouldn't be if anything happened to her or my kids?"

Emma recoiled from him. "You know I didn't mean that."

Jeff stood up from his chair. "Pete, don't take your frustration out on her."

"You're right. It's not her fault. It's your fault!"

"How's it my fault?"

"Do you want me to tell you?"

"Go on then."

"It's your fault, because you're a poor excuse for a man. You're a pussy!"

"How'd you come up with that?"

"It's obvious. You're more concerned about styling your pretty blond hair, than trying to save your wife. If you were any kind of a man you wouldn't have needed my help to save her. And then I wouldn't be here, I'd be with my wife and kids."

"That's bollocks, Pete!" I said.

Jeff sighed and looked at me. "No, Dean. If that's what he thinks then there's no point arguing with him." He then looked back at Pete. "Of course I'm grateful for what you both did earlier. But that really isn't the point here."

I nodded. "He's right, Pete. It isn't."

"The point is that it is far too dangerous for you to leave now."

I took another step towards my brother. "Pete, I'm sure that they are fine at Mum's. Graeme and Steve will both be there and you can bet anything that they would have secured the place. You can leave first thing in the morning and I will go with you."

"Fine," he said as he walked back into the spare bedroom and shut the door.

I turned around and looked at everybody in my living room, "You all better get comfortable, it looks like it is going to be a long evening."

I went over to Jeff and put my arm around him. "Don't listen to him. He's angry and upset. He couldn't have chatted more shit if he tried."

He looked at me and smiled. "Thanks, Dean. But maybe I should have got us back here safely myself."

"Don't be ridiculous! You did all that you could and you're here now. No harm done. We're family, for God's sake! You would have done the same for me."

—◁— —▷—

Everybody except for Pete was crammed into my living room watching the news on my forty-seven inch flat screen TV. Pavel, Magda and Otis had strategically placed themselves next to the radiator, which was manfully trying to keep the cold November air at bay. Sarah and I were squeezed in between Sheila, Jeff and Emma on the large brown leather sofa. Derek was in the armchair, feet up on the foot stool and remote control in hand. All of a sudden he muted the TV and stood in front of it.

"Is everything okay?" Sarah asked.

He ran his hand through his silver hair and straightened his regimental tie. "I'm fine, dear. I just wanted to say that I think that we should reinforce the barricade and wait for the army to do their job."

"But how long can we wait for, Dad?"

"For as long as we have to. It's not safe out there. For any of us."

"Well, Derek, for what it's worth I totally agree with you. But I've already promised Pete that I will go with him in the morning."

"It's a fool's errand, Dean."

"That may be. But I did it for you and Sheila."

"True, but there's no way we would have held it against you if you didn't come."

"But I would have held it against myself though."

Derek snorted. "You got me there."

"Talking of Pete. I'm going to go and check on him."

I walked into the hallway and knocked on the spare room door. I waited for a good ten seconds and knocked again.

"Come in."

I opened the door. He was sitting at the desk fiddling with the computer. I sat down on the bed. It was still a little damp from Frank's sweat.

"Bloody thing can't get online."

"I'm not surprised. No phones, no internet, I guess. But I suppose it was worth a go."

"That's what I thought. Anything interesting on the news?"

"More of the same. We've already been involved in far worse."

"Yeah, I suppose so. How is everybody doing in there? Is Jeff okay?"

"Everyone's fine, all things considered. Although, you really did upset him. It was bang out of order."

"I know it was. I just saw red. To be honest I wasn't thinking straight and my head has been spinning ever since Otis pretty much confirmed your 'ridiculous' zombie theory. I will apologise to him in a bit."

I got up to leave. "I think all of our heads are spinning at the moment. Come and join us in the living room. I'm sure Sheila is gasping to make some more tea!"

Pete smiled at me, but he didn't get up. "Dean, you know that it could have been me bitten instead of Frank, don't you?"

"Yeah, I know. But it wasn't you. There is no point worrying about it now. It's done. And this might sound bad, but I would trade one hundred Franks everyday just so long as you are okay."

"But he is dead because of me. It's my fault." His voice broke as he finished the sentence, his eyes started to water and a single tear fell down his right cheek.

"Pete, it's not your fault at all."

"Of course it is. If I didn't pick her up she would never have been able to bite him."

"You had no way of knowing that she was one of them. And anyway, if you didn't come out with her, he would have just gone further into the store to find her himself. And she would have just bitten him in there."

"But I should have known. And to make things worse I made you bring him up here. I put everybody at risk, all because I didn't believe you."

"In fairness, you were just being rational. Before today how many people would have said that zombies are real?"

"I should have listened to you and Jeff."

"For God's sake. Don't worry about it. I'm your little brother; you've never listened to me! And no one in the history of the world has ever paid attention to Jeff!"

My witty comment briefly put a smile on his face. "I won't make that mistake again. I'm serious, okay. I don't think that I'm geared up for this."

I didn't say anything I just looked at him.

"Ever since Dad died I've been used to being the man of the family. Mum has got a great bloke in Graeme, but he has always just let us get on with it. Whatever family matter I have decided on, you, Steve and Emma have always gone along with it. And I was mostly right. Wasn't I?"

I nodded.

"I never got much wrong... until today. Do me a favour, will you? Look outside."

I walked over to the window and peered through the blinds. Soft street lighting illuminated a dozen or so zombies just milling around Court Road. "This isn't my world, Dean. I'm like a fish out of water. But you… you seem to be doing okay. You've not cracked up; you've dealt with everything that's been thrown at you. I wish I was like that, but I'm not. Whatever you decide upon, you can count on me. I want you to promise me that if I start talking crap, come up with a bad idea or am just being a dick head, then let me know."

"I think you might be overreacting a bit. I'm not any more prepared for this than anybody is. I'm just going on instinct."

"Exactly! You have the instincts. Now promise me, Dean. I mean it. I don't want to make the same mistakes again."

I stared at my brother long and hard. Eventually I nodded.

"Well I'm glad that we got that sorted. One other thing, do you think that it is a stupid idea to want to go to Mum's tomorrow?"

"In all seriousness, going to Sidcup may not be the most sensible thing in the world, but it won't stop us from doing it."

He jumped up and gave me a massive bear hug. "Thanks, Dean. I just want to be with Julie and the kids."

"Yeah, I know. I'm sure that they are all fine there. They've got Graeme and Steve looking after them."

With that he left the room and called out Jeff's name. I didn't follow him out straight away. To be honest I was a little taken aback by that conversation. It took a minute for me to get my head around what he had just said. At first I was worried that he seemed to have lost his self-confidence and swagger. It did not sound like Pete at all. But eventually it clicked. He hadn't lost confidence in himself; he had actually gained confidence in me.

CHAPTER SEVEN

S arah sat bolt upright in her chair. "Everybody shush. Dad, turn the TV up."

Derek had somehow managed to squeeze onto the sofa next to Sheila, leaving even less space for the rest of us, but it didn't matter how little space there was, he still kept an iron grip on the remote control. He complied with Sarah's request by turning the TV up ridiculously loud.

The exhausted-looking newscaster stared at us down the camera. He no longer wore a suit jacket or a tie and his white shirt sleeves were rolled up past his elbows. His usually immaculate façade was now a thing of the past. "The BBC has received video footage showing that the dead are coming back to life and attacking people. These images depict graphic violence and anybody of a sensitive disposition should look away now."

Sensitive disposition or not, none of us were going to look away. Otis and Pete stopped chatting at the dinner table and turned their attention to the television. In fact the only two people who weren't watching it were Pavel and Magda. They had seized upon the recently vacated armchair and were now snoozing silently; blissfully unaware of what was happening on the screen right before our eyes. Even Troy was now awake, although I doubt he was paying attention to the TV.

The newsman's face was replaced by a grainy black and white security camera recording of an Intensive Care Isolation Ward. It looked like the camera must have been in the top corner at the back of the room as you could clearly see the bed and the door in the shot.

Sarah pointed at the screen. "Look, this is from two days ago."

Sheila scratched her head. "How can you tell, dear?"

"There's a time stamp at the bottom of the screen."

"It's not the best picture quality, is it?" Jeff said. "I can hardly make out their faces."

Derek shifted in his seat. "It will do me. I used to love my old black and white telly."

"Otis, you're the man to ask this question," I said. "Have you ever seen a good quality CCTV recording?"

"I've been a policeman for four years and I can honestly say that the answer to that question is no."

I laughed. "Thought so, I've been watching Crimewatch for as long as I can remember and they're always piss poor!"

Sarah nudged me and smiled. "Shush."

The room's only bed had a man lying in it who was obviously in serious discomfort and it was an easy guess to see that he was on the verge of dying. Despite not being able to see his face, he didn't have the appearance of a particularly old man. The room had seven other people in it and they appeared to be a mixture of family members and health care professionals. After sixty seconds or so the man stopped moving and everybody looked at the heart rate monitor.

"He's flat-lining," Pete said.

"Why isn't anybody doing anything?" Emma asked.

"They know it's too late."

The doctor pressed a button on the monitor, touched the man's neck and then closed the dead man's eyes. He looked at his watch. He then walked over to whom I assume was the widow, put his hand on her shoulder, said something and left the room followed by another doctor and two nurses.

I looked at the time stamp. "21.07, if he is anything like Frank, he will turn at 21.12."

The widow was hysterical; although there was no sound I could tell that she was distraught and that she was wailing. Each cry consumed her whole body and it looked like she was convulsing. She eventually rested her head on his chest and continued to sob. Her shoulders kept on going up and down.

"She's devastated," Sarah said. "We shouldn't be watching this."

She was right. It was very uncomfortable viewing. I felt dirty, like some kind of sick voyeur, but I couldn't take my eyes away.

Another three people (two women and one man) were also in the room, they were obviously relatives as they were crying and hugging each other, and also in a great deal of pain.

Sarah put her head on my shoulder. "Those poor people."

I watched the time stamp change from 21.11 to 21.12. "It's going to happen in a second."

The widow raised her head and looked at the man on the bed.

I squeezed Sarah's hand. "This isn't going to end well."

Despite it not being the best quality recording I could see the confusion on her face; and within a few seconds this confusion had turned to joy as it was replaced by a massive smile. She motioned for the other three to come and take a look at what she had seen. As they approached, the man lifted his body off the bed and looked at everybody in the room. He raised his arms out towards the widow and she took this as a sign to hug her beloved.

"Bloody get out of there!" Jeff shouted at the TV.

Pete shook his head. "They can't hear you, Jeff."

The widow leaned in to him, he appeared to grab her and pull her towards him, she didn't struggle, she gave herself to him as if every one of her wishes had come true.

Sarah closed her eyes. "I can't watch any more."

His mouth went directly to her neck and within the blink of an eye he had ripped her throat out.

"Fuck me!" Pete said.

The three other people just stood there in shook.

Pete pointed at the TV. "Fucking move then!"

"They can't hear you, Pete," Jeff said.

I think that one of the women instantly wet herself as a dark patch appeared on her trousers. None of them had any idea of what was going on. The man (I mean zombie) then reached over to the woman who was closest to him and pulled her towards him and within another second she had no throat too. That was enough for the other two to work out that hanging around was not a good idea and they legged it. I mean they literally flew out of the room. The zombie slowly got out of the bed and started feasting on the first woman that he had killed. The footage ended as a doctor and a security guard came thundering into the room. The screen was then filled by a close up of the stunned, slack-jawed newsman.

Jeff shook his head. "The geezer wasn't expecting that, was he? All the colours drained from his face!"

Now that was must-see TV. If broadcasting ratings still mattered, then I'm sure the Beeb would have won the contest outright with that clip. Game, set and match. It didn't matter that I'd already seen zombies, it didn't matter that I already knew that the dead were coming back to life; the bloke tore his wife's neck out, for God's sake. And that is messed up whatever way you look at it.

I think that the clip led to the shit really hitting the fan, as soon after the broadcast the BBC wheeled out a whole series of 'experts' to try and downplay the footage. The so-called experts said that the video was an obvious fake; 'a hoax that had been made up by a bunch of students who wanted to get famous'.

Jeff stood up and pointed at the TV. "The bloody liars!"

Emma looked up at him. "How many people are going to die because they won't admit to what's really going on?"

I sighed. "I don't know. I really don't. But at least we know what the truth is."

Derek shifted uncomfortably in his seat. "Do you think this is the end of the world?"

"Maybe," I said. "But even if it is, that doesn't mean we're just going to give up."

❧

"Everyone knows where they are staying then?" Sarah said to me in the brightly lit hallway.

"I think so, babe," I said as I stared at our wedding picture on the wall. "We just need to sort out some kind of guard schedule and then we can get some rest."

She nodded and then pointed at the wedding picture. "Happier times."

"Easily the best day of my life."

"We didn't scrub up too badly, did we?"

I looked her up and down. "You look even more beautiful now."

She smiled and shook her head. "Don't be silly, I don't even have any make up on! Are you sure you didn't take a bump on the head earlier?"

I laughed as I wrapped my arms around her slender body and kissed her pale cheek. "You're the second person to ask me that today!"

Moments later I was standing in the living room doorway looking at everyone. Otis noticed me first. "Are you okay?"

I nodded. "I'm fine. I'm just thinking about how we should do this."

Derek rose from his seat and looked at everyone still in the room. "Sun Tzu."

"Sun who?" Jeff said.

Derek shook his head. "Really, Jeff? The Art of War."

Jeff stared blankly at him.

"Sun Tzu was an Ancient Chinese General who said that first you should know your enemy."

Pete looked around the room. "If it's all the same to you, Derek, I don't want to know them."

Everybody laughed apart from Derek. "This is serious, Pete!"

"I know it is. Sorry, Derek."

"Apology accepted. Now, we know that they want to kill and eat us. But do we know what they can do in order to achieve this?"

Otis raised his hand. "What do you mean exactly?"

"Do you think that they will be able to climb up a drainpipe to get to us? Can they open doors? Will they be able to break through the barricade? And then depending on those answers we will know what kind of guard duty schedule we need to work out. If we even need one at all."

I found myself nodding along with him. "Good points, Derek. Well from what I can tell, they probably can't climb and have no idea how to open a door. So I think that it is unlikely that they will be able to break through the barricade. But even so, I think that we will all feel safer if someone is watching out just in case."

"I totally agree, Dean," Otis added, "It makes sense to be prepared."

Derek nodded vigorously. "In my experience of being in similar situations I must say that people always work best in pairs. I remember during the Falklands—"

"Great point, Derek," I said, interrupting him, "we probably should keep the shifts short too."

"How about Pavel and I take the first watch?"

I looked at Pavel and he didn't say anything, so I took that as a sign of agreement.

"Okay, then. How about Jeff and Otis for the second shift and me and Pete for the last one?"

"Fine with us," Jeff said, looking at Otis.

"Me too," Pete said as he lay back on his makeshift bed.

Derek cleared his throat. "Otis, I don't suppose you can finish your story off from earlier, can you?"

"Why not? I'll only play it over in my mind again anyway."

"Good man."

"So, as I was saying, Jumbo and I were just about to leave the canteen when six lads came rushing into it and barricaded the doors with some tables and chairs. As you can imagine there were more than a few of us who wanted to know what they were playing at. And that's when they told us that Sarge had bitten the paramedic. A few lads went into the room to try and restrain him and help the paramedic out. Sarge bit them too. One of the guys said that he saw Sarge literally tear someone's face off. No matter what they did they couldn't get him to stop. He was like a wild animal, biting and scratching."

"After a few minutes one of them finally decides to shoot him; just like I did to that woman. Only they didn't hit him in the head. When they saw that it did nothing to him, they just turned and ran."

Otis paused for a second and shook his head, "I still can't believe that they gave us guns without any proper training. Anyway, they passed a few lads in the hallway and got them to follow too. I think that there was maybe ten or so of us in that canteen. I felt sick, when I thought of Sarge being like that woman."

"Then what happened?" Derek said.

"Well, opinions in the room were divided... A few of the lads, the ones who hadn't seen those things, wanted to go downstairs and sort the situation out. They said that they didn't become coppers to hide from the bad guys. I agreed with them, in principle, but these weren't normal run of the mill bad guys."

I found myself nodding at Otis.

"Anyway, Jumbo and I both agreed that we didn't want Sarge to suffer any more than he had to. And as he got hurt with us then maybe we should be the ones to put him out of his misery. The lads that saw it all happen told us that we were mental and that they weren't leaving the canteen for anybody. Well, we probably were mental, but six of us still agreed to go."

Derek nodded. "Very brave. Exactly what I would have done."

"Before we left the room I told everybody that we had to shoot them in the head. I was a bundle of nerves as we walked down the stairs and headed back towards Sarge. I was at the rear of the group, and thank God that I was. From out of nowhere the two lads at the front of the group were jumped on by Sarge and a bloke with no face. They were growling and snarling and tearing these two lads to pieces. Before the rest of us could process what we saw, more of them started coming out of the surrounding rooms."

"How many of them were there?" asked Jeff.

"I don't know. The rest of us just started shooting."

"Did you get many of them?"

"No. The truth is we couldn't shoot for shit. We might have hit a couple of them in the head but I really don't know. When we realised how well and truly screwed we were, we ran back to the room. Myself and this other lad were quite quick and we were already on the stairs, but Jumbo and this other bloke, Perkins, were quite a bit slower. It didn't seem to matter though as the zombies weren't too fast themselves."

He paused to search for the words.

"I thought that the four of us would be okay, but in one second everything came crashing down around me. Jumbo tripped on the first step and knocked himself out cold. Me and Perkins tried to pick him up, but we couldn't, he was a dead weight. So we started to drag him. But as we dragged him, Sarge started to gain on us. Perkins just turned and ran, leaving me with Jumbo."

Derek's face contorted. "The coward!"

"That's easy to say, Derek, but I can't blame him. It was terrifying. I wanted to run myself, but I couldn't because Jumbo was my friend. I wasn't going to just give up on him."

"You're a good man, Otis. A damn good man."

"I tried to pull him up the stairs, I really did. I put my arms around his torso and tried to pull him up step by step. He was a heavy bloke and I was making slow progress. When Sarge got to the stairs, Jumbo started to stir, I was screaming at him to wake up, but by the time he'd opened his eyes it was too late. Sarge grabbed hold of his ankle and plunged his teeth into his leg. Jumbo screamed with pain and I dropped him. I ran to the top of the stairs, pulled out my gun and fired off two shots. I put my two friends out of their misery. I turned to run down the corridor, but all I could hear were the others tearing into Jumbo."

"I hope you gave Perkins what for!"

"I was going to. I really was. I was running up the corridor when I saw Perkins and the other bloke going through the canteen door. I was getting ready to give Perkins a piece of my mind, when a zombie came from the opposite end of the corridor. I have no idea how it got there, but there it was, just following them into the room."

I shook my head. "Jesus Christ. What did you do?"

"I heard screams and gunshots and I panicked, I had nowhere to go. Luckily I was standing right outside the Gents, so I threw myself through the door and closed it behind me. I put my whole weight against it and strained to listen to what was happening. I heard them come up the stairs and I was waiting for them to start banging on the door... but they never did."

Pete raised his head up. "How long were you in there for?"

"All night. I slept upright against the door. I don't know how long I slept for but when I woke up they were still shuffling around in the corridor. I was terrified and glued to the spot. At about midday, I decided that I couldn't wait around any longer, so I opened the toilet window, climbed onto the ledge and scooted down the drainpipe. I then spent a few hours running all over town, dodging zombies and trying to find somewhere to hide. I started to be followed by a large pack of them and just when I thought I couldn't go on anymore Dean saw me."

Pete let out a long whistle. "You are one lucky bastard."

"I suppose so. But I didn't feel too lucky at the time."

"And on that note," I said, blowing air out of my cheeks. "I'm going to bed."

Sarah was waiting for me. She smiled when she saw me.

"We've got a visitor;" she pulled the duvet back to reveal Troy on my side of the bed. In all the years we had had him, he had never been allowed in there. But fuck it; it was the end of the world after all.

CHAPTER EIGHT

I woke up at four-thirty am, exactly thirty minutes before my guard shift was due to start. I got out of bed as quietly as I could as I didn't want to disturb Sarah. It didn't work.

"Dean, what's wrong? Are you okay?"

I kissed her. "I'm fine. It's just my turn to do guard duty. Try and go back to sleep."

I left the room to find Jeff and Otis playing a game of cards by the front door. They both looked up at me and smiled. I acknowledge their greeting and trudged into the bathroom. I came out a new man ready to start the day and sat down with them both.

Jeff looked at me. "You're up nice and early, Dean."

"I'm nothing if not punctual. Anything happening?"

"Not really. We haven't heard any movement in the block and the last time we looked out the back we couldn't see any of them walking around."

"That's something at least. You two get some rest, I'm sure Pete will emerge in a minute."

Otis handed me the pack of cards as he followed Jeff into the lounge. I was pretty sure that I wouldn't need to wait too long for Pete, and he was sitting next to me only five minutes into my game of solitaire. We spoke a bit, but we pretty much sat there in an easy silence. The kind of silence that only family can share. It was reassuring to hear the light snoring coming from the other room, but every so often I swear I could make out the faint moans of the dead moving around outside. By the time dawn broke, I'm sure that I could sense where they were in relation to the building.

As soon as daylight started to break through, Pete was on his feet and getting his leather trench out of the cupboard. "Come on then. Let's go."

"Easy, tiger. It's still too early. Let's just give it a little while longer."

He sat back down and draped his coat over his lap.

"Let's just be patient. We will go as soon as we can."

He nodded in a reluctant kind of way, but I could feel the impatience emanating from him.

The flat started to come back to life at around eight am. Sarah drifted out of the bedroom and sat down next to me in the hallway. Pete took this as his cue to leave and within seconds he'd woken up the rest of the flat by putting the TV on.

Sarah hadn't slept well and the dark circles around her eyes really gave it away. She just sat there with her head resting on my shoulder. At some point Sheila had conjured up breakfast and before I knew it I had a tray full of tea and toast put onto my lap.

I looked at Sarah. "How much food do we have in here?"

"We did a big shop last week. That's fine for us for a couple of weeks—"

"But probably won't last eleven of us that long."

Sarah got up from the floor and walked to the living room. "Hold on a sec. I've got an idea."

She started to speak to Derek and after a few minutes they both came out of the room. "You don't have to worry about that, Dean. Sheila and I will start cataloguing supplies today. I'm sure we will know where we stand before lunchtime."

"Thanks, Derek. That's good to know."

"I didn't get where I am today without learning a thing or two about rationing."

I finished my breakfast and called out for Pete, it was time to leave. I didn't want to go anywhere, but I swallowed my apprehension and picked myself up from the floor.

Pete came into the hallway followed by Otis, Jeff and Pavel. "We've got company."

"That's great, guys. But you don't need to risk it. This might not be the most sensible of things to do and anyway we need to make sure that this place is safe."

Derek stuck his head out of the kitchen. "He's right, you know. Five of you shouldn't leave."

"Well I'm going," Jeff said, putting on my duffel coat (I had to get used to the fact that my wardrobe was now Jeff's). "Pete helped me and Emma get back here yesterday. The least I can do is help get him back to Julie and the kids."

"Thanks, Jeff," I said. "But you should stay here with Emma."

Emma popped her head out of the room. "Don't bring me into this. He's going with you."

Otis pulled on his black uniform jacket and attached his telescopic baton and his handcuffs to his belt. "Count me in too. I probably wouldn't be alive right now if it wasn't for you lot taking me in. It will help me repay the favour."

I looked at Pavel. "It might be best if you stayed here."

Magda then said something in Polish to him from the kitchen that I obviously couldn't understand. Pavel nodded at me. "Okay. I stay and help Derek."

"Okay then. Us four it is." I patted Jeff on the arm. "I'm glad you're backing us up."

I wanted to speak to Sarah privately before we left, so we went into the bedroom. As soon as I walked in

Troy put a big smile on my face. He was still living it up in the bed. He knew that I was leaving and looked at me with his big, brown eyes. I gave him a big hug and said, "Look after Sarah for me." He rubbed his head into my chest and I took that as a yes.

I smiled at Sarah. "He'll make sure you'll be fine."

She nodded, tears welling in her eyes. "Come back to me."

I took her in my arms. "You know I will. Nothing can keep me from you."

She nodded again and this time the tears came down her cheeks.

"I love you."

She kissed me on the lips. "I know and I love you too."

I had a knot in my stomach the size of a cricket ball as I went back into the hall.

"Are you ready?" Jeff asked.

"Let's get this done."

"All clear," Derek said as he looked out the bathroom window.

I firmly gripped the crowbar and opened the front door. The cold metal felt good in my hand. I was tooled up and I was ready. "Come on then."

Pete hesitated. "Are you sure it's clear, Derek?"

"As much as I can be, but I can only see so far. The damn view's obscured by next door's block."

About ten seconds passed.

"Pete, are you okay?" I asked.

He buttoned up his leather trench coat and nodded. "Let's go."

We filed out onto the landing and slowly walked down the stairs. The front door slammed shut behind Jeff and the noise echoed throughout the hallway.

Pete jumped. "Jesus, Jeff! Are you trying to give me a heart attack?"

"Sorry," Jeff said.

I turned to Pete. "Are you sure you're alright? You seem nervous."

"Of course I'm fucking nervous. I'd be mad not to be."

I nodded. "Fair enough."

Eddie opened his front door as we reached the first floor landing. He took a step onto his welcome mat and nervously ran his fingers through his thin white hair. "What's going on out there, Dean?"

"Nothing has changed since I spoke to you yesterday."

He was still wearing the same moth-eaten cardigan and he nervously tugged at his sleeve. "I tried calling for help, but the phones aren't working. What are we going to do?"

"I've told you everything that I know. Just don't go outside."

"Why are you telling me not to go outside when you're going out yourself?"

I sighed. "Fine, go outside if you want. I don't have the time to argue with you."

"There's no need to be like that."

"Look, Eddie, if you or Iris need anything just go up to Sarah and she will help you. I've really got to go."

We left him standing on the landing, and carried on down the stairs. The smell outside Mr Trotters hadn't got any better; I'm sure that Frank's body had made it worse. The door hadn't been touched and the barricade was still in place. I instinctively had another look through Flat Two's letterbox; it still stank of stale smoke.

The time had finally come for us to leave the safety of the block. We moved the furniture out of the way, raised our weapons and exited the building. I shivered as the cold air hit me. The first thing that I noticed was Patrick Stewart and his friend entangled in some kind of grim zombie embrace.

I looked up and down the path. "Come on, it looks like the coast is clear."

The two blocks of flats and the tall brick boundary wall loomed over us, and although the path was a good four metres wide, I couldn't help but feel slightly claustrophobic. Side by side we slowly walked along the pathway and within seconds we had got to Mrs Johnson's festering body. A fine frost had formed over it. Otis stopped and looked at it. "Who did she upset?"

Pete pointed at me. "Who do you think?"

My heart rate increased as we approached the car park and I had an overwhelming feeling that I was being watched. I heard a noise coming from behind me. "Lads, hold on," I said.

We all stopped. I spun around, trying to ascertain where the noise had come from. I craned my neck up to see somebody from the other block trying to get our attention by tapping on the window. I pointed to them. "Up there."

A young boy on the first floor was pointing towards the car park and furiously shaking his head. "What's he trying to tell us?" Pete asked.

The boy suddenly disappeared from the window. "Where's he gone?"

I looked around and saw Jeff put his finger to his lips. He then slowly pointed to the car park. I followed the direction of his arm and I saw a group of zombies. They were no more than twenty metres away from us and they were standing right in front of Pete's X5; thankfully they hadn't noticed us.

I heard Pete tut behind me. "We haven't even got off the fucking property yet."

I raised my crowbar. "Don't fret, okay. We're just going to have to fight our way out."

Otis nodded. "Can you see how many of them there are?"

I shook my head. "Not exactly. But I can tell that we're outnumbered."

Sweat beaded on Pete's forehead. "We can't fight that many!"

I looked at him. "I promised you we were going to Sidcup today. Don't make me into a liar. Just let me think."

The seconds ticked by as I racked my brain. I could see the pain in Pete's face as he contemplated turning around. I was at a loss.

After a few seconds we heard shouting coming from the other side of the block.

"Oi, ugly! Come over here!" I heard a woman shout.

That was then closely followed by a younger voice yelling, "You too, worm face!"

The pair of voices kept on shouting second rate jibes at the zombies and it didn't take long for them to move towards the noise.

I winked at Pete. "I told you I'd think of something."

He shook his head and smiled. "Yeah, I suppose you did."

Within two minutes the car park was just about clear, aside from a couple of stragglers.

I took a step closer to the car park. "It's now or never."

"Either's good with me," Jeff said.

Pete's face reddened. "Not funny, Jeff."

"Come on, Pete," I said. "It is a little funny."

"Can we just fucking go, please?"

"On three. One, two... three."

We all bolted towards the vehicle. The gravel crunched under our feet and one of the stragglers turned around just in time to see Otis's telescopic baton clatter into its own face. The zombie fell to the ground like a sack of rancid spuds. The impact's sickening crunch alerted the rest of his group to our presence and they forgot about the amateur taunts and turned their attention back towards us.

The zombie's desperate moans were drowned out by the sound of the BMW's engine roaring to life. Otis was well into finishing off his second victim by the time that Pete had pulled up beside him. Jeff threw open the back door and Otis jumped in. Pete's wheel-spin covered the advancing zombies in dust and gravel as the car sped off the drive. I looked up at the first floor of the neighbouring block and saw a woman standing next to the little boy who had warned us just moments before. The little boy was smiling and waving us on our way.

Jeff whistled. "We owe them big time."

I nodded.

"Who are they?"

"I've seen them around, but I don't really know their names."

"Do you know anybody where you live, mate?"

"I should probably know more of them. Bad, isn't it?"

"Well I'm sure you'll get to know them all better now."

"Every cloud and all that..."

As we drove along North Park I couldn't help but stare at the zombies that had made one of the most desirable roads in Eltham their own. A few of the beautiful detached homes had already been penetrated by them, with open front doors revealing stripped carcasses and blood-stained walls. Immaculate front lawns were now the final resting spots for whole families and half eaten bodies lay discarded on the road between parked cars.

Jeff stared out the window. "These million pound houses didn't stand a chance against them."

"I still can't believe what's happening," Otis said.

I turned in my chair to look at him. He tried to pre-empt what I was going to say, "Don't worry, Dean, I'm fine."

"I'm glad, mate. But what about the poor zombies back there? Talk about police brutality!"

Raucous laughter filled the car and for a few moments at least I think that we actually forgot what we were facing.

It took us about ten minutes to get to Mum's house in Sidcup. Her four-bedroom semi was the first on her street. It was on a corner plot, had a large front garden and was surrounded by a six-foot-high wooden fence. Large brick pillars supported big electric gates that controlled access to the driveway, and as we approached it I was heartened to see Julie's car parked on the side of the road.

Pete looked relieved. "Thank God, everything looks normal."

I clasped his shoulder. "I told you Graeme would take care of everyone."

The tree-lined suburban street was crammed full of vehicles of all shapes and sizes, and sweat started to bead on Pete's forehead. "Why can I never find anywhere to park on this fucking road?"

"Just go wherever you can," Jeff said. "It's not like you're going to get a parking ticket."

Pete parked the car about one hundred metres away from Mum's under a large tree. He shook his head as he got out of the car. "Under a fucking tree. It will be just my luck that a bird will end up shitting on it."

"I don't think you will have to worry about that," Otis said.

"Why not?"

"Because all the birds have gone."

"Eh?"

"Listen, there's nothing. No chirping, no anything."

Jeff started to slowly nod. "He's right, you know. That is really creepy."

Pete smiled. "Maybe it is, but at least I won't get any shit on my car now."

It took about twenty seconds or so for us to jog over to the house. I could see that some of her neighbours had already boarded up their windows and doors. Just because we couldn't see them now, didn't mean that they weren't around.

At the gate Jeff tried to push it open but nothing happened. "He's only gone and welded it!"

Otis inspected Graeme's handiwork. "Your step-dad isn't taking any chances, is he?"

I looked at Pete. "I'm sure that I mentioned something about Graeme taking care of everything."

Pete rolled his eyes at me.

"Over the wall it is then," I said.

I hadn't climbed that fence for at least fifteen years, so I felt quite nostalgic as I put my hands on the top of it and pulled myself up. Once there the nostalgic feeling made me turn my body around and sit on the top facing the street, just like I used to when I was a child. I watched as Jeff and Otis quickly joined me, but Pete just stood there tentatively looking at it.

"Come on, Pete, you never had any problems doing this when we were younger."

He ignored me.

Jeff laughed. "We don't have all bloody day!"

Pete scowled at him as he pulled his bulk over it. The front door opened before our feet had even touched the ground. Standing there were Julie and the two boys.

"Daddy!" they both squealed as they ran over to him.

My two little nephews, Pete Junior (PJ) and Justin, were mini copies of him. Two little rugby props in the making. He picked them both up in his big arms, kissed their dark hair and carried them back to the front door.

He put the boys down and pulled Julie's large body into his arms. He stroked her strawberry blond hair. "I missed you, love."

I squeezed past Pete and Julie into the narrow hallway, and when I saw Mum, Graeme and Nan behind them relief surged through my body. It was only after we had introduced them to Otis that I noticed that something wasn't right.

"Mum, where's Steve?" I asked.

Her brown eyes went wide with fear. "What do you mean? I thought he was with you!"

CHAPTER NINE

There was no time to waste, no time to panic and least of all no time for recriminations. My brother and his family were in danger and I needed to find them. We had to leave.

"You can't leave us again!" Julie said, pacing around the narrow hall, tears streaming down her pale, freckled face.

Pete looked at the hardwood floor. "I have to. He's my brother."

"I'm your wife and these are your children!"

"Steve needs me."

"We need you!"

Julie started to wail and she buried her head in Pete's chest. He ran his fingers through her hair. "I have to."

She violently pulled away from him. "The only thing that you have to do is protect me and your children."

"Listen to your wife and stay, Pete," I said. "We came here for you to be with them."

Pete gasped. "Dean, I can't let you three go out there whilst I stay here."

"You can and you will. They need you and I'm not taking you away from them."

"But what about Steve? I can't just leave him. He's my brother too."

"Listen to him, Pete. Listen to him!" Julie begged. "He's telling you to stay! Don't leave us!"

Pete ushered Julie into the front room and closed the door behind them. I walked into the recently decorated dining room and admired the new patterned wallpaper; it wasn't my taste, but then it wasn't my house. I leant against the mahogany sideboard and shrugged my shoulders at Jeff and Otis who were both sitting at the matching grand mahogany table.

Jeff whistled. "It didn't sound good out there. Julie's in a bit of a state. Isn't she?"

I nodded. "You can say that again."

"Do you think Pete will come?"

"I have no idea. He wants to... but he doesn't want to let Julie down."

My mum walked into the room from the kitchen. I looked at her. She was still wearing her dressing gown and worry was etched into her soft face. I'm sure that her curly brown hair had gone greyer in the last ten minutes and that her brown eyes lacked their usual sparkle.

"Julie's not in her right mind. The poor thing's been worried sick all night."

"Pete has been too. I think he should stay here." I looked at Jeff and Otis. "Sorry... are you two alright with that?"

They both nodded. I hugged my mum. I had to stoop as she was barely five foot tall. "Don't worry, we'll be back soon with Steve, Sandra and Abby."

My step-dad Graeme came into the room and put his strong arm around Mum's back. "I'll come instead of Pete."

I looked at him. "There's no need. We'll be okay."

He scratched his thick blond beard and shook his head. "But, Dean—"

"Graeme, you're needed here. I know that everyone will be safe with you around. No one will protect Mum like you."

"Only if you're sure."

"I am."

I looked at Otis and Jeff; I could see the resolve in their eyes as we walked into the garden. They weren't the biggest and they weren't the strongest but I knew in my gut that they would never let me down. As I climbed back over the fence I heard shouting coming from the house. I turned to see Pete, machete in hand, jogging over to us. He never said anything; he just looked at me and climbed. All I could see was anger in his eyes; I just hoped it was for the zombies.

As we approached the car, we saw three bedraggled bodies slowly walking down the middle of the road towards us. It didn't take too long to realise that they were zombies. None of us panicked, we just stood there waiting for them to come closer. When they were about fifteen metres away, I realised that I recognised them. It was the Kershaw brothers.

We'd grown up on the same street as the Kershaws and throughout our younger years they were a constant thorn in our sides. Pete was in the same class as Sean, Steve was in the same one as Rob, and Greg was in the same one as me. Each of them was the biggest and strongest member of their class. And let's just say that they didn't use their size and strength for the good of the school community. They were bullies, plain and simple, and each of them took it upon themselves to try and torment all of the kids in their class.

We were quite lucky I suppose, as we didn't really get it that bad from them. They liked to target far smaller and weaker children. There was an incident in primary school when Sean seriously injured Pete's best friend. Sean got into some trouble for it, but not enough, and Pete had hated him with a passion ever since. Pete had been upset that he had never been able to settle that score. As we grew up we kind of contented ourselves with the fact that they were either too stupid or too lazy to succeed in life and none of them ever left home. When Pete recognised them or rather who they were, thirty years of pent up rage plus his immediate anger exploded from within him.

"I'm going to kill the bastards," he seethed.

He charged towards them and swung his machete at Sean who was leading the way. Pete slashed the giant knife at him and it cut into the right hand side of his neck. Gooey blood poured out of the wound, but he wasn't dead. Pete had got the angle all wrong and the machete had got lodged in his collarbone. Pete attempted to pull it back out but he couldn't get a grip on it. Jeff, Otis and I raced towards him.

"Just move. Forget the bloody machete!" I screamed.

The Kershaw brothers ignored the rest of us as they homed in on Pete. To my utter dismay, he tried one more time to grab the machete.

"Pete, no!" I shouted.

Pete was making himself an easy target. The three zombies each went into attack mode and pounced at him. Pete finally gave up on the machete and turned to run. He was far enough away from Rob and Greg, but still too close to Sean. Diving full stretch, Sean's outstretched zombie hand grabbed hold of Pete's calf.

"Ahh!"

"Pete!"

It was pulling him to the floor and its teeth were perilously close to tearing into the back of his calf. The other two were side by side and inches away from helping their sibling bring Pete down.

Fuelled by the fear of my brother's imminent demise, I lost all sense of self-preservation and charged head first into the back of the two chasing Kershaw brothers. The force of my impact skittled them both to the ground. Pete was now on the floor and must have been waiting for his skin to be torn into. I never broke stride as I launched my right foot at Sean's head. His skull crumbled as my size ten Timberlands piled into it. My kick's follow-through ripped the head from the neck and I'm not ashamed to say that I have never heard a more satisfying sound. The initial crack followed by the tear; I swear it could have been the climax to the Proms. It was spectacular; Sean's head must have landed a good twenty metres away.

But I didn't stop there. I just kept on kicking the body. My legs were covered in blood and guts, but I couldn't stop myself. Jeff and Otis had to pull me away from the bloody corpse. I was screaming and cursing. I was filled with rage.

Pete smothered me in a bear hug. "I'm alright, Dean. I'm alright. It's okay. Calm down."

I slowly began to regain my composure. I extricated myself from Pete's grasp and saw that Jeff and Otis had taken care of the other two. Relieved, I purposefully walked over to the car. On the outside I tried to project my normal, calm demeanour, but on the inside I was a mess. Of course, I was elated that I saved Pete's life, but I was also furious with him. He nearly died because of his own recklessness. But it wasn't just that. I was also angry with myself. I had put myself into huge danger with my own actions and I was lucky to be alive too.

Steve and his family lived in Bexley Village, which isn't too far away from Mum's, maybe only another ten minutes or so. I was hoping to find them all safely locked away in their beautifully restored terraced home on the high street. It didn't take much longer for me to fully banish my anger and by the time we had got to the end of Mum's road, I was okay and conversation was in full swing.

Jeff leant forward in his seat. "It doesn't seem as bad round here compared to what it was like on the Old Kent Road or even back in Eltham. We've not seen that many zombies knocking around. Where are they all?"

I nodded to myself, but carried on staring out of the windscreen at the suburban homes. Most of the curtains were drawn and the blinds were pulled shut, but I still saw a few shadows lurking in the windows. "You're right about that. It looks like most people either had enough time to get out of the city or to lock themselves into their homes."

Otis shifted in his seat. "Yeah, most of the early reports I heard about were coming from north of the river. Maybe it started over there and has been working its way down here. Perhaps south London is less affected, then."

"It would make sense," Pete said. "I mean you're the only copper we've come across around here, maybe everybody else has been redeployed to where it's really bad?"

"I hope so, Pete. I really do. But after what happened at the station I bet there aren't that many of us first responders left."

"Fucking hell, Otis. You're a proper optimist, aren't you?"

I looked at Pete. "My heart hopes you're right, but my head's telling me he is."

"It's not all bad news though, is it?" Jeff said.

Pete shook his head and tutted. "How'd you work that out?"

"At least we now know that south London is better than north London then."

I turned in my seat and looked at Jeff. "As if that was ever in doubt!"

﹥﹦﹦﹤

We got to the beginning of Steve's road without a hitch. Don't get me wrong, there were bodies on the roads and pavements but everywhere else was deserted. Cars weren't on drives, some windows and doors were boarded up but on the whole the streets were devoid of all life. It was like a ghost town. The closer that we got, the more we became aware of the silence. The only thing that I could hear was the purr of the X5's engine as we made our way down the narrow Victorian high street and came to a stop ten metres or so from Steve's house, just behind his family car. The four of us got out of the X5 and congregated at the boot with our weapons at the ready. Forgive me for the cliché but it was quiet, almost too quiet.

Everything appeared to be normal, as normal as you could expect considering the situation we found ourselves in, as we approached Steve's car. The pavement was very narrow so Otis and Pete walked in the road (the bigger blokes needed more room), whilst Jeff and I walked along the pavement in single file. Steve's cars were always immaculately kept and I smiled as I couldn't help but think of this as his white Seat Leon glistened in the winter's sun. As I continued my approach I saw a decapitated body covered in broken glass sitting on the pavement by the driver's door.

I looked at the body and started to scan the pavement for its head. Bile crept up my throat as I couldn't help but imagine the worst. Was that Steve's body? It looked roughly the right size. My blood turned to ice when I saw the head. It wasn't facing me, but it had the same short dark hair. I needed to see the face; I needed to confirm my fear. I stepped over the body and my feet landed on the broken glass. Then the moaning began.

A bloody, but well-manicured hand shot out of the car window and started swinging around trying to grab hold of me. Fortunately it wasn't close enough for it to get me. I forgot all about the head, as I instinctively swung the crowbar as hard as I could at the arm. The crowbar connected just below the elbow, tore through the flesh and broke either the ulna or the radius into two (I was never very good at biology so I'm not sure which). The broken bone was poking out of the gaping wound, whilst the rest of the arm hung at an unnatural angle. The zombie just carried on its incessant moan and unhampered by the blow, the broken arm kept on flailing around. I took a step closer and could see the side of its head, I wound up for a second swing and then I heard a high-pitched scream calling out.

"Stop!"

I recognised that voice. But in the moment I couldn't quite place it.

"Uncle Dean! Please stop!"

It wasn't a random someone begging me to stop. They'd called out my name, and I now knew exactly who it was.

I lowered the crowbar and looked up to the first floor of my brother's home. Staring out of the sash window was my six-year-old niece, Abby, crying uncontrollably. At that moment I knew what I had done. I turned back towards the car and immediately confirmed what I had feared. It wasn't just any old zombie. Was it? I mean who else would it be buckled up in Steve's car? It was Sandra; Steve's wife, my sister-in-law and worst of all, Abby's mum. The reality of the situation hit me like a punch to the gut and I stumbled backwards into the wall. Pete and Jeff charged past me and headed to the front door.

Pete banged on the door. "Abby, let us in!"

But Abby didn't move; she just sat there staring at the thing that was her mum. It was still moaning, it was still writhing but worst of all it still was trying to get me with its broken, gimpy arm.

I looked at the thing that used to be my sister-in-law. It was trying to pick itself up and get out of the chair, but it lacked the rudimentary intelligence to undo the seatbelt. I forced myself to look at it and take the scene all in. It still had the bleach blonde hair and was wearing the same designer clothes, but it was no longer her. I saw a bloodied bandage on her left arm and knew that was the injury that took her humanity away. She was no longer human and could never be so again.

I heard Pete and Jeff kick their way into the house and after a few seconds Abby was no longer at the window. I knew what I had to do. I thundered the crowbar into her forehead. The merciless metal cut through her temple and tore into her frontal lobe. Her black eyes rolled into the back of her head and she let out one final moan. Blood seeped down her face as I yanked the crowbar away. And like a doctor pulling the plug on a brain dead patient, I'd put Sandra out of her misery.

"God help me."

I felt Otis's hand on my shoulder. "It's not your fault, Dean. You had to do it."

"Thanks, Otis. But it doesn't make me feel any better. That was my sister-in-law, for God's sake."

"I know how you feel. I had to do the same thing to Jumbo and Sarge. Just remember that it wasn't her."

I nodded; logically I knew that he was right and that it wasn't my fault. I never started this plague or whatever it was, but the pain in my heart was immeasurable. I never killed my sister-in-law; she was dead long before I came across her, but still I felt an overwhelming responsibility for it. Call me selfish, but instead of worrying about Abby's grief; I started to worry about what she would think of my actions; I hoped that she would understand.

As I turned from her body, I saw the head on the floor looking up at me. I must have knocked it in the skirmish. I stared at it and was overwhelmed with relief as I realised that it wasn't Steve. But whatever relief I felt was short-lived as I looked up to see two people limping towards us, being followed by goodness knows how many zombies. The zombies covered the whole width of the road and their numbers went back as far as the eye could see. They were relentlessly pursuing their prey, and it wouldn't be too long before Otis and I were on the menu too.

"We need to get out of here," I heard Otis say behind me.

"Shall we take those two with us?" I said pointing at the two desperate people in front of me.

"What people?"

Otis and I must have turned around at the same time, because his jaw dropped when he saw what was behind me and I very nearly shit myself when I saw what was behind him. Both ends of the street were filled with zombies. We had no choice but to run into Steve's house. On the face of it that may not seem too bad, but the only problem was that Pete and Jeff had pretty much smashed the door off its hinges trying to get to Abby. It wasn't going to be too long before the house was going to be full of unwanted guests.

My flight instinct replaced the guilt and we sprinted into the house. As we entered, Pete and Jeff were coming down the stairs with Abby's bags. I could hear the zombies' moans getting closer and closer. Pete and Jeff must have heard them too as they simultaneously lost their colour. Pete threw a bag at me and ran back up the stairs. He reappeared seconds later carrying Abby in his arms. She immediately flinched at the sight of me. I put it out of my mind.

"Follow me," I said.

I ran into the kitchen and thanked God that the back door key was sitting in the lock. When the five of us were in the garden I slammed and locked it shut. The back door wasn't much, but at least it was some kind of barrier. I looked around and assessed our options. Steve's back fence was massive and there was no way that we would all be getting over it without help. We had to go garden-to-garden and hope that the brick walls and fences would be enough to slow the zombies down if they got through the back door.

We used a plastic chair from Steve's patio set to help us get over the first fence. Pete and Otis had already got Abby over it when I heard the first crash on the back door. Jeff and I tried to ignore it, and we almost did until we heard a woman scream.

"Help!"

We ran back to the door and I saw her scared eyes peering at us through the glass.

"Hurry up!" Pete shouted at us from the neighbouring garden.

"Obviously!" I shouted back.

Her petite body was shaking and her short blonde hair had a couple of broken twigs and leaves in it. I opened the door as quickly as I could and she fell through it and into the garden. I slammed the door shut and relocked it in the process.

I pointed to the six foot tall creosoted fence. "We're going over that now!"

Jeff and the woman had just climbed over when I heard more banging and shouting coming from the kitchen. I ran back to the door to see a scruffy young man who I immediately recognised as the woman's companion.

"Hold on!" I shouted as I put my hand on the key.

"No!" I heard the woman say. "He's been bitten."

My arm froze as I processed what she said.

"Let me out. Please hurry!"

I could see the zombies entering the house behind him. I quickly looked at him and saw that the bottom half of his t-shirt was covered in blood. I didn't want to believe her, but at the same time I couldn't take any chances.

"Lift up your shirt."

"I can't hear you," he lied. "Hurry up!" He started pounding on the door with even more force.

"Lift up your fucking shirt!"

He raised his shirt to reveal a bite mark on his torso. He started to cry. "Please let me out! Please!"

"I'm sorry," I said as I took a step back from the door.

He started banging with even more force, but it was no use. He was out of time. The back of his neck was torn out as he stared into my eyes. He held my gaze as his blood spurted all over Steve's back door. He finally fell to the ground as a pack of them converged on him. I walked away from the gruesome scene and climbed the fence as the zombies stripped his carcass clean.

There was no time for introductions as we went from garden to garden. We must have gone through seven or eight of them before a massive red brick wall stopped our progress. We frantically looked around the overgrown garden for something to stand on, but there was nothing of any use.

Otis shook his head as he looked at the wall. "It's got to be a good ten feet high. It would be easier for someone to get out of Belmarsh than it would here!"

Pete kicked the wall. "Well, what now then?"

I pointed at the tired old house of the garden that we were in. "We've got to get in there."

Pete took the initiative and tried to open the faded lime green back door. It was locked. Undeterred, he calmly knocked, but there was no answer.

Somewhat agitated, the newest member of our group started to speak. "What are you waitin' for? Just smash the window for fuck's sake," she said in a high pitched south-London accent.

Otis turned to her. "We can't just break in. We're not criminals. Just give them a minute to look us over."

"Yeah, alright, but what if no one is in there? Are we gonna wait out here like Muppets for the next 'arf hour?"

Otis nodded. "Of course we understand your point. Just give it a little while longer."

As if on cue a face appeared at the dirty window. A bald man looked us over and slowly opened the door. "Shush," he whispered, and with his cane motioned for us to follow him.

The six of us tiptoed into his dated home and my nostrils were immediately overcome by a pungent scent that can only be described as old man's musk. We followed him as he limped up the stairs into a dingy bedroom situated at the back of the house. Torn orange and brown wallpaper hung from the walls and a matching threadbare carpet was underfoot. No doubt the room was last decorated in the seventies.

The man was short, but he was quite broad and in his day probably would have been quite imposing. "You stupid bunch of bastards. You brought them back here. I hope it was worth it!"

I held my hands up. "I don't know what you mean. We didn't bring them with us. We came here for our family."

He looked straight at Otis. "I can't say I see much of a resemblance."

I was just about to snap back at him, when Abby stepped out from behind Pete. His demeanour changed as soon as he saw her. "Hello, Abby dear, is this your lot?"

She nodded. "Yes, Bernie."

He looked at Otis. "I'm sorry, son. That was uncalled for."

Otis nodded at him. He really was a good bloke.

"Where are your mum and dad then?" Her soft blue eyes instantly welled up and Pete took her in his arms and tried to comfort her. She buried her face in his chest and Pete stroked her long blonde hair.

"She's our niece," I said.

He rubbed his face and signalled for us all to sit down. Everybody but me complied. I walked into his front bedroom and peaked through the ugly, floral curtain. There were scores of zombies still coming from both directions; they were all heading into Steve's. Only God knew how many of them there were. I ran back into the other room and looked out of the rear window. Steve's garden was full of zombies. It wouldn't be long before his wooden fences would collapse under the weight of them and they would spill into the next garden. On the plus side at least there were another seven gardens between us and them.

We had found sanctuary; but for how long?

CHAPTER TEN

The tension was unbearable and conversation was fraught. It didn't really bother me as I was preoccupied with the zombies' progress; I found myself checking on them every five minutes. The ones at the back had broken through two wooden fences, but they were now pinned back behind a sturdy-looking brick wall. There must have been more than five hundred of them. The ones at the front were still coming, but thankfully there seemed to be fewer of them now.

When I wasn't thinking about zombies, I was thinking about Steve.

It turned out that Bernie knew Abby quite well. His wife had been her babysitter before she had passed away the year before. Abby seemed to like him and he was trying his best to make us all feel comfortable. I had tried to make eye contact with Abby on a few occasions but she was ignoring me. I can't say that I blamed her; I suppose it is what you would expect. The woman that we rescued hadn't said a word since Bernie had taken us in; she just sat on the floor propped up against the wall.

Jeff joined me on one of my numerous visits to the front window. "Are you okay about the whole Sandra thing?"

I obviously wasn't okay, but now wasn't the time to talk about my feelings. So, I gave him the classic male response that was guaranteed to shut him down. "I'm fine."

I could tell by his face that he didn't believe me; but he responded in the only way another man can reply to the classic male response. He nodded and said, "Okay."

As we walked into the back room Jeff asked the question that was on everybody's lips, "What are we going to do?"

"We have to wait, mate. We can't go anywhere until we can get to the car."

Pete looked at me. "How long do you think that will take?"

I shrugged my shoulders. "I really don't know. There's more of them still coming. Do you have any idea, Bernie?"

Everybody in the room looked at our host. He seemed to be confused that he might be the oracle of this information. "How am I supposed to know?"

"You might not. But just tell us what happened yesterday. It might shed some light on things."

Bernie started to nervously tap his foot. "I noticed that things weren't right yesterday morning when I went up the road to get my newspaper. People were acting strange and on the way home I thought I saw someone get mugged. I'm only an old man so I thought the best thing to do would be to call the police."

I snorted. "Let me guess. A recorded message?"

"Yes, that's right. I tried over and over again, but I couldn't get through. I went outside to see if they were okay, but that's when I realised that it wasn't a mugging. I can't really describe it. It was like a free-for-all. People were screaming and I saw people biting each other."

He paused. Otis put his hand on Bernie's shoulder. "It's okay, Bernie. Take your time."

"I'm ashamed of what I did really. I just locked all of my doors and windows and came up here as quick as I could."

"You did the right thing."

"That's kind of you to say."

"No, it's the truth."

"Well, I eventually put the radio on and I started to hear the reports about what was going on. I only went downstairs to get something to eat. I was as quiet as a church mouse. I didn't want them to know I was in here."

"What happened next?" I said.

"I don't know when exactly, but at some point in the evening, they seemed to move off. They only came back after I heard you come here in that tank of yours."

"Come on, Bernie, I really need you to think about this."

"I don't know, they left after about five or six hours."

"That's good. Do you have any idea why they left?"

"Everybody either drove off or locked themselves in their homes, I suppose."

I nodded. "No one was left for them to eat."

Otis exhaled deeply. "That makes total sense. Why wait around when nothing is for dinner?"

The late morning sun shone as Jeff rubbed the condensation from the back window and looked down at the gardens below. Zombies were still piling through Steve's back door and the gardens were becoming more and more congested. "That brick wall is going to buckle soon."

I joined him at the window. "You're right and that means that we don't have five or six hours."

"What are we going to do then?"

"You're not going to like it."

Pete stood up. "Try us."

"You realise that we don't have many options."

"Just spit it out!"

"It's pretty simple. We have to wait for the tide of zombies coming into the street to slow down and then we have to make a break for the car."

"You're right, I don't like it."

"Listen, if any of you can think of anything better then I'm all ears."

Pete smiled. "Dean, I think that you can safely assume that if we think of anything better, then you will be the first to know!"

Around an hour or so later I was in the front bedroom sitting in Bernie's faux leather armchair staring out the window. A tired-looking Pete joined me and sat down on the bed beside me.

"What's going on out there?"

I turned to face him. "There aren't that many more of them coming. It's just a trickle now."

"That's good, right? It means we'll be able to go soon?"

I got up from my seat. "I think so. But…"

"What about Steve?"

I nodded.

"What do you want to do?"

"What I want and what I think we should do, are two totally different things."

Pete stood up and patted me on the arm. "He'll be okay. He's Steve, he's always okay."

"I hope so."

"Come on, Dean, you're meant to be keeping my spirits up here. Not the other way around!"

I smiled. "You're right. He'll turn up. He always does."

"And he'll probably have a handful of joke sweets on him too."

I laughed. "I can't believe he still finds that funny."

"Neither can I. What a—"

Jeff ran into the room. "You two have got to see this."

We followed him and saw everybody looking out of the back window. "What's happening?"

Otis moved out of the way so that I could have a look. "They've broken through the brick wall, but that isn't the problem."

Pete looked out the window. "Well, what is? Oh shit!"

Hanging out of a back window three houses down, a fat middle-aged man wearing a Burberry cap was throwing petrol bombs at the large group of zombies that would soon be gaining access to his garden.

I shook my head. "What is that idiot doing?"

Bernie looked at me. "At least he's doing something."

"But, Bernie, it's not killing them! Look they're still trying to get through the bloody wall."

Scores of zombies were ablaze, but they were oblivious to it. Don't get me wrong; I could see this guy's thinking. Eventually the fire would burn them to death; but not quick enough. The more he threw the more of them he set on fire. But even a ten-year-old could see the catastrophic chain of events that he had started. The zombies were so close together and within minutes the fire had spread back into Steve's house. The zombies didn't care, still they came, and still they went garden-to-garden. The ones at the front were getting crushed by their brothers behind them and as the next garden fence fell, the ones that fell with it got stomped into the ground.

The unrelenting zombie inferno grew larger and more perilous every minute. The lack of space and the sheer quantity of zombies had meant that other homes were now on fire. The human clothes on their zombie bodies were fuelling the blaze. Man-made materials were sparking up and melting all over their dead grey flesh. Bernie's old windows could not stop the smell of burning flesh and acrid smoke from permeating into the house and up all of our nostrils. It smelt like a rancid barbeque. I couldn't help but wonder if that was the smell of Hell. I watched a zombie in a shell suit burn and melt to nothingness, it was stomach-churning and it was hideous. The image seared itself onto my retinas and it joined the pantheon of horrors that I had witnessed since everything had begun.

The street that had only hours before been devoid of life, was now full of people running for their lives. They fled their tightly packed terraced homes, carrying suitcases and other cherished possessions as they fought to get into their vehicles. Chivalry was forgotten as terror-stricken men bundled women and children out the way in order to save their own lives. Panic grew as families were separated in the melee leaving those who were too old, too frail or too slow to fall into the clutches of the grateful zombies that hadn't yet made it into Steve's.

I picked up my crowbar and looked at everybody. "We've got to go."

Bernie grimaced. "I can't go out there."

"If you stay here, you burn."

"But my life is here."

"I'm sorry but we don't have time for this, Bernie," I looked at Pete. "Get everyone ready to move. Jeff and I are getting the car now."

We charged out of Bernie's front door straight onto the narrow street. The smoke spread down the street shrouding the old homes in darkness. The air was toxic and it burnt my lungs with every breath. I could feel the heat emanating from the houses as I ran past them. My ears were assaulted by a cacophony of roaring engines and screaming people as I desperately tried to fight my way through the tail of the desperate mob. When I finally got into the car I started to heave.

I tried to hold it down, but I couldn't. I decorated Pete's dash with bile. The combined smell of burning flesh and my bile was too much for Jeff to handle and he was sick too.

"Hurry up, Dean!"

We had attracted an unwanted visitor coming towards the car. I put the car into reverse and fully locked the steering wheel. The car slammed into the zombie and crushed its body against one of Steve's neighbours' homes. I pulled away from the house and the zombie's crumpled body fell to the floor. Within seconds I was outside Bernie's.

I leant over the seat and opened up the door. "Get in!"

Everybody piled out of the house and into the car. Bernie was the last one out and he made sure to slam his front door shut on the way out.

I looked in the rear view mirror and saw Burberry Bloke run out of his house; he saw the car and ran towards it. Even though he was an idiot and the car was full, I couldn't leave him. I reversed the car. He stopped running when he saw the car reversing towards him; it was as if he'd hailed a cab.

"Hurry!" Otis shouted.

"I'm going as quickly as I can!"

Otis pointed at the man. "Not you. Him!"

Otis opened the car door as the car screeched to a halt about six inches ahead of him. Burberry Bloke casually approached the car and smiled as he stuck his head in the door. "That was a close one."

Pete covered Abby's ears. "Just get in the fucking—"

But before Pete could finish his sentence a pair of flaming hands grabbed onto Burberry Bloke's shoulders and pulled him to the ground. His screams made my blood run cold. They could be heard over Abby's cries, the slamming door and the roar of the engine. They could be heard over the burning buildings and the moans of the dead. Words can't describe the sound of his screams; all I can say is that they pierced my soul. He was being eaten alive by fire and zombies. I don't know what killed him first, but at least it stopped his screams and his suffering was over.

I watched the macabre scene unfold all around me as I drove away behind a queue of other cars and vans. People were still fleeing their homes, still desperately trying to get away. More and more blazing zombies appeared from the black smoke emanating from Steve's front door, oblivious to their own impending doom, just focused on finding food. The fire raged and started to burn harder, blowing out downstairs windows and covering unfortunate people in glass, leaving the flames free to lick the narrow kerb.

We made slow progress along the road passing Victorian terrace after Victorian terrace; dodging people unfortunate enough not to have a car and the zombies trying to get to them. But then I saw something odd. I saw someone running past us towards the blaze. Tall and broad. Short dark hair and wearing double denim. It could only be one person.

I buzzed the window down. "Steve!" I shouted.

But he couldn't hear me. He was too far away. He was running full throttle down the narrow winding road deeper into the smoke, towards his home, on a mission to rescue Abby. I needed to get to him, but I couldn't reverse as there were cars behind me. I slammed on the brakes and the car behind me roughly banged into the back of the X5.

"Jeff, move over and drive!" I screamed as I jumped out of the car.

I was oblivious to everything apart from Steve. I tuned out my companions' pleading voices and I ran. A man got out of the car behind and tried to confront me. I swiped my crowbar at him and he dived back into his car. I swear to God that I would have killed him if he didn't get out of my way.

I ran on the foot-wide pavement and passed the same terraced homes on my way back towards Steve's. Red brick home after yellow brick home, after red brick home, I indiscriminately pushed past person and zombie alike. Discarded personal possessions crunched under my feet as I tried to catch my brother.

"Steve," I called out again and again, literally saying it with every breath. The acrid smoke burned my throat and I was becoming hoarser every time I called his name. But he still couldn't hear me. There were no other people around now. It was just me chasing my brother in between a host of normal and flaming zombies. He had no idea that I was there. He was on his own mission; he was calling out for his daughter.

"Abby!" he cried.

He must have thought that she was inside his burning home. He would never be able to hear me. My hoarse, tired voice was no match for their moans. I needed to physically get to him. I carried on running and I was gaining on him. The closer that he got to his home the slower he became as more and more fire zombies started pouring out of his house. He was wielding a metal pipe and he hit anything that came near him with it. I now was only a few metres away from him, but still he couldn't hear me.

I managed to grasp his shoulder and shout, "Steve!"

But he didn't know it was me. Why would he? He swung the metal bar as he turned. I tried to jump back, but I wasn't quick enough. The top of the metal bar hit me in my side, sending me flying backwards. I tried to say his name but I couldn't speak. I clutched at my ribs as I tried to stand up. He must have thought that I was a zombie and he carried on going forwards towards his burning home.

I got back onto my feet. Using all of my strength I tried to follow him. God, the noise was so loud.

He was now less than ten metres away from his house. I couldn't go much further, the heat was unbearable and the pain in my side was intolerable. I used all of my strength to call out to him one last time. "Steve! Abby's safe."

He turned around. His eyes focused on me and a smile appeared on his face. He started to move towards me, but he'd gotten too close to his house. I saw a fiery hand come towards his shoulder. I tried to get to him, but I wasn't quick enough. The hand pulled him back towards the flames and I saw a flaming head open its mouth and tear into his throat. My brother didn't have a chance to scream, as his torn vocal cords could no longer make any sound. I desperately wanted to get to him, to somehow try and save him, but the fire was too hot and I couldn't get close enough.

The smoke was getting heavier and heavier. I could hardly breathe and I could barely see. I couldn't walk away. I was in shock. My brother had died before my eyes. I had failed him. I was consumed by grief and I forgot who and where I was. I forgot about Sarah, I forgot about my mum, I forgot about Pete, I forgot about Emma and I forgot about Troy. If I was going to give up, if I was going to let myself be taken, then this was the moment. I don't know how long this went on for. It could have been for three seconds, it could have been for thirty of them. All I know is that if it went on for any longer than I would have joined Steve and Burberry Bloke as the last meal for a flaming zombie.

Then right before my eyes, I saw a zombie crawl out of the flames and stand metres before me. I knew that this was the thing that had just killed my brother. My grief instantly turned to rage. It exploded out of me like a volcano erupting molten lava. The smoke no longer stung my eyes and it no longer burned my lungs. I could no longer feel the searing heat nor could I feel the pain in my ribs. The crowbar became an extension of my arm and I pummelled the bastard thing to a pulp.

No sooner had I killed it than another one was upon me. Fuelled by my fury I made short work of it. I didn't want to escape, I wanted to kill more of them. I was no longer the hunted, I was the hunter. I had gone temporarily insane with my grief-driven blood lust and for ten minutes I slaughtered everything that I came upon. Ten, twenty, thirty; I don't know how many I killed but I slowly came to my senses as the bodies piled up around me. There were now too many of them and I was trapped.

I was standing five metres away from the fire with a wall of bodies protecting me from the flames, but there were twenty more of them slowly walking towards me from everywhere else. I was now starting to feel the heat, and the smoke was starting to burn my lungs again. My only option was to try and fight my way out, but I was now once again the prey.

They advanced on me and were getting closer and closer. I knew that this was it; I was done for. But then the incredible happened. Out of the corner of my left eye I saw that Steve's white car was covered in a sea of flames. I don't know what came over me, but I ran at a diagonal towards one of the zombies that was still about fifteen metres away. When I was only about five metres from it I dived to the floor. I think the zombie must have thought that all of its Christmases had come at once, because something close to a smile came upon its face and it upped its pace towards me.

When the zombie was less than a metre away from me the car exploded. Thank God that zombies are brain dead, as it didn't have any clue about what happens to petrol when you mix it with fire. I don't know if I felt it or heard it first. All I know was that the shockwave pinned me to the ground and the back of my body was sprayed with flying glass. I looked up to see that the explosion had thrown all of the zombies to the ground. Some of them were trying to pick themselves back up, but the majority were dead, their brains leaking out of the back of their cracked skulls.

I slowly picked myself up. I could feel everything. My lungs burned and my ribs ached as I hobbled down the high street, dragging my crowbar beside me. My ears were ringing and I couldn't hear myself think.

Luckily, I wasn't too near any of the zombies that were still standing and even in my injured state I was still faster than them. It was like I was the leader of a morbid marathon. I was slowly pulling away from them, but I knew that they would never give up. I allowed myself a look behind and I saw Bexley Village burning; without a fire service I doubted the small village would survive.

The stench of burnt, putrid flesh stuck to me as I made my way onto Hurst Road. I couldn't go on much further and I was starting to slow down. In fact, I was running on empty and I knew that I wouldn't be able to fight off any more zombies. I kept on walking up the road and I finally saw it. It was Pete's crumpled grey car parked on the verge. I started to weep. I don't know if it was for me or for Steve. But the tears cleansed my smoke-damaged eyes. Jeff, Otis and Pete jumped out of the car and embraced me in the manliest group hug that the world had ever seen. Two minutes later, I was crammed into Pete's car with everybody else heading back to Mum's. Despite my relief at being safe, I felt numb inside. I had failed.

Steve was dead.

CHAPTER ELEVEN

I had been back at my mum's for at least an hour, and in that time I had managed, with great difficulty, to tell everybody what had happened with Steve. Mum and Nan held Abby and the three of them cried from the second that I started to speak. Pete's eyes filled with tears and Jeff, Graeme and Otis just stood there with grim looks on their faces. Thankfully, Julie was seeing to our two new guests, Bernie and Natalie (that's Natalie with a silent 'T' by the way) and the two boys were watching today's equivalent of Button Moon or something. Nobody blamed me. I was the only one who did. Of course I know that it wasn't my fault, but even so I still can't help feeling that I should have done more.

As soon as I had finished my story everything started to hurt. I don't know if my mind had managed to hold it back until I had told my tale, but the pain started with a vengeance as soon as I did. I could see the cuts, scrapes and abrasions that were all over my arms, but I didn't dare to look at my ribs. I knew that at best they were bruised and at worst they were either cracked or broken. I didn't want to make any fuss because as hurt as I was, as numb as I felt, all I wanted was to get back home to Sarah. I swallowed five or six Ibuprofens and prepared myself for the inevitable argument that would accompany my leaving.

I anticipated a heated debate and for me to do a 'Pete'. But it never came. My mum fully expected me to go back home.

"Just be careful, love," she said.

"You should all come back with me."

"I've been here for over thirty years. I'm not going anywhere."

"Mum, please think about it. I think that we will be much safer at mine."

"How's that? We've got a tall fence and big gates."

"That won't stop them."

"Do they have a tank or something?"

"Mum, you should have seen what these things did to the walls around Steve's. Your fence will not be able to stand up against a thousand of them pushing against it! We have walls at ours too, but we're on the second floor of a block of flats. I'm telling you that it will be much safer being high up."

"Anybody can get into your car park there. I've got a gate here."

"I can fix that. All I need to do is block off the car park entrance. I'm telling you, the flats will be safer."

"Dean's right," Pete said, "he's been right all along. I promised him yesterday that I would follow his lead. If he thinks that we will all be better off at his, then I think it too."

Jeff nodded. "Please reconsider, Rose. Emma wouldn't forgive me if I came back without you."

"What do you think, Graeme?" she said.

"I know you love this place and will be upset to leave, but you will be more upset being separated from your family. We've already lost Steve and Sandra; let's not lose the rest of them. If this is the end of the world, then I would rather us face it together. We should go back to Dean's."

She stood there thinking. Now wasn't the time to interrupt her. Eventually she nodded. "Let's go back to yours."

It was coming up to four pm and we now had to somehow pack and transport thirteen people, all of the food in the house and anything else that could be useful, before daylight ran out. We put everybody to work; even the three children. I had never seen so much stuff in all of my life. We literally packed everything but the kitchen sink. Food, clothes, blankets and tools. You name it, we probably had it. Graeme's white Transit van was jam-packed first and it didn't take much more than thirty minutes in total before Mum's faded black Toyota Corolla, Nan's ancient grey Mini Metro and Pete's less than pristine X5 was too. My mum said goodbye to her home and locked it up tight. She attached a piece of paper to the front door that had three words on it: 'Gone to Dean's'.

I led the way with Nan and Bernie in the Mini Metro. The tiny hatchback groaned as it hauled the combined weight of the three of us and the supplies. Pete and his family were next in the X5, followed by Otis, Jeff and Natalie in the Corolla with Mum, Graeme and Abby bringing up the rear in the van. I looked at Nan in the passenger seat. She was in her Sunday best and her brown perm was as pristine as ever. No one ever said you couldn't look your best at the end of the world.

"What way are we going, Dean?" Nan asked.

"The normal way through Blackfen."

"Have you thought about the traffic? I know all the back doubles."

I glanced at my nan and smiled. "We probably won't need to take any shortcuts, Nan. It was pretty clear on the way here."

We headed towards Blackfen passing the well-maintained chalet style semis as we went. They were all built in the 1930s, big homes with front gardens and driveways. In essence this was south east London's middle class suburbia. Yes there were no people around, and yes all the homes looked like they were locked up, but the funny thing was that the casual observer wouldn't have been able to tell that there was anything wrong. It was just very quiet, much like Christmas Day or Easter Sunday.

"That doesn't look good!" Nan said, pointing ahead to a tail-back of cars at the upcoming crossroads.

Bernie rubbed the back of his bald head. "I thought you said there wouldn't be any traffic?"

I slowly brought the car to a stop about twenty metres away from the first car. "That's not traffic, Bernie. It looks like the cars have been abandoned. Something's happened up ahead. Both sides of the road are blocked."

"Well, what are you going to do about it then?"

"We have to turn back. There's no way through."

"We don't have to turn back," Nan said. "We can take the back doubles and get past all of this."

"Are you sure, Nan?"

"I've been driving around here for sixty years. Of course I'm sure. Take the next left."

I followed Nan's advice and slowly headed into the leafy side street. The homes were the same, but the street itself was much smaller. Cars were parked either side of the road, vastly reducing the driving space. I carefully drove about one hundred metres down the road and I was forced to stop the car when we came across a mishmash of vehicles blocking our way.

Bernie sighed. "Oh terrific! Another pile-up."

I shook my head. "This wasn't an accident."

Cars and vans were parked two deep across the pavement and road, essentially forming a barrier wall-to-wall, from one side of the street to the other.

"Why would they do that?" Bernie asked.

"It's for protection," I said. "They don't want anything getting past. Zombie or otherwise. We're going to have to go back and start again."

Nan put her hand on my arm. "It's okay, Dean. I know another way."

It might not have been the most direct of routes, but know another way she did and ten minutes later we had finally bypassed Blackfen. The detour had cost us time and the sky was now charcoal and getting darker with each passing minute. We really needed to get back home.

We made good progress along the main road that headed straight towards Eltham. It was very wide and we were able to easily glide past the abandoned vehicles that littered the way.

"Things seem to be worse here," Bernie said, pointing at a house with a smashed front window and a garden full of dead bodies.

Nan turned in her seat and looked at Bernie. "It shouldn't be too long now. It's only one straight road to Dean's. Isn't that right, love?"

"Pretty much, Nan."

The Mini Metro's weak headlamps fought against the black winter sky as we headed past the large Greenwich University campus on Bexley Road. The engine howled as it tried to pull us up the shallow hill.

Bernie leant forward and stuck his head through the front seats. "Why don't you put your foot down?"

"It is down! It's on the floor."

"It doesn't feel like it."

"We're going uphill in a car with a one litre engine that's stocked to the gills. It's pretty impressive that we're moving at all."

"It's not much of a hill."

"I think you're doing really well, Dean," Nan said.

"Thanks, Nan."

I kept the accelerator on the floor even after we got to the top of the incline. The car finally started to pick up some speed as we came down the other side. "That's more like—"

My mouth stopped working as soon as my eyes registered exactly what was ahead of us. Zombies. Hundreds of zombies. Arms outstretched walking towards us. It was the largest group of zombies I'd ever seen. More than at Steve's. This was insane. The group was as deep as it was wide. They took up the whole road and there was no way past them. Even a tank would struggle. Bernie had baited me into speeding up and here I was driving downhill towards an army of zombies that were barely fifty metres away from me.

Bernie's hand slammed onto the headrest of my chair. "Stop!"

I ignored him and I attempted something that I had only ever done about fifteen years earlier in an empty car park.

I turned the steering wheel to the right and engaged the handbrake.

Bernie shrieked as the rear wheels locked. I can't blame him, because if I'm honest I totally lost control of the car. The adhesion between the tyres and the road surface vanished as the car spun around and around. The steering wheel was flying all over the place and I can only think that the additional weight in the car stopped us from flipping over. I somehow managed to gain control with the car facing at a diagonal from Pete's decelerating X5. With the zombies behind me I released the handbrake and accelerated the vehicle; the passenger side wheels mounted the kerb as I managed to right the vehicle, just before we hit a lamppost. The air was filled with the pungent smell of burning rubber as we zoomed past the rest of our retreating convoy.

"You're a bloody madman!" Bernie shouted.

Nan turned around in her seat and gave Bernie a dirty look. "That was brilliant driving, Dean."

I looked at her and winked. "Sébastien Loeb, eat your heart out." (Now before anybody judges me, at the time I had no idea that the nine-time World Rally Champion was indeed eating somebody's heart out.)

My heart rate didn't drop until we were settled into the second detour of our trip, heading along another wide main road towards New Eltham. I'd learnt my lesson and wasn't driving anywhere near as fast as I was before. I passed the homes slowly, scanning the road ahead so that I wouldn't be caught short again. The architecture was pretty similar to Sidcup's with most of the buildings being built in the 1930s, they perhaps were not as well maintained, but still nice nonetheless. They were only spoiled by boarded-up windows and doors, but I suppose that aesthetics weren't that important at the moment.

The generic suburban homes were replaced by little independent shops as we turned into New Eltham's main road. Convenience stores, estate agents, nail bars, that kind of thing. Nothing that you would travel any great distance for, but essential to the local community. Every one of them had their lights off and shutters down. That was apart from the little Co-op supermarket.

Its windows were smashed and a small group of people were helping themselves to its contents. The whole scene made me very anxious; we were only on the second day of this disaster and the looting had already begun. I had no idea if this had happened quickly or if people had shown remarkable restraint. In any case as we got closer to home I found my anxiety turning into annoyance; I couldn't decide if the simple act of theft had upset me or if it was because I wasn't the one getting all of those precious supplies.

I was still on autopilot wrestling with my conundrum, when we finally approached the car park. The sight of about ten or so zombies hovering around it put me onto high alert. They noticed our cars and slowly made their way towards us. Even if we could get all of our vehicles past them and onto the driveway, there was no way that we could all sprint past them unscathed. And even if we could I had no idea if there were any of them waiting for us by the block's communal entrance. Thankfully we had planned for this eventuality. I pulled up twenty or so metres from the car park's entrance and signalled to the others with my hazard lights. One by one the other cars started to flash; it was time.

I got out of the car and my ears were assaulted by the zombies' desperate moans. I firmly gripped my crowbar and within ten seconds I was joined by my tooled-up posse of Pete, Graeme, Jeff and Otis. Five of us against ten of them. I saw the resolve on everyone's faces and at that moment I liked our odds.

They kept on walking towards us, totally oblivious to the fight that we were going to put up. The five of us stood there, waiting for the right moment. I raised my crowbar like a Major Leaguer coming into bat and zoned in on my two victims. I knew the first one of them. It was Mehmet from the local kebab shop. He was a lovely man with a fantastic Magnum PI-esque moustache who always used to give me a free can of Coke whenever I went in there. I hoped that he might recognise me, but of course I knew that he wouldn't. His apron was covered in blood and he had a long thin piece of meat hanging from the inside of his mouth. I really hoped that it was a piece of doner meat and not a piece of his family.

Within the blink of an eye the street was engulfed in chaos as we went onto the offensive. Graeme took to the violence like a duck to water as he nailed his first zombie right between the eyes with his pickaxe. The pointed steel tore through its skull and it was killed instantly. His blond beard and shaggy hair gave him the look of a modern day Viking. Otis dished out his own form of justice with his telescopic baton to anything that came near him. Pete was proficient with his machete, and Jeff made every shot count with the nail gun and his ninety millimetre projectiles.

As Mehmet came into range I swung the crowbar with all of my might. It cannoned into his head and sent him flying backwards into the zombie behind him. They both fell to the ground in a tangle. I approached them cautiously, careful not to get hit by one of their flailing limbs. They were both pretty much in the throes of death, Mehmet thanks to my crowbar and the other thanks to the road surface. I could have left them there to suffer and die slowly as they surely wouldn't have survived much longer, but that just isn't me, so I wasted no time in ending their suffering.

It was all over very quickly and the five of us walked towards the car park. We signalled for the cars to follow us in, and after another sixty seconds or so all of the vehicles were safely parked up.

Pete stayed back with the convoy as the rest of us swept the block's communal gardens. On the way round I looked up at the flats and saw that all of the curtains and blinds were drawn. Nobody wanted to draw any unnecessary attention. There were a few zombies milling around, but we made short work of them and were back at the car park, quietly confident that if we were quick we would all be able to get safely into the block.

By now it was far too dark to try and empty all of the vehicles and get our supplies upstairs. We took what we could and parked the van next to a large brick wall at the back of the car park. We then parked the other supply-laden cars side by side, making it as difficult as possible for someone to try and get into them.

I walked up the communal staircase with twelve pairs of feet trudging along behind me. I was spent; an emotional and physical mess. My mind was awash with conflicting thoughts and emotions as I climbed each step. I felt an overwhelming guilt about losing my brother and my sister-in-law; but I felt joy at having saved my niece. I was filled with pride that my family had put their faith in me; but was scared that I may not be able to protect them. But most of all I was filled with relief at nearly being home; nearly being back with Sarah.

My heart nearly burst when she opened the door and I saw her face. Before I knew it she was in my arms. I had been gone for over eight hours. She had worried about me for every second. Relief coursed through our veins as we embraced. We laughed and we cried. I was finally home.

Troy got involved in the action too; he jumped up on his powerful hind legs and licked my face. I don't know how long it took for the three of us to come inside, but it was enough time for everybody else to get into the living room. My brown leather sofa had been turned into a makeshift bed and you couldn't see the pale oak floor through all of the blankets and pillows. It would be an understatement to say that it was a tight squeeze.

My sister started to look around the room. Her dark eyes finally searching the empty hall. "Where's Steve and Sandra?"

The room became silent. I started to hear Abby's breathing change.

Emma looked at me. "Dean, where's Steve and Sandra?"

A lump formed in my throat and I could feel my eyes welling up. "They didn't make it."

My words caused Emma to gasp and Abby to burst into tears. Both Jeff and my mum instantly leapt into action.

I couldn't face the inevitable questions, or bring myself to listen to what felt like my own failure. So I left the room and went into the kitchen. Sarah squeezed my hand as I walked past. She knew I needed a minute, but Derek followed me out. I put the kettle on to try and style out my discomfort.

"I'm sorry about Steve. He was a good man. I liked him a lot."

"Thanks, Derek."

"I know this may not seem like a good time, but I want you to know that we made progress here today."

"Great."

"We've catalogued every item of food that is in this entire building."

"How did you do that?"

"Everybody helped out. And I hope you don't mind, but Pavel let himself into Flat Two and we've taken what was in there."

"Why would I mind? I don't think the owners will be back anytime soon. Waste not want not, and all that."

"I'm glad you approve. In any case I think that we maybe have enough food to last us for about three days."

"It's not great. But I suppose it isn't a total disaster. Especially as we have all of my mum's supplies too."

"I wouldn't count on that. It might be extra food, but there are now extra mouths too."

"Very true."

"You'll also be pleased to know that Pavel and Magda have made up their spare room for guests and we've prepared the unoccupied flat across the hall. Even Eddie and Iris have offered up their own spare room to the group in case it's needed."

"That's great, Derek. I think we could all use a bit of space in here."

"Just happy to help. You can always count on me."

CHAPTER TWELVE

An image of the Prime Minister filled the TV screen. He was sitting at a desk in what I assumed was his office and he looked like he hadn't slept in days. In fairness to him he probably hadn't. His tailored blue suit was dishevelled and his grey hair lacked its usual verve. He looked directly at the camera and started speaking in his crisp Etonian voice.

"People of Britain, please let me start by apologising for interrupting your viewing. All is not well in our country this evening, nor is it in the rest of the world. The international community is facing a crisis the likes of which it has never seen before."

Pete scoffed. "No shit."

Mum glared at him.

"You will have heard news reports of a narcotic that is turning people into murderers. Let me tell you now; these reports are not entirely accurate. These people are not drug addicts, they are normal people like you and me, who have just had the misfortune to be infected by some form of virus that induces mental illness. As a result these people are not in their right minds and are not responsible for their own actions. They are extremely dangerous and should not be approached or spoken to for any reason."

I nodded to myself. A virus made sense, but they were more than just mad. They were dead, for God's sake.

"The latest figures that I have been given show that only a few thousand people have been infected—"

Jeff shook his head. "That can't be right. Can it?"

"But due to the nature of the illness and because we take public health matters extremely seriously, the House of Commons, after taking advisement from National Health Agencies, has reached a cross-party consensus to confine everybody throughout the entire United Kingdom to their homes until further notice so that the Emergency Services, reinforced by the Armed Forces, can protect the country and get the infected individuals the help that they so badly need—"

Graeme nodded. "At least they're doing something."

"We do not foresee too many problems with the operation and we are all very confident that the illness is treatable and that normality will be restored before the weekend is out. I have spoken to other world leaders and they are taking similar steps in their own countries. You may think that these measures are extreme but there is nothing that I take more seriously than the wellbeing of the citizens of this great country."

Jeff got to his feet. "Bloody hell! I can't believe that this is happening all over the world."

"Please be safe and heed this advice. I will ensure that our progress is relayed to you all as and when we have any news."

The transmission finished and the room was in total silence.

Jeff stepped in front of the TV. "Was it just me or did it seem like he was speaking to us like we're idiots? I mean things are blatantly worse than what he's saying. Aren't they?"

"Maybe, maybe not," Otis said. "Anyway, what do you expect him to say?"

"The truth would be nice, mate."

"Maybe he is telling the truth," Emma said.

"Don't be so naïve," Pete said. "He's definitely holding things back."

Emma glared at Pete.

"There's no need to be nasty, Pete," Derek said. "But it is true that the PM would know far more than anyone else does about what's going on. He probably doesn't want a full-on panic on his hands. But that isn't to say that this won't all be under control soon."

Mum looked at Derek. "I don't know, Derek. It's close to a full-on panic anyway. We saw people looting on our way here."

Derek's brows arched. "Really? My goodness."

"It might be close to it," I said, "but they'd want to avert it for as long as possible. It will be nigh on impossible for them to get things back to normal if people were going mad in the streets."

"People are already going mad in the streets," Jeff quipped.

Nobody laughed.

"All the PM wants," Pete said, "Is for us all to sit back, stay safe and let them do their thing."

Graeme's knees cracked as he raised his large frame out of his seat. "Isn't that what we pay our taxes for? Anyway that doesn't sound like a bad idea to me. The PM said it will all be under control by the end of weekend. It's Thursday today, so we've only got to stay here until Sunday. Another three days at the most."

Jeff cleared his throat. "I'm not being funny, Graeme, but you're kidding yourself. What are the authorities going to do? The only copper we have come across since this whole mess started is Otis; and he was running for his bloody life!" Jeff made eye contact with Otis. "No offence, mate."

"None taken," Otis said.

"So what should we do then?" Graeme asked to no one in particular.

"Although I don't like it that he's held things back, I understand why he's done it," Pete said. "So I just think we should just stay up here and wait for it all to blow over."

Graeme nodded. "That sounds good to me. I think that we're pretty okay up here. We just need to make sure that the downstairs barricade holds."

"I'm afraid that it isn't that simple," Derek said.

"What do you mean?"

"It's not just about safety. We need to think about supplies too. We've only got enough food for three days."

Pete looked shocked. "Are you sure, Derek? What about everything that we brought from Mum's house?"

Derek straightened his tie. "I have already discussed this with Dean. There may well be extra food, but there are also extra mouths to feed too."

"Blimey, three days isn't that long."

"But that's still okay though," Graeme said. "Because the PM said it'll be all over by the end of the weekend and that's three days. Same as the food."

"Look, I think that we're missing the point here," I said.

"Food's really important, Dean," Pete said. "How can we be missing the point?"

"We have enough food for at least three days. So it isn't the priority."

"Of course food is a priority!"

"I never said it wasn't. It's just not our first one. Graeme's right, the first thing that we need to do is to protect ourselves. But it can't just stop at the block. We need to secure the whole of the grounds. That has to be our main concern and that is what we have to do tomorrow. Only after that is done, do we need to think about the next priority; which in my opinion is food."

Sarah put her hand on my knee and smiled at me. "You're right. First and foremost we need to make sure that the zombies can't get anywhere near us."

I looked around the room. "Does that make sense to everyone?"

Nearly everyone nodded.

At least that was kind of sorted then.

Later in the evening, most people were either settling in to their new accommodation or getting on with their evening chores; leaving me sitting around my large wooden dining table with Pete, Jeff and Otis.

"That was hard work earlier," Jeff said.

I nodded at him. "At least we know what we have to do tomorrow now."

Jeff looked at Pete. "You nearly shit yourself when you thought we were going to run out of food."

Pete scowled at him. "Can we take things a little more seriously please? Otis, do you think the PM was right about Sunday?"

"I want it to be true, but I can't see it."

"Me too," I said. "It's absolutely mental out there."

"But you don't know for sure," Pete said. "They might have a cure. Modern technology moves at an incredible pace these days."

"No way. It would be impossible to find a cure and administer it to everybody in a few days. And anyway, how can you cure death?"

"Anything's possible!"

"Yeah, okay, I suppose anything is possible. It's more likely that they will get the army to try and wipe them out one by one."

"That'll work too."

"It could work. But think about it. Every time they bite someone they infect them. That means that their numbers will just keep on increasing. We must have seen over a thousand of them and that's only in three or four small areas in south London. We've seen news reports from all over the country, there has to be tens of thousands of them. The PM's figures don't stack up and in my opinion that means that Sunday is a massive long shot. It's more likely that it will take longer than that."

Pete sighed. "Just because you seem to have half a clue about what to do, doesn't give you the right to kill my hope."

I rolled my eyes at him. "I'm not killing hope; I'm just trying to be realistic. Look, I obviously don't know what is going to happen tomorrow nor do I know how long this situation will go on for. I just don't want us to rest on our laurels. Our best chance of surviving is by being proactive."

Otis put his hand on Pete's shoulder. "We have to be prepared for Sunday to come and go and us still be in this same situation."

"That's all well and good," Jeff said. "But how do we do that?"

"Well, we're already taking the first step tomorrow by securing the grounds."

"That's the key to everything," I said. "But it doesn't stop there. We need to clean up and get rid of the dead bodies that are out there too. Who knows what germs are festering in them? We also need to make sure that next door is safe too."

Jeff nodded. "Yeah, meet the people. We might even be able to pool our resources and buy us another day of food."

"We've also got to get the rest of the stuff out of the cars. There's still a lot of gear out there."

Pete nervously scratched his head. "I do understand where the three of you are coming from, but I still think that we should just stay here for the next couple of days and let it all play out. Safety first and all that. If we don't leave the building, we don't get hurt."

"We have no idea how many of them are out there now. But what I can guarantee is that there will be more of them tomorrow, and more again the day after that. We need to do this whilst we can."

"We've already been through this. You don't have a crystal fucking ball! You can't see into the future. And the PM did say it would all be under control by Sunday."

Exasperated, I threw my hands in the air. "You accused Emma of being naïve earlier. You're being even more so now."

Pete slammed his large fist on the wooden table, causing it to shake. "I've got two children to protect!"

"You're missing the point, Pete. The only way to protect your children is by making the grounds safe! And you know what? It doesn't stop there. What happens when we have no food to feed them? What happens when we have no heat to keep them warm? You can pin your hopes on everything being alright on Sunday all you want to. But I won't do it. I'm not that stupid!"

Pete's round face went a very dark shade of crimson, but he remained silent.

I took a deep breath. "I don't want to pull rank on you, Pete. But yesterday you sat in my spare room and said that you would back my judgement. I'm not saying we should do this for a laugh. I'm saying that we should do this because we have to."

His face softened a little as he slowly nodded. "Okay, let's say that I agree with what you're saying about securing the grounds. But I bet we can make our supplies last longer than three days. Are you sure we really need to go back outside?"

"The supplies could last three days, they could last for four days or maybe even five days, but that isn't really the point. We already saw some looting going on this evening. If we wait too long to go back out there, there might not be anything left. I've said it before and I'll say it again. We need to be proactive here."

Jeff sat back in his chair. "I don't know about you, Otis, but I'm convinced. It makes sense to me."

Otis nodded. "Yeah, me too. If I had my way, we wouldn't need to go back outside. But it isn't really an option."

I touched my brother on the arm. "I know it's a lot to take in. But we need to all pull together if we are going to get through this."

Pete shrugged his shoulders at me. I could tell that he wasn't happy, but at least he'd stopped arguing with me. I think that the fact that Otis and Jeff seemed to agree with me made him a little less vocal.

"So in summary, all we need to do," Otis said, smiling, "is block off the entrances, kill God knows how many zombies that happen to be in the grounds, dispose of the dead bodies, properly introduce ourselves to the neighbours and bring the rest of the supplies in from the cars and van."

"And don't forget a supermarket run too," Jeff said.

Jeff, Otis and I laughed.

"You three should be taking things a bit more seriously," Pete said. "The whole thing isn't a joke."

"Don't jump down our throats!" Jeff said. "How are we treating it like a joke?"

"I lost my brother today!"

"Oi, Pete," I snapped, "There's no need to bring Steve into this. How much more seriously can we take it? We're trying to plan for our very survival!"

He stood up and took a step towards me. "Your laughing and joking shows a distinct lack of respect for the dead."

I jumped up from my seat. "What did you say?"

"I said you should grow up and have a bit more respect for the dead."

"Are you taking the piss? You stayed in the car, when I tried to save him. I watched him die! If I can try and hold it together, then you can too!"

"Hold it together! Hold it to-fucking-gether! I'm your older brother, you little bastard. You're lucky I don't put you on your arse!"

I squared up to him. "Just try it."

Otis and Jeff jumped in between us at exactly the same moment Sarah came into the room. "Julie and the kids have settled down now, Pete."

"Have a think about what I said," he said, never taking his eyes off me. "I'm going to spend the rest of the evening with my wife and kids."

He then slammed the front door as he stormed out the flat.

Sarah looked at the three of us. "What was that all about?"

Jeff scratched his head. "He's a bloody child."

"Look, I obviously don't know Pete very well," Otis said, "But in my opinion this is just the grief and pressure getting to him. It is understandable. I bet he just needs a little time to adjust."

I took Sarah's hand and squeezed it. "I hope so. We're going to need everyone pulling together if we are going to pull this off."

"He's always had a bit of a temper," Jeff said. "He was like that with me yesterday. Remember? I'm sure he will be fine in the morning. You might even get an apology."

I chuckled. "An apology? Not biting my head off will be enough."

CHAPTER THIRTEEN

Anybody who has ever experienced a traumatic event will tell you that the first second of consciousness after sleep is the cruellest trick that a mind can play on itself. That first half second is bliss as your mind is ignorant of the trauma; for those milliseconds all is well and nothing will feel better than that. But as the brain kicks in and starts to process the world around it again the rest of the second becomes gut-wrenching torture. The trauma starts to cascade into your consciousness like a tsunami flooding the shore. After only a few seconds your mind has been enveloped and all is no longer well; you are back in reality.

I warmed my hands on my cup of tea as I watched the morning news in the living room. Troy was sprawled out on the brown rug, oblivious to everything, and Emma was brushing her dark hair over by the large oak-framed mirror at the side of the room.

"Are you okay?" I said to her.

"I'm trying to be. So much has happened... What with Steve and everything."

"I'm trying not to think about it."

Tears started to well up in her brown eyes.

Jeff came in from the communal area wearing my black duffel coat. He took it off to reveal another one of my England shirts, this time it was a white one. "It's bloody cold out there. Oh babe, are you okay?"

Emma dabbed her eyes with the sleeve of her jumper. "Yeah, I'm okay. I'm fine."

"Are you sure?"

She nodded and pecked him on the cheek. "Sort your hair out, blondie, you look like a mess!"

He used his fingers to try and sort out his unruly hair. "Give me a chance, babe, I've just got back in."

Emma playfully shook her head. "It doesn't take much to have a little bit of pride in your appearance."

He smiled at her as she left the room. "How are you doing this morning, Dean?"

"I'm okay, mate. Anything interesting happen during your shift last night?"

"Nope, all quiet on the Western Front."

"That's something. Have you seen Pete?"

"No, me and Otis didn't see anyone."

The toilet flushed and Derek appeared in the hallway. Suited and booted like it was any other day. "Didn't mean to earwig but I saw Pete about ten minutes ago. He came in here looking for you when you were otherwise indisposed."

I smiled at Derek. "Otherwise indisposed, you make it sound so sinister. I was having a shower!"

Emma popped her head back into the room and pointed at Derek. "See, Jeff, look at Derek. He's still making an effort."

"You cheeky mare," he said, following her back out of the room.

"What was Pete like?" I asked Derek.

"He seemed fine to me. Why, is there something wrong?"

"We had a difference of opinion on something last night and we didn't part on good terms."

"Perhaps he just wanted to apologise. He wants you to go next door when you're ready."

"He can wait. I'm not doing anything until I've finished this cup of tea."

As if on cue, Sheila came out of the kitchen wearing a floral apron. "Did somebody want a cup of tea?"

"No thank you, Sheila," I said. "I've still got this one. By the way, where did you find the apron? I didn't realise we had one."

"I had it in my bag. I never know when I'm going to need one. Any tea for you, Derek?"

He smiled at her. "You know I can never say no to one of your brews."

"Why don't you two watch the TV? Have a look to see if there is any more on the news."

Derek and I sat down in front of the TV. It didn't take too long for me to lose myself in the horror of the images. After about ten minutes or so Pete came into the room.

"I've been waiting for you," he said.

"I was just coming."

"Yeah, I'm sure. Anyway, I can't blame you for not coming right away. I was a bit of an arse last night. I know you weren't being disrespectful or anything. I'm just finding this situation... difficult."

"Thanks, Pete. It means a lot. I know it's tough. We're all just trying to do our best."

"Well, as I said a couple of days ago, you're handling this better than me. So tell me, what's the plan for today?"

"There's over twenty of us. We need to occupy every single person here, even the kids."

"The kids?"

"They can look after Troy or help Nan and Sheila prepare food. There is lots to keep them occupied. The way I see it is that if someone is busy then they not going to be able to do something stupid and end up putting the rest of us in danger."

Pete nodded. "I like your thinking. What do you need me to do?"

"Just make sure you're ready to go outside when we get some daylight. We've got a lot of work to do."

We disassembled the barricade piece by piece and one by one we stepped outside into the crisp air. It was getting colder every day. I couldn't hear anything; no groaning zombies, no birdsong, no nothing. We walked slowly towards the car park. Thank God it was empty. We quickly set about blocking off our two entrances. We used Graeme's van to block the car park entrance and Nan's Mini Metro to block the small pathway on the other side of the grounds. It was by no means perfect and it wouldn't stop a person from getting in, but I was fairly certain that it would hold back any zombies that wanted to partake in a spot of trespassing.

As we were now relatively safe we split up into two groups. Graeme and Pavel started unloading all of the supplies from the vehicles, whilst Pete, Otis, Jeff and I went into the other block. The block was in itself exactly the same as mine, with six flats in total and two on each floor.

Otis stepped into the block. "What door first? Seven or Eight?"

"Does it matter, there's only two of them?" Pete said.

"Course it matters," Jeff said. "We don't need any more bad luck."

Pete shook his head. "Whatever."

"Seven," I said, looking at Otis, "it's my lucky number."

"Not you too!" Pete said, clearly not amused.

Otis knocked on Flat Seven's door and we all collectively held our breath. There was no answer. The door had a big frosted glass window in the middle of it and we couldn't see any movement behind it. Otis knocked again and again and there was nothing. He looked at the three of us and we all nodded. We had already made up our minds. If there was no response, we were going in.

My hands were sweating as I gripped the crowbar. I swung it hard into the frosted glass and the crowbar thudded against it, but it only cracked slightly. It was toughened and it wasn't going to go down without a fight. In the end I must have hit it about five times before it shattered and could be pushed through. I made a hell of a lot of noise trying to get in there. We would have made awful burglars, that's for sure. Luckily the place was empty. Whoever my neighbour was, wasn't fortunate enough to have been home when this thing started.

Just as we started to leave the flat we heard multiple footsteps coming down the stairs. The four of us fanned around the communal hallway with our weapons at the ready. It took us a few seconds to realise that the footsteps were far too light to belong to zombies, but we didn't stand down until we saw that it was a group of seven regular people, including the woman and little boy who had helped us escape from the car park the day before. She instantly recognised us and with a wave of her long slender hand, she put the rest of the group at ease.

The little boy furrowed his dark brow. "Do you know how much noise you made?" He was genuinely confused by how stupid we'd been.

The lady's pale skin reddened. "Theo! Don't be so rude."

I smiled and looked down at the young boy. He was short and skinny and had an Iron Man top on. "Sorry, that was my fault. I had no idea how strong the glass in the door was."

"That's okay. You didn't wake me up or anything. It was just really loud."

"Thank you for being so understanding, young man. My name is Dean, by the way. I live in Flat Five. And this lot are Pete, Otis and Jeff."

"I'm Tammy and this is my son Theo. We live on the first floor in Flat Nine. Why are you breaking into that flat?"

"We need to make sure that there are none of those things in them."

Theo's face lit up. "You mean zombies!"

"Well yeah, I suppose I do."

Tammy tucked her auburn hair behind her ear. "That makes sense. If I'd have known, I could have saved you the trouble though. The people who live there are on holiday at the moment."

I pointed across the hall to Flat Eight. "Do you know if anybody is in that one?"

A short, round man wearing a suit and a large lady in a green and purple dress popped their heads out from behind Tammy. The man started to speak and he had a heavy Nigerian accent. "My name is Harold and this is my wife, Blessing. We live in there. Tammy and Theo have been very kind in allowing us to stay with them, during this difficult time."

"Lucky you told us, Harold," Jeff said. "We were just about to break your door down next!"

"I would be most grateful if you didn't."

Jeff tried to suppress his grin. "Of course not, Harold."

"So where next then?" Otis asked.

"You don't have to worry about Flat Twelve," a young man with glasses said.

"That leaves Flats Ten and Eleven then," Pete said, "Have any of you checked on them?"

The young man laughed nervously. "Well, no. We've been staying in Tammy's, to be honest."

"Sorry, I didn't catch your name, mate," I said.

"Oh yeah. Sorry, that was my bad. I'm Jon and I live with these two lovely ladies," he said pointing behind him, "Tara and Poppy. We all go to Greenwich University."

"Okay, you lot, get back into Tammy's and we will check the last two flats out."

"Yeah, that's a great idea," Jon said.

They quickly went back into Tammy's flat, leaving the four of us standing in the hallway.

Jeff slapped me on the back. "Jesus, you didn't need to tell them twice, did you?"

"What do you know about the two other flats, Dean?" Otis asked.

"I know that the Johnsons live in Number Ten and a middle aged couple live in Number Eleven."

"That sounds straightforward then."

"Kind of... But, you know the body that is outside next to the broken squash racquet?"

"Yeah."

"Well, that was Mrs Johnson."

"I see. Well if Mr Johnson is okay, it probably won't be a good idea to tell him that you kind of killed his wife."

Jeff looked at me. "On the other hand he could be dead too."

"Or he could be a zombie," Pete said.

"Lads, all of those are distinct possibilities," I said, "But there is only one way to find out."

We climbed the one set of stairs to the first floor and stood outside of the Johnsons' flat. The door was big and heavy-looking and a silver number ten proudly sparkled above the small window that was in the middle of it. We knocked a couple of times but neither Mr Johnson nor anybody else came to answer. The crowbar was not going to be much help smashing the window as it was too far away from the latch. Already semi-prepared for this eventuality, we looked at Pete. He was our secret weapon, our very own 'battering ram'. I admit that it wasn't a great plan, but it didn't seem like we had any other options.

Flat Nine's door opened and Theo stuck his little head into the hallway. "Why don't you use this?" he said, tossing a key at Pete. "Mum looked after their plants when they went on holiday a few weeks ago."

Pete caught the key and put it in the lock. "Thanks."

"You're welcome."

Theo couldn't take his eyes off the Johnson's front door, he was mesmerised by it.

"Go back inside," Otis said to him in his most official voice.

Theo ignored him and carried on watching.

"Theo. Shut that door," I heard his mother say. The door instantly closed. No sane person messes with their mum.

We stood with our weapons at the ready. Pete slowly turned the key and pushed the door. The door opened into an immaculately kept hallway. We walked in. Slowly. Unlike Mr Trotter, the Johnsons kept a beautiful home. Nothing was out of place. As I looked around I saw Mr Johnson. Well, some of Mr Johnson anyway. His stripped carcass was lying by the living room door, there was no meat left on him.

I stopped in my tracks. "This doesn't feel right, lads."

"Of course it doesn't feel right," Pete said, "The poor bloke was eaten by his missus."

"But he couldn't have been. She was outside, there is no way a zombie could have opened the front door and—"

I noticed something that cut me off mid-sentence. Slowly walking towards us from inside the living room was the Johnson's four-year-old granddaughter. She had her hair in pigtails and couldn't have been much more than three foot tall. There was dried blood all over her hands and face, even her once yellow party dress was now stained a crimson brown. She was covered from head to toe in her granddad's blood. A morsel of her granddad's flesh fell from her mouth as a crooked smile appeared on her grey face; she was still hungry.

Since this all started I have seen some shit. Some absolutely terrifying shit, and my bones have been chilled more times than I can remember. But that moment; that moment was easily the worst. It is the most fucked up thing I have ever seen. A four-year-old girl, for fuck's sake. Seeing that girl literally knocked the wind out of all of us. But she was no longer a four-year-old girl and it was no time to get sentimental.

Pete gulped. "I don't think I can do it."

"Neither can I," said Otis.

"We have to," Jeff replied.

I approached her more than a little tentatively and swallowed hard. "We do."

Her black eyes locked in on me and I'm certain that she was looking forward to tucking right in. When she was only a few metres away from me she suddenly pounced. She had great speed and was easily the quickest one that I had come across. She came at me arms outstretched and I was lucky enough to just about side-step her. She thrashed at thin air as she hurtled past me. My good fortune was bad news for Pete, as she was now face to face with him. The fact that she was only a child had shocked him and left him totally unprepared for this eventuality. He was helpless and I was too far away to do anything about it. One cut or scratch and my brother was as good as dead.

Pete managed to take one step back. From out of nowhere Jeff had leapt into a flying kick and had somehow managed to connect with the little girl's body, sending her off course and crashing into the wall. Otis reacted the quickest and before she could pick herself up he had already started pummelling his baton into her small skull. Mercifully, it didn't take him long to kill her.

My big brother just stood there looking at her body; he was in a daze. "She was so young. I need to get back to my kids." And with that he left. Jeff started to follow him out.

"Leave him," I said. "He needs some time."

Jeff nodded. "Jesus, that was fucked up."

"I know, mate," Otis replied.

"She was only four," I said, "The worst thing is that I can't even remember her name."

Otis shook his head. "You're wrong, Dean. The worst thing is that I had to smash her head in."

Touché! I looked at her lifeless body. Even before all this had started I knew that it was a cruel world. Now it was even crueller.

As we left the Johnsons', Graeme and Pavel came up the stairs.

"What's wrong with Pete?" Graeme asked.

"We just had to kill one of them in there," I said.

"I don't want to sound heartless or anything, but so what?"

I looked at Jeff and Otis for a little help, but they remained silent. "Yeah well, the thing is, Graeme, it wasn't really like the others."

Graeme was a good few inches taller than me. He seemed to loom over me. "Well?"

"It was a young child. She'd already eaten her granddad and she was coming for us next... Pete's just taken it hard. That's all."

Graeme's face lost all colour and he seemed to shrink with my words. He rubbed his shaggy blond hair. "Blimey. No wonder he's run off. I never thought of kids getting infected too. That's scary, isn't it, Pavel?"

Pavel didn't say anything; he just adjusted his blue beanie hat and shrugged his shoulders. He didn't really show much emotion and so I wasn't really surprised that he didn't now. The guy was a machine.

"If you two are all done, do you mind stepping in for Pete please?" I asked.

"Is fine for me," Pavel said.

"Yeah no problem, Dean. Doesn't sound like it can be any worse than what you've just described," Graeme said.

The five of us stood on the second floor ready to go into Flat Eleven. Graeme armed with a hammer and Pavel with one of my bread knives. We could hear a dull thud coming out of the flat.

Otis look puzzled. "What's that noise?"

Jeff shook his head. "I don't know, but it does sound familiar."

I racked my brains trying to work it out. Was that music? It wasn't too loud to disturb the neighbours but it was definitely there. "I think it's music."

"You're right. It sounds like dance music," Jeff replied.

"That's not what I call music," Graeme said.

"Someone must be home then."

Otis looked at all of us and shrugged his shoulders. "Here goes." He knocked on the door. Nobody answered. "Hello, is anybody in there?" But there still wasn't any answer. He shook his head. "This is not good, lads. Nobody would be partying at a time like this."

"Maybe someone just left the radio on," Graeme said.

"Someone is definitely in there," Jeff replied. "I'm sure I can hear them moving around."

I knelt down and tried to peer through the letterbox. I couldn't see a thing as it was one of those premium ones with brushes on it.

Graeme examined the door and nodded. "A shoulder in the right place will open that."

So, this was it. This was the final flat. We were one flat away from relative safety. Graeme took a few steps back. He was a powerful man and I was certain that he was going to make short work of the door. He blew out his cheeks and launched himself at it shoulder first. The doorframe splintered under his weight and the door opened with such force that it slammed into the inside wall. Graeme, not being totally prepared for this, lost his balance and fell into the flat. The noise of the door slamming into the wall was incredible. We'd lost the element of surprise. The four of us leapt over him ready to face the unknown.

I heard them before I saw them. My ears were confronted by a mixture of techno music and moaning zombies. I swear it was that Zombie Nation tune blaring out of the living room as a group of leather-clad male, make-up wearing zombies in various states of undress came straight for us, followed by another load in dirty white vests and stonewash jeans. It was like we had gate-crashed a joint Kiss and Right Said Fred convention. I was expecting a lot of things when that door opened, but I certainly wasn't expecting that.

There were twelve of them and the first few came at us pretty quickly. The first zombie lunged at Otis, it was naked from the waist up and there was a large bite mark on its shoulder. Otis swung his baton into the side of its head. He sent it crashing to the ground, Pavel then hacked at its neck with my bread knife like a crazy man. His hands were covered in blood when the head eventually separated from the body. I clubbed the next one in the face with my crowbar and Otis finished it off as it lay dazed on the floor. We had less and less room to manoeuvre in as the rest of them came into the hallway. It got to the point where there wasn't enough room for any of us and we had to split up.

I'm not exactly sure where everybody went, but Jeff and I ended up in a brothel-like master bedroom, which was covered in black and red flocked wallpaper, with a naked Gene Simmons and two fully clothed Richard Fairbrasses. Gene Simmons had most of his left calf missing and was dragging his left leg behind him and was easy pickings for me to smash into oblivion. Jeff tried to fire off a few rounds from the nail gun, but it jammed and was useless. He threw it at Richard Fairbrass number one and despite hitting him in the head, didn't do him any damage.

Jeff and I both climbed onto the bed to put a little distance between them and us. I could hear shouting coming from outside the room, but I couldn't tell who it was coming from. Jeff was frantically looking around the room for a weapon but he couldn't get his hands on anything. I passed him the crowbar and he looked at me like I was mad.

"Get ready!" I shouted, picking up the duvet.

"Eh?"

It was too late for me to answer. I was already flying through the air with the duvet underneath my outstretched arms and body. I landed on top of Richard Fairbrass One and we both crashed into the ground, with only the duvet in between us. It did the trick as it was thick enough to stop me from getting scratched or bitten.

Lucky for me, Jeff is more than just a pretty face and he immediately realised what I was on about. He quickly took care of Richard Fairbrass Two and sent it to the floor. My Fairbrass was still thrashing around under the bedcover and it was all that I could do just to keep it there. I somehow managed to straddle its chest and I knew that I now had my chance. It managed to uncover its head just as I drove my elbow into its temple. The ferocity of the blow caused my elbow to scream with pain, but it was worth it as the zombie was momentarily stunned. Like a flash I got to my feet and with absolutely no hesitation whatsoever I drove the heel of my foot into its nose. Its nasal bone ruptured under the force and then the blood came. It started thrashing around on the floor as the blood gushed out of its nose. It stopped moving after my next stamp. But it wasn't dead just yet, so I kept on going until I was absolutely certain.

In the living room I saw Otis finishing off another member of Kiss with his baton, whilst Pavel and Jeff were busy with the last one in the flat, but I couldn't see Graeme anywhere. I ran into the communal area and that's when I saw him. My step-dad was lying dead on the floor with two zombies gorging themselves on him. His entrails were hanging out of his body and I was enveloped by rage. I saw his hammer on the floor and I grabbed it. I screamed as I charged into them.

The first one of them was too busy eating to acknowledge my presence and I struck the hammer into the back of his head. The tool crashed into its skull and when I pulled it out its liquefied brains started to leak out of the hole. In the same backwards motion I then slammed the hammer into the other one. However, with my back to the beast I wasn't able to connect properly and I only managed to hit it in the shoulder. The blow had no effect on it and I didn't have enough time to reset myself and strike it again.

It jumped on me and forced me up against the wall. The impact winded me and I dropped the hammer. I was face to face with pure evil. I couldn't free myself from its hold; in fact it was all I could do to just keep its mouth away from me. It had impressive strength and it didn't take long for me to tire. I could feel its fetid breath against my face as it got closer to my throat. I honestly believed that this was it; that this was the end. It tried to sink its teeth into me and I struggled against it one last time. It took all of my resolve and my last ounce of strength, but I was able to hold it off. In the corner of my eye, I saw Jeff come out of the flat. I will always be grateful to him for clobbering it with the crowbar. The impact caused it to loosen its grip and then Jeff sent it into the next life.

I looked at Graeme's mutilated corpse and slumped to the floor. I had failed Steve and now I had failed him. Another member of my family was dead.

CHAPTER FOURTEEN

My mum was distraught. Yesterday she lost a son and a daughter-in-law and today she lost her husband. Nan stayed with her in the vain hope that she could comfort her. To be honest the rest of my family wasn't faring much better. Graeme was a good man and he had been a father to all of us. I couldn't help but wonder who was going to be next.

"Let me see him, Julie," I said as she opened Flat Six's front door.

She used her large frame to block my path into the flat. "Pete doesn't want to see anyone."

"I know he thinks this is his fault. I just want to tell him that it isn't."

She looked exhausted and her curly strawberry blonde hair was not looking its best. "I know you mean well. But he isn't up to it. He's in quite a state."

"That's exactly why you should let me in. Please, Julie. I just want to help him."

She nodded. "Okay. But if he gets annoyed, you better be the one taking the blame."

I followed her into the flat. Layout wise, it was the mirror image of my own. Decorating wise, it couldn't have been more different. Where my flat had oak flooring, this one had a blue, threadbare carpet. Where my walls were covered in light and airy colours, these walls were papered in dark blues and purples.

I opened the bedroom door without knocking. Pete was lying in the double bed, his bulk hidden by the covers that were pulled up to his neck.

He looked at me with red eyes. "I told her that I didn't want to see anyone."

"She tried to stop me, but I wouldn't take no for an answer."

"Graeme's dead because of me."

"It's not your fault, Pete. It really isn't."

"I fucked up again, Dean. Just like I did with Frank. Only this time one of us died."

"You didn't fuck up. I was the one that asked him to help. Not you."

"Don't be a prick, Dean. You only asked because I walked off."

I shook my head. "Don't do this to yourself. It won't help you and it won't help the situation."

"Our Mum's husband is dead because I can't handle the pressure."

"Come on, Pete. The zombies killed him, not you!"

"The man who brought us up is dead because of me."

"Fine, whatever you want to think. Maybe you're right. Maybe if you kept it together, then Graeme would be okay. But maybe, just maybe, we would all be mourning your loss instead."

Pete was silent.

"I loved Graeme, but I'd trade him for you in a heartbeat. You're my brother, Pete. I'm devastated that he's gone, but I'm thankful that I still have you…. And you know what? I think that he would have made that sacrifice for you if he was given the choice. You said it yourself, he brought us up! There is no way that he would want Mum to lose another son, or PJ and Justin to lose their father."

Pete was crying now, but I managed to fight back my own tears.

"Do you think that I'm okay? I'm not, Pete. I'm a mess too. I want to curl up into a ball and just grieve for Steve, Graeme and Sandra. To be honest, I want to grieve for the whole bloody world. But I can't, because we're not safe and we still have so many things to do."

I paused and let my brother continue to cry. It broke my heart. This beast of a man, somebody I spent my whole life idolising, was beaten. He was a shadow of his former self.

"I don't care how bad things get and how awful that I feel; I'm not giving up. I don't want to lose anyone else. Take the rest of the day and try and get your head straight for tomorrow, because I need you, Pete. I need you to be the man that I always thought you were."

Organisation was always going to be the key to our survival and we all needed to work together. Emma, Otis and Sarah went flat to flat and invited everybody to a meeting at twelve-thirty pm in my flat. They did that whilst Jeff and I took on the solemn task of burying Graeme.

"Any idea where?" Jeff asked as we walked back into the green communal grounds.

"I'm not sure, mate, but we will know it when we see it."

And I was right. As soon as I saw the spot I was sure. "Over there," I said pointing at a large tree right by the middle of the perimeter fence.

Jeff started to nod at me. "An oak tree. Very apt."

We dug for a good hour. Now that was hard graft. I don't think that we managed to dig the full six feet down, but we got close. We marked his grave by nailing two pieces of wood into a cross. When everything was in place I went back into the block to get everyone. I found Emma comforting Mum in my living room.

I went up to my mum and put my arms around her small body. "We're ready."

She nodded against my chest.

"I tried to help him, but I was too late."

She nodded. "I know you did."

"I'm really sorry, Mum. I wish I could have done more."

Everyone except for Pete, Julie and the children gathered around Graeme's final resting place. Derek led with a small prayer as we tried to ignore the zombies shuffling along outside, banging into the wooden fence. It was a truly surreal experience. My mum sat by his grave for some time after and it was only my nan's prompting that eventually got her to come back inside.

By meeting time, the flat was packed. Most people came and our little group of survivors amounted to twenty-eight people. Julie took all of the children across the hall into Flat Six and it was nice to see Abby and Pete's children make Theo feel welcome. We started off the meeting by introducing ourselves, and Sheila made herself busy by preparing drinks for everybody.

It really is a black stain on city living that you do not know your neighbours. I had only seen the other people from the next block on a few occasions and before that day I never even knew their names. As first impressions go, I think that we all acquitted ourselves well.

Tammy raised her hand. "I just want to extend our thanks to you all for making this place safe."

"You're welcome, Tammy," I said.

"I also wanted to say that I am sorry for your loss. Graeme will be in my prayers tonight."

Mum smiled weakly at her. "Thank you."

Harold raised his hand. He was immaculately dressed in a suit and tie. My first thought was that Derek would like him. "I would very much like to echo what Tammy has just said. Dean, can you guarantee that nothing will get through the fence?"

"I'm afraid that there are no guarantees here, Harold. We could certainly try and do more to it over the next few days."

Derek cleared his throat. "I would like to raise the issue of food now if I may?"

"Of course, Derek, go on."

"I think that we should pool all of our supplies."

Harold, Blessing and Tammy all nodded.

"What about you three?" Derek said, pointing at the students.

Jon was jolted into the moment. "Yeah, yeah of course," he said pushing his glasses up his nose. "It's just that we don't have that much in."

Derek eyed him suspiciously.

"Whatever you've got will be fine," I said. "We're probably going to need to go on a supply run at some point."

"But didn't the like, Prime Minister say that everything was like going to be okay by Sunday?" Poppy asked as she twiddled with her long red hair.

I nodded. "He did, but it doesn't mean that we can't make plans. Just in case."

Derek stood up from his chair. "I agree, Dean. It makes perfect sense. If there are no objections I would like to volunteer to be the camp's quartermaster. I have experience in this kind of thing."

I looked around the room, there didn't look like there were any. "Go for it, Derek. Get whoever you want to help you."

We discussed a few more matters and by the end of the meeting everybody had a job; if you weren't down to count or cook, then you were cleaning.

Cleaning up mutilated bodies is not for the faint-hearted and the less said about it the better. Needless to say there was a lot of work to be done. We cleaned blood off the walls and we ripped up a lot of carpet. We even removed all of the rancid food from Mr Trotter's place. The reality was that if we were all going to be here for a while then we needed to make the most of all of the available space. It would be an understatement to say that we had a lot of rubbish, and as we knew that the dustman wouldn't be turning up anytime soon we were responsible for getting rid of it all ourselves.

Burying Graeme's body was bad, but that was nothing compared to having to carry the festering zombie bodies out of the block and into the makeshift fire pit situated in the car park. The remains of each zombie consisted of a demolished skull, sagging grey skin and contorted limbs. They were not pretty sights. As bad as they all were, I found Mr Trotter's body the worst by quite some distance. I don't know if it was because he had been dead the longest or because he was the first one that I had killed. I was actually doing okay until I saw his Thomas the Tank Engine Cap on the floor; looking at it was like having a scab ripped off a wound as it brought the whole episode from that day back to me.

Without question the worst and easily the most haunting part of that afternoon was trying to burn their bodies. It is not as easy trying to burn a human body as what you might think. The average body is nearly sixty percent water and it takes a long time for all of that to evaporate and leave the rest of it to turn to ash. A proper crematorium burns at about eleven hundred degrees centigrade for over a couple of hours and even then some portions of the pelvis, skull and teeth may not be totally gone. Obviously we didn't have a proper crematorium; but what we lacked in facilities we more than made up for in petrol.

It took a while for the fire to properly take hold, but eventually it did and a few of us stood by and watched it set about its work. I couldn't help but stare as the flames ravaged Mr Trotter's body. It took about twenty seconds for his face to melt away and become unrecognisable but his body was still pretty much intact for a good hour. We needed to burn a lot of bodies that afternoon and I honestly couldn't tell you how many of them there were. For a while I was actually quite worried that our rancid bonfire might attract more unwanted guests, but it didn't and we carried on adding bodies and petrol to the fire.

It didn't take long for the atrocious smell of putrid burning flesh to take me back to the day before in Bexley. As I looked at the flames I couldn't help but think of Steve being pulled back into the fire at the same time as being eaten alive. My thoughts were only interrupted when I heard a loud crash coming from the other side of the gardens.

"Bloody hell! What was that?" Jeff said.

"God knows," I said. "But whatever it was it came from the other side of the grounds."

We all stopped what we were doing and ran from one side of the grounds to the other to where the noise came from. We gathered in a line and gawked at the scene. Somebody had driven a brown Vauxhall Cavalier into the back of the Mini Metro. The large saloon car made short work of the small hatchback and pushed it back into the gardens, taking its place in the process. The bigger car had only some minor damage on the bumper, but the Mini Metro looked like it had been totalled. We'd be lucky if it could be driven again.

"What a dick!" Jeff said.

We were lucky that the makeshift barrier still appeared to be in place. Wedged in between the two cars was a half crushed zombie. It didn't seem the least bit concerned that it no longer had the use of its legs, as it kept on waving its arms around trying to get the person that had crushed it with the car. That person was already out of the car holding a baseball bat. He was less than average height, no more than five foot seven, but he was as wide as he was tall, full of muscles, with tattoos all over his arms and a closely shaved head. I was trying to place him as he swung the bat through the zombie's head, but I couldn't quite do it. It wasn't until he looked at us all and I saw his face that I knew who he was.

"What are you doing, Shane?" I shouted.

"A thank you for killin' that thing would be nice," he replied in his gruff cockney accent.

"You've destroyed my nan's car."

He climbed over the cars and stood directly in front of me. "Don't get your knickers in a twist, Baker. It's a piece of fucking shit!"

"You're lucky that the barrier is still in place."

"Am I? And what would you do if it wasn't?"

I didn't say anything. I just stared at him.

He started to laugh. "Cheer up, Baker. Where's me mum and dad?"

"They're fine. They're upstairs in their flat."

The rest of the group continued to stare at him as he walked past and headed towards the block.

"Who was that?" Jeff asked.

I shook my head. "Shane, he's Eddie and Iris's son."

"Looks like I was right a minute ago."

"What about?"

"He is obviously a dick."

Shane's arrival might have been good for Eddie and Iris, but it certainly wasn't going to be good for the rest of us. He wasn't what you would call a stand-up guy; he was a loutish bully who would take advantage of his mum and dad and belittle anybody else around him. A few years before all of this, he got in the habit of harassing Mr Trotter whenever he saw him and he only stopped after the police had got involved. He had always been quite wary of me and his leering had always made Sarah feel quite uncomfortable. Like most parents they put up with it because he was their child, but they surely must have known what kind of person he was. I was not looking forward to him being around.

In any case, not long after Shane's dramatic entrance we all got back to work and I soon forgot all about him. The fire had reduced all of the bodies to a large pile of ash. I looked on at the embers slowly burning themselves out and felt a strange combination of relief and sadness. I eventually turned my back on the smouldering ash and walked upstairs.

It had been another bad day and every one of us could have given their own reason as to why. The day had been filled with killing, cleaning and burning and because of this, despite all of Sarah, Sheila and Magda's hard work in the kitchen, eating dinner felt more like a chore rather than something to be enjoyed. Don't get me wrong, the food was good but not even Gordon Ramsey's Michelin-starred cuisine would have been able to lift the mood. We ate in shifts and during this time the TV and the BBC's news team in particular were our constant companions. Reports of people coming back from the dead had intensified and fires were being reported all over the country; Bexley Village (or what was left of it) was one of the locations mentioned. I wouldn't say that the country was on the verge of collapse, but it was bloody well close.

Shane's arrival had seen Bernie evicted from Eddie and Iris's and he decided to set up home on the ground floor in Flat Two, directly opposite Mr Trotter's. He didn't care about the smell of stale smoke and was happy to be by himself down there. He was a brave man, as there is no way that I would have wanted to have cozied up on the ground floor.

All in all we had got to the end of another awful day. I'm not sure what time I went to bed or at what time I finally fell asleep. Grief and guilt plagued my dreams all night long, as I relived Steve's and Graeme's deaths over and over again. When Steve's cries faded they were instantly replaced by Graeme's and vice versa. At some point my subconscious must have grown tired of torturing me as all of a sudden I was standing in front of the smouldering fire pit. The fire had left its mark on the ground, but the events of the last few days had left their mark on the deepest reaches of my soul.

CHAPTER FIFTEEN

S arah and I (don't forget Troy) woke up at around
six am on Saturday and joined Jeff, Emma and Otis
in the living room watching the news.

"You guys should see this," Otis said pointing to
the TV.

"What's going on?" Sarah asked.

"Just watch."

I turned my attention to the screen. The high-def-
inition image did nothing for the newsman's appearance as you could make out every line and wrinkle on
his face. His crow's feet were more like spider legs and
the bags under his eyes resembled bin liners.

"How long has that bloke been in the studio?" I asked.

"He's been there since day one," Jeff said.

"And now back to our breaking news story. The BBC has received a leaked government document that explicitly states that the dead are coming back to life and attacking people. The Prime Minister had previously stated that a viral infection was the cause of serious mental illness, but doubt has now been shed on his comments by the revelations found in this document. The government are yet to comment on the veracity of this document, but the BBC has no reason to doubt its authenticity. These are worrying times—"

Jeff whistled. "Now that's an understatement!"

I shook my head. "This is really bad."

"Of course it is. But it's not like we didn't know what was happening already."

"That's not the problem, mate. Now other people know and that's going to make it even more difficult for us to survive—"

"Because more people are going to try and get the supplies," Otis said, finishing off my sentence.

"Our only hope is that the government keep their mouths shut about it. The whole country will go into meltdown as soon as it's confirmed."

Sarah put her hand on mine. "You need to go out again, don't you?"

"I'm afraid so. Eltham is full of people and if we don't try and take what we can now, there might not be anything left later."

Jeff stood up. "Let's just hope we're not too late."

Otis and Jeff went knocking for volunteers, whilst Pavel and I sorted out our transportation. We needed to use Graeme's van, but we also needed to keep the integrity of the perimeter.

I looked around the car park. "How about we just put a couple of cars side by side, whilst we use the van?"

Pavel shook his head. "No, Dean. Is not safe."

"I don't really want to use the cars though, as we won't be able to get enough food into them."

A smile came across his face. "I have better idea. Give five minutes."

With that he went off and left me standing in the car park. It didn't take long for me to walk over to the fire pit. I was struck by just how much ash there was in it. I know we burnt a lot of bodies, but what was left just didn't seem real.

True to his word, Pavel was back in less than five minutes. He was holding a large screwdriver. "Look over fence."

I followed him and peered over the fence.

Pavel pointed at a rusting beige Volkswagen campervan that was about one hundred metres down the
road. "We use that."

I was startled by Pete's voice coming from behind
me. "What are you two up to?"

I turned and saw him bounding towards me wearing his trusty black leather trench coat. A large smile
spread across my face.

"What are you smiling at?"

"I wasn't expecting you to come."

"Well here I am."

"I'm glad you're here."

"Stop acting like a bird and tell me what you're up
to."

"Oh yeah, sorry. We've just spotted our wheels."

"Aren't we using the van?"

"No, don't think of it as a van anymore. Just think
of it as a giant gate."

"Whatever you say."

Before I could reply, Otis appeared in his full uniform, followed by Jeff, again wearing my black duffel
coat. No doubt he had another of my England football
shirts underneath it too.

"Great news," Jeff said.

"What is?" Pete asked.

"Jon and Shane are coming with us."

"What, Shane's coming?" I said.

"Yeah, he said he wanted to help."

"I never saw that coming."

"Jeff told me that you didn't like him," Pete said. "You could be wrong about him, you know?"

Jeff laughed. "Meow!"

"What? He could be!"

"Let's hope I am," I said. "We need everybody pulling in the same direction."

Pavel tapped me on the shoulder. "Dean, coast is clear. We must go now."

"Let's do it."

Pavel and I walked up to the back of the van and got into position. Jeff moved it just enough for the pair of us to get through and within seconds we were on North Park covering the hundred metres or so to the campervan as quickly as we could. Our presence caught the attention of eight zombies that were standing in the garden of a large detached house that the camper was parked outside of. Two of us against eight of them were not good odds, so time really was of the essence. Pavel instinctively pulled the handle on the driver's side door and it opened up straight away. He got in, leant over and unlocked the passenger door and I quickly joined him in there. We should have realised that something probably wasn't quite right as nobody leaves a vehicle unlocked in London.

I heard a noise coming from the back of the vehicle and I quickly turned around. Someone or something was lying underneath an old blanket.

Sweat instantly beaded on my brow. "Fuck!"

Pavel turned toward me in the seat. "What, Dean? What?"

"Just start the thing, Pavel. I will deal with this," I said as I climbed over the seat.

Pavel set about his work as I approached the blanket. There wasn't enough room for me to stand up straight, so I ended up doing some kind of weird, squat walk, which I'm sure wasn't very dignified. As I got closer I unwittingly kicked a glass bottle into the blanket and I heard a groan. Reflexively, I raised my crowbar, ready to strike the bejesus out of whatever was under there. As I went to bring it down I heard a dry, croaky voice come from under the blanket.

"Who's there?"

I was taken aback by the voice. I was pretty certain that zombies didn't speak, but I didn't yet lower my crowbar. My silence caused the person under the blanket to shuffle around and poke his head out from underneath it. The man had a shock of salt and pepper hair and was seriously pale. He looked like he was frozen through. He saw my crowbar at the ready and I could see the fear in his bloodshot eyes.

He instantly sat up. "I didn't mean to use your van, man. You didn't lock it. Those things were everywhere and I needed somewhere to crash."

His breath reeked of alcohol and that's when I noticed that I had kicked a whisky bottle into him.

Ignoring him, I looked out of the window and I could see that we were on the radar of quite a few more of the local zombies. It wasn't going to be long before we were surrounded.

I never took my eyes off the man. "How much longer, Pavel? We are running out of time here."

I heard some commotion as he busted the ignition lock out of the column. "Dean, is time to sit down."

I sat on the dirty orange camper sofa as Pavel inserted the screwdriver under where the lock used to be. He turned the screwdriver and the old van somehow spluttered to life.

"Where the hell are you taking me?" the man asked.

Before I had a chance to reply, Pavel was already turning the vehicle into the communal drive. I opened the camper door and looked at the man. "I'm Dean and this place is my home."

Pete came over to see who I was talking to. "Who's the tramp?"

I don't think that I could have described him any better myself. He was wearing a crumpled suit under a large dirty overcoat and his white shirt had all sorts of stains on it. His voice was a little less croaky when it replied, "The name's Gerry and until a couple of days ago I was the absolute opposite of a tramp."

"Sounds like you have a tale to tell then. How did you end up in this campervan?"

"Well, you're right about that, I do have quite a tale. But to cut a long story short let's just say that the good people of Eltham weren't willing to open up their doors to me. I needed to hide from those things out there and thank God that the camper was unlocked."

He'd spent over twenty four hours in the van with only a bottle of whisky for company and he was not in good shape at all. He stank of booze and he didn't look too good, but it didn't feel like there was anything threatening about him. He just seemed like somebody that needed our help. And one thing was for sure; I would have wanted somebody to do the same for me and mine if we were ever in that situation. I know that I didn't know him from Adam, but I felt compelled to take him in. In fairness, him being in the camper had kind of already made the decision for me. Call me crazy, but what else could I have done? It's not like I could have just turfed him back out on to the street.

I didn't have the time to run the rule over him myself, so I did the next best thing and took him to Derek, who was just about to take Troy out for a quick walk around the grounds.

Troy smelt Gerry and wagged his tail.

"Gerry, that's Troy and this is Derek," I said.

"And what rock did you crawl up from under?" Derek said, extending his hand and smiling.

Gerry took Derek's hand and shook it vigorously. "Ah, it's a long story. Listen, I don't mean to be rude or anything, but I'm desperate for the bathroom."

I pointed at my front door. "Go into the hall and it's your first door on the right."

He pushed the door open, but turned around before he went inside. "Look, Dean, I just wanted to say thank you for taking me in."

"Gerry, you don't need to say a thing. Just get yourself cleaned up and we can catch up later."

After he walked into the flat, I motioned Derek to come closer to me. "I know he looks a bit rough, but I think he's okay. Can you check him out please?"

"Leave it to me, Dean. You don't have to worry."

Less than five minutes later I was sitting in the campervan on the way to the local Sainsbury's.

"At least it's going to be quiet for a Saturday," Jon said as he played with his glasses.

Jeff and I laughed and I found myself warming to the young student.

"What are you talking about, you bell end?" Shane said disgustedly, not really understanding Jon's joke as he rubbed his runny nose.

"Saturday's usually the busiest shopping day of the week, isn't it?" Jon said.

"That's true," said Jeff, "I'm gutted that the football's cancelled!"

It was Jon's turn to laugh at Jeff's joke, but Shane didn't find it remotely funny. "I can't believe I volunteered to help you mugs."

Very awkward. Nobody said another word for the remainder of the journey, which was luckily less than two minutes as the Sainsbury's was pretty much on our doorstep and that was definitely one of the benefits about living so close to the high street.

The campervan and the X5 sat side-by-side idling in the middle of the large tarmac car park about fifty metres away from the old supermarket. Two untidy rows of shopping trolleys were parked in front of the run-down two-storey red brick building. Its once proud glass entrance was destroyed.

Somebody had already beaten us to the place.

Pete shook his head. "Some bastard has only gone and ram-raided the place."

I turned to face Pete. "I know it doesn't look good but it's a big place. There's no telling how much stuff is still left in there."

We parked the camper and Pete's X5 as close to the building as we could and everybody except Jon got out; he was on lookout duty. There were mutilated bodies all around the front of the building; some had their heads cut off, but most were just the spent leftovers of what the dead didn't eat. There were no flies or maggots to be seen. Whatever had gone down here had happened recently. We grabbed our trolleys and manoeuvred past the bodies. As I struggled to get past one, I got half a number plate caught under one of the front wheels of the trolley. Aside from my cursing, the only noise that could be heard was our own footsteps on the broken glass as we walked through the smashed front entrance and into the supermarket.

The foyer was no better. We were greeted by tens of slaughtered bodies, some lying on beds of blood-stained newspapers and others just on the cold white tiled floor. There was even a body propped up against boxes of special offer washing powder. Blood had pooled in the middle of the entryway like a giant red welcome mat and multiple red footprints led away from it and into the store.

"Everybody be careful," I said as I walked through the puddle and we went our separate ways.

We were all on high alert as we went deeper into the store. The further we went into it, the less bodies that we came across, but there was something off about them; something that wasn't quite right. I couldn't quite put my finger on it so I just got on with the task at hand and started to fill my trolley. A lot of stuff had already been taken but there was still an awful lot there for us too. Tinned food, bottled water and medicine were our priorities, but we took pretty much anything else that could have been kept indefinitely. Things were progressing quite well and I was really pleased with how everybody was working together, even Shane seemed to be working for the cause.

I bumped into Otis in the middle of my fourth trolley load just as the uneasiness about the dead bodies returned to me.

I looked at the corpse of a middle-aged female shop assistant. "Something is not quite right about some of these bodies."

"I know. I've been having the same feelings myself," he replied.

Otis stopped filling his trolley and stared at the body. She was lying face down in a pool of her own blood. He bent down and with some effort rolled the body onto its back. It was awful, her neck had been slashed and her face was contorted with terror. After only a few seconds he spoke in a very serious tone. "This woman wasn't a zombie, and she wasn't killed by one either."

As soon as he said it I realised what had been staring me in the face all along; I took a deep breath. "Jesus Christ, Otis! She was killed by a person. A proper fucking person!"

"We have to hurry up. These people weren't messing around with her. They probably killed her and anybody else who was in their way. Look how much stuff is left. They could be back any minute and God knows how many of them there are."

I nodded. "Ok. The camper has a lot in it anyway and we've surely got enough food for a couple of weeks."

We both filled the rest of our trolleys with whatever was on the shelf next to us and we hurried back to the entrance. Jeff and Pete were the only two still inside when we got back to the vehicles. I went back inside to get them, whilst Otis and the others put the rest of the goods into the van.

"Jeff. Pete. Hurry up! We've got to go," I shouted.

"What's the rush?" I heard Jeff say.

"I'll explain later. We've just got to go!"

Jeff came running down the aisle with a half filled trolley, but Pete was nowhere to be seen.

"Jeff, where's Pete?"

"I don't know. He's in here somewhere."

I shouted again, "Pete! C'mon, hurry up!" and then looked at Jeff. "Get that stuff into the camper and make sure that it leaves as soon as it is full. Pete and I will follow in the X5."

Jeff nodded and headed towards the exit. I called Pete's name again and walked along the middle of the supermarket methodically checking each aisle. Where the bloody hell was he? I saw a door behind the deli counter and I noticed something move behind it.

"Pete, fucking hell! I can see you behind the door. Hurry up! We've really got to go."

He never replied. But there was no more movement behind the door. I did not like this one bit. In my rush to go back inside and get Jeff and Pete I'd left my crowbar in the trolley. I looked around the counter and I saw a pretty useful looking meat cleaver. It must have been about eight inches long and about three inches wide and when I picked it up it certainly had some weight to it. I crept closer to the door and strained to look through the window. It was dark in there so it was difficult to make anything out. Then out of the corner of my eye I saw some movement.

It wasn't much, but I now knew something was definitely in there. I put my hand on the handle and slowly opened the door. The door creaked as it opened and I saw a bit more movement in the same area again. I heard muffled breathing, so I raised the meat cleaver in my right hand and searched for the light switch with my left. When I found it, I instantly turned it on. The brilliant white light immediately lit up the room and I saw exactly where Pete was. He was sitting on a chair in the corner of the room with two women standing behind him; both of them were holding pretty large knives with the older one holding her blade to his throat. They looked like sisters, as both of them had the same skin tone and were wearing headscarves. That wasn't the only similarity as both of their Sainsbury's uniforms were covered in blood. Neither of them were particularly big; combined, they probably wouldn't have weighed as much as Pete, and it just showed the advantage that a couple of good weapons can give you.

I surveyed the scene, paying careful attention to Pete. He didn't seem to be injured, but he was clearly scared. I didn't blame him, the one holding the knife looked like she had a touch of crazy in her eyes. Pete was trembling in his seat, but she was steady with her blade.

"Look, we don't want any trouble," I said. "We just came to get some food. All we want to do is to get back to our family."

Neither of them said anything; they both just stood there, staring at me.

"Please just let him go. He's got a wife and two little boys that are counting on him."

The eyes of the younger one started to soften, but the older one's grip remained steady. I pressed on.

"Our mum has already lost one son since this all started, please don't take another one away from her."

I was sure that I was getting through to them; they clearly weren't killers, but something had happened here.

"Whatever happened here before was nothing to do with us. We've only been here for twenty minutes or so."

The two of them exchanged glances; they were obviously weighing up my words.

"I think whoever was here before will be back and I have no idea when that will be. I need to get my big brother out of here and get back home. Please let him go."

They looked at each other again and the one with the knife to Pete's throat slowly started to lower it. That was until she heard Jeff calling out to me and it went straight back into position.

"There you are. I bet Pete's in there eating all the luncheon meat. Come on, let's get going. The others have already left in the campervan."

I didn't say anything. I just stood in the doorway with my back to him; he had no idea what he had interrupted. "Well come on, what's the hold up?"

"Jeff, can you give us five minutes please?" I said as calmly as I could.

"Five minutes. What do you need five minutes for? You said we needed to get out of here." He walked up behind me. "What's going on in there?" As he spoke he squeezed past me and into the room. "Bloody hell!" he croaked when he saw Pete with the knife to his throat.

I ignored his profanity and carried on speaking to the women, "Excuse our brother-in-law's interruption."

Jeff looked at Pete's captors and recognition appeared in his eyes. "Are you two Tony Hassan's girls?"

The older one replied, "No," immediately, but it was clear that she was lying.

"I used to come in the dry cleaners all the time, I'm sure I've seen you both in there before."

It was clear the younger one wanted to say something, but she didn't want to upset her older sister. Undeterred Jeff continued, "I was very sad when he passed away, he was a really lovely man."

That comment cracked the younger one; I could see the tears form in her eyes. Jeff was on a roll. "Selma, isn't it?" he said pointing at the older one, "Didn't you used to go to school with my wife, Emma? Yeah that's right, she's Emma Wilson now, but she was Baker then. Your dad always used to make a fuss of her when we came in the shop."

He'd done it, she removed the knife from Pete's throat and my older brother bolted out of the seat and ran to our side of the room. Jeff was a master. He'd taken the fight out of both of them, but he wasn't finished there. "You might think that I'm going to say something strange, but Emma would never forgive me unless I asked this. Do you want to come back with us?"

Pete's eyes nearly bulged out of his head. "What the fuck are you saying? They're both fucking mental; they were going to slit my throat, for fuck's sake."

I interjected. "Pete, I understand what you're saying but if they are friends of Emma's we've got to give them the offer." I looked at the sisters and said my next words directly to them. "I know you didn't want to hurt him and that you were only trying to protect yourselves after what happened here before. I've got no problem with you both coming back to ours, if you want to."

"What do you mean, what happened here before?" Pete said.

Selma averted her gaze. "There were ten of us hiding in here until early this morning. Loads of those crazy people were outside. Then a few hours ago a group of men drove a van into the front of the store. They killed all of the crazy people in the car park and we thought that they were here to rescue us... but they weren't. They took what they wanted and killed the people that were here with us. So we just hid in this room. We heard you all arrive and we were afraid that they were back and that they would find us. When he came in here... We just panicked."

Jeff nodded. "I think we can understand why you did what you did. You can come back with us if you want to. Can't they, Pete?"

"I suppose so."

"Look," I said. "We really need to go now, because those animals could come back at any minute."

Selma looked at us. "We don't know you. We're going to take our chances here."

Her younger sister looked shocked at her response. "But, Selma—"

"Be quiet, Semra."

I looked at Jeff and shrugged my shoulders. "Okay, fine. Good luck to you both. Thank you for not slitting my brother's throat and everything, but we're off."

Pete and I turned around, but Jeff faltered. "Jeff, we can't force them. We've got to go."

He eventually turned around and followed us out of the room. We could hear the sisters arguing behind us. Jeff looked gutted, but to his credit he never wavered as we got back to the X5.

As Pete started the engine, Jeff just sat there shaking his head. "We can't leave them in there."

"We can't force them, mate," I said as we sped to the exit.

CHAPTER SIXTEEN

It's amazing what guilt can do to you; it is an incredibly unstable emotion. Sometimes it doesn't set in for years and other times it hits home straight away. The guilt associated with leaving those two girls was the latter. Logically my conscience should have been clear, we had offered to take them with us, but they had sent us away. They made their own beds, didn't they?

Sarah, Emma, Jeff and I were all in the living room. The trusty TV was still on, but we weren't paying it any attention. Jeff paced the room and his heavy footsteps disturbed Troy's nap as they relentlessly pounded against the wooden floor.

"We should have made them come with us," Jeff said.

Emma's eyes followed him around the room. "How could you have done that?"

"I don't know."

I stood up and put my hand on Jeff's shoulder. "We couldn't have done anything more. We offered and they said no."

He shook his head. "We should have tried harder."

I sat back down on the leather sofa. "Yeah, maybe."

Sarah squeezed my hand. "Don't be silly. You did all that you could."

"Look, Jeff," I said. "It was the right thing not to force them, but it was also the wrong thing to leave them. We couldn't win."

A smile appeared on his face. "Does that mean what I think it does?"

I took a deep breath and stood back up. "I think that it does. We've got to try and bring them back here. It's not safe for them there."

"What, really?"

"Let's go now."

"Yeah... great... okay."

Emma looked at Sarah and frowned. "I don't know if that is such a good idea. They already said no and what if those people go back there?"

Jeff stroked her brown hair. "The chances are that we will need to go back there at some point. I don't think that I could live with myself if I went back there and found them dead."

"I couldn't have put it better myself," I said.

She nodded. "I understand, but if they say no again you've got to leave them."

"They won't say no again. We will make sure that we're very persuasive."

"What about the others?" Jeff said.

"Ask them, mate. Just be quick, we need to get back there as soon as we can."

⇒⊹⇐

Pavel, Otis and I sat in the X5 waiting for Jeff.

"Do you think he will be able to convince anybody else?" Otis asked.

"I don't think so," I said.

"Not even Pete?"

"Especially not Pete. He's still in shock after what happened back there."

"They weren't going to hurt him though. Were they?"

"It was touch and go. Anything could have happened. The one with the knife looked crazy."

"I didn't realise it was so bad."

Pavel fidgeted with his blue beanie hat. "Pete... I don't know how you say... is not in good mind."

I turned in my seat and looked at him. "You're right. He's totally lost. He doesn't know how to deal with what's happening."

Jeff opened up the car door just as I finished my sentence. "It's just us."

"No Pete then?" I asked.

"He didn't want to come."

"What about Jon and Shane?"

"They're not coming too."

"Any reason?"

"Shane said that they were stupid birds and they weren't his responsibility. And Jon, well him and Shane seem to have become fast friends as they're hanging out together in his flat."

"Shane couldn't stand him earlier," Otis said.

I laughed. "Yes, but he has probably realised that Jon is his ticket to two single ladies."

Otis nodded. "Of course he is."

We couldn't have left the supermarket less than an hour before, but when we got back to the car park, it was clear that we had been gone an hour too long. A large black van was parked at the front of the store and seeing it filled me with apprehension. It had its back facing the building entrance and the front facing towards us. As soon as I noticed that only half of its number plate was still intact, my apprehension turned to full-on dread.

Jeff noticed it too. "It's them. It's blatantly them. They're back and we left those two girls in there to get slaughtered."

"They've parked with the back of the van right up to the entrance," I said. "That means that they're not there for the girls, they just want to stock up on more supplies. They don't even know that they exist, so as long as they don't do anything stupid they will still be safe and sound in there."

I slowly drove the eight hundred metres or so past the front entrance and parked the car at the side of the building outside of one of the emergency exits. We had to go in the front, but I had a feeling that we wouldn't be coming back out that way.

I turned in my seat and looked at my three companions. "Lads, we don't have to do this."

"Yes we do!" Jeff said.

Pavel nodded his agreement and then Otis said, "Well what are we waiting for?"

As we got out of the car, I saw a lone zombie enter the car park. It was too far away from us to cause any immediate harm, but I was understandably wary of it all of the same. We skirted around the side of the building in single file and waited at the corner. I heard voices, so I slowly peeked around it to see what was happening.

There were two of them leisurely loading the back of the van up with beer and they were having a right old laugh. I was glad to see that they had their priorities straight. They really were taking their time and it was making me more nervous as another zombie had decided to make its way into the car park. I heard shouting coming from inside the store. I couldn't make out what was said, but the two men stopped what they were doing and rushed back into the building.

This was it; we had to follow them in.

We crept to the front entrance and slowly made our way into the store, being careful not to step on any of the shattered glass. We could hear loud cackling laughter coming from deep inside the building. We followed the sound, being careful not to make any noise ourselves. Every twenty seconds or so the laughter would die down, but would start back up again soon after. I did not like it one bit and the closer I got, the more nervous I became.

We stopped in our tracks as soon as we could hear voices and a dull sob over the laughter.

"Not so mouthy anymore, are you, bitch?" His sentence was punctuated by a cracking sound followed by a louder sob. "What are you crying for? I'm only playin'." Another crack and more sobbing followed.

"She's really upset, isn't she, lads," the voice said with mock concern.

"You're right, Bill. Why don't you cheer her up?"

Feigned surprise filled Bill's voice, "That's a really good idea, Tom. And I know just the thing to do it." When he finished speaking the laughter reached even higher decibels.

We were now in the next aisle. Bill's voice was filled with anger as he spoke, but his friends' laughter didn't stop. "Stop struggling, you whore; Tom, get over here and give me a hand, will ya." I heard an even louder cracking sound and then a scream.

Tom replied, "My pleasure, Bill," and the sobbing abruptly stopped.

I glanced up the aisle. Selma was being held down on the floor by a short, fat man with long black hair, he had his arm across her throat and he was practically choking her. In front of her stood two other men, both had their backs to us, and then the man whom I assumed was Bill started to undo his belt and drop his trousers. "Yeah, that's better, baby, now we're gonna have a party," he shouted out merrily.

"Oh fuck!" I whispered.

"What is it? What's happening?" Jeff said.

"They're going to rape her!" I gasped.

The colour instantly drained from his face.

Bill then playfully shouted, "It's alright, Tom, let her have a breath, I like my women with a little fight in them." The three of them started laughing again. "Anyway, you and Lee are gonna want a go too, aren't ya?"

Otis looked at us. "I've got a plan."

Jeff and Pavel went to the top of the aisle, whilst Otis and I remained at the bottom of it. When Jeff and Pavel were in position, Otis stepped around the corner holding his police warrant card in one hand and his telescopic baton in the other. "Police."

Bill stopped what he was doing and turned around, he looked at Otis and sneered, "You're havin' a laugh, ain't ya? You're the only copper in London and you think that you are gonna stop this little party?"

"I'm giving you one chance to stop this yourself, because if you won't, I will."

Bill laughed as he pulled his trousers back up. "Eh, Tom. Can you believe this spade copper?"

"No, Bill, I can't. Who does he think he is?"

"This wog needs to know his place, doesn't he, Lee?" Bill said to the man next to him.

"He does, Bill," Lee replied.

Bill pulled out a large knife and started to walk towards Otis. "Perhaps us two should do it for him."

I came out from next to the aisle and stood beside Otis clutching my crowbar.

Bill laughed. "Oh look, the spade's got a friend."

Jeff and Pavel appeared from the top of the aisle. "He's got more than one friend," Jeff shouted.

Bill stopped laughing. He could see that he was now outnumbered. I could tell he was working out whether the three of them could take on the four of us. From the outside watching in, I wouldn't have bet against him to be honest, but how much would it cost him? And that is exactly what he was weighing up. He was at an impasse and thankfully, he knew it. "I don't like filthy Turks anyway, Tom, let the slag go."

Tom took his arm away from Selma's throat and she scurried away to the side. Her face was swollen; they had really slapped her around.

"Let's get the fuck out of here," Bill said, trying to save face in front of his men.

Tom responded to Bill's command and stood. I have to say that he was very well trained! He didn't know it, but getting up from the floor and extending himself to his full height would be the last thing that he ever did. Without warning and like a flash, Selma picked up a discarded knife that was lying on the floor and lodged it into the side of his throat. To say that I was shocked would be the understatement of the century. But the worst thing about that moment was that now I truly knew that there was no turning back.

I looked over at Jeff and saw that his jaw was resting on the floor (figuratively speaking of course); like me, he couldn't believe his eyes. Pavel looked normal, like he saw this kind of thing all the time. But Bill and Lee hadn't yet seen it; they only knew something was wrong when they heard Selma's guttural war cry, coupled with the shocked expressions on both mine and Otis's faces. They turned around to see their friend writhing on the floor with his hand trying to cover the fatal wound. The blood flowed freely, ruining his once white vest, and eventually pooled next to him in the middle of the aisle. Selma retrieved her knife by yanking it out of the wound and Tom continued to struggle for every last breath.

Bloody knife in hand, she beckoned her two remaining former captors over to her. "Come on then, you spineless wankers!"

Neither one of them said a word. They just stood there dumbstruck; five minutes earlier they thought that they owned the place. There is no way on God's green Earth that they ever could have imagined such a dramatic turn of events.

"Come on, which one of you wants to party now?"

Bill was looking around trying to work out all of his options, he had faithful crony Lee, standing beside him awaiting his orders. Directly in front of him was the knife-wielding Selma and the writhing body of Tom, his soon to be dead other crony. Not forgetting the menacing figures of Jeff and Pavel further down the aisle, and Otis and me standing ten metres behind him.

"What the fuck, Lee? You're gonna just stand there?"

Lee shook his head. "Nah, course not, Bill." He approached Selma, swatting his own blade in her direction.

Selma only lost a little of her bravado as the man twice her size started inching towards her, and to her credit she did not take one step back. But there was no way we could let this go on. I didn't care how angry (or mad) she was; at the very least Lee was going to hurt her. I exchanged glances with my three friends and we all knew what we had to do.

Otis and I charged at Bill. Otis went high and I went low. Bill turned around just in time for his chin to meet Otis's fist, he then stumbled into the perfect position for my textbook rugby tackle, which sent him hurtling to the floor with a loud thud, his own knife clattering into the floor before him. Otis then went into police mode and within two seconds flat, Bill was lying face down on the floor with his hands cuffed behind his back.

Both Lee and Selma took their eyes off each other to see what had happened, and that gave Jeff and Pavel the time they needed. They put themselves in between them both; Selma may well have been safe, but they were now only a few metres away from Lee's blade themselves.

"Drop the knife," Jeff shouted.

Lee didn't do anything.

"What should I do, Bill?" he said in a panicked voice, looking backwards and forwards between Bill and Jeff.

Bill was still too winded from being punched, rugby tackled and handcuffed to say anything.

"Just drop the knife," Jeff repeated with more force.

Lee was becoming increasingly agitated and was now even more frantic. It looked like he could go off at any moment. "What should I do, Bill?"

Bill lifted his head and spat some blood from his mouth. "Just kill—"

Before he could finish his sentence Pavel executed the fastest punch I have ever seen. He brought his left fist up from the side of his body and struck Lee in the side of the head with more force than I would think could be possible. The man didn't see it coming. In fairness to him, I don't think that any of us did. He was spark out as he instantly hit the deck.

"Bloody hell, Pavel!" Jeff said in awe. "Where did you learn to punch like that?"

"Is normal. Everybody in Poland punch like that," he replied.

I looked over at Selma. She too was stunned by what had just happened. It took a few seconds, but I could tell that the anger was starting to build up in her again. Her knife started to shake in her hand as she fixed her gaze on Lee's unconscious body.

"Selma," I said, trying to snap her out of it.

She didn't listen, but at least Jeff and Pavel took a step back and gave her a little extra space.

"Don't do it, Selma. You will regret it later."

She ignored me again and I could see the rage start to cloud her eyes.

"Where's Semra?"

"She's in the store room."

"You better get her as you two really need to come back with us now."

She took her gaze away from Lee. "Why do we need to come back with you?" She said it as more of a genuine question than with any hostility attached to it.

"Because this lot have more friends and they could be coming by any minute to join them here."

She slowly nodded. "You're right."

She ran to the storeroom with Jeff following behind, leaving Otis, Pavel and me to keep an eye on Bill and Lee. Lee was still in a land far away, but Bill had managed to get himself into a sitting position up against a shelf, with his hands still cuffed behind his back.

"What should we do with them?" I asked.

"I don't know," Otis said, "it's not like I can take them back to the nick."

"Well they're not coming back with us. I suppose we could just leave them here and forget all about them."

"We must kill them," Pavel said.

"Fucking hell, Pavel," Otis said, "we can't just kill people!"

"They kill people here before. They kill us, no problem."

"Help me out here, Dean, please?"

"Jesus! I don't know, Otis," I replied. "If we leave them here, all that will happen is that their friends will come looking for them. And then they get away with it. They get away with killing all of these people. They get away for nearly raping that girl."

Bill started to laugh. "Hey, nig-nog, you better kill us. Your Polak mate is right. If you don't, I'm gonna hunt you down and kill ya like the animal you are!"

I felt my cheeks redden. "Oh shut up, you prick," not that witty, I know, but it was the only thing that I could think to say to him.

"What are we, four days into this shit storm? Me and my lot, we don't give a fuck and we're gonna be just fine. We take what we want, when we want and don't let anybody get in our way. And that is what these stupid supermarket cunts found out earlier. We're all sitting pretty, with enough food to last us for months. We just came here to pick up some booze, so we could have a bit of fun."

I walked over to him and looked him in the eyes. "I just told you to shut up."

"He is rapist, Dean," Pavel continued. "He is how you say, 'lowest of low'. If we don't do this, we will regret."

Otis finally spoke, his voice cracking under his words. "Pavel might be right, you know. But I'm still a copper. I can't advocate this and it's not for us three to decide who lives or who dies."

"Otis, he just admitted to killing these people earlier and now he's saying that he's going to kill us if given the chance. It might not be for us to decide who lives or dies, but it's up to us to protect ourselves."

Bill shook his head and started to laugh. "Otis, is it? I always thought that us white folk were superior to you blacks. Even the fucking plumber knows the right answer! And you're confirming it all for me. You're weak and that's why you're not going to survive. Listen to him and don't make me think you're an even bigger cunt than I already do."

Otis just stood there. He was conflicted by this and who could blame him. It didn't matter that this bloke was a racist murderous thug; he couldn't sign off on murder. He looked at Pavel and me. "We're not vigilantes. We don't have the right."

"Otis, listen to him," I implored. "He's fucking mad. He's bloody insane and before this week I would have had him carted off to the loony bin. But we don't have that any more. Look around us, mate, society is dead. We can only survive and hope that we have one again some day."

Otis just shook his head.

"I suppose it's kind of like self-defence really," I said, trying to convince myself as much as him.

Otis looked at us both with a new resolve. "You're not talking about self-defence, you're talking about an execution and that is too much for me. If it's a consensus you're looking for then you're not going to get one. If you want to have a vote then it is a 'no' from me."

"Is okay, Dean, I will do," Pavel said.

"Whoa, whoa! I don't mind dying but I'm not having a dirty Pole do it," Bill said.

"Hold your horses, Pavel," I said. "I'm not one hundred percent yet and I need to be one hundred percent."

Otis put his hand on my shoulder. "You may never be—"

He was interrupted by Bill. "Got a wife have ya, Deano? I can tell by your wedding ring, unless it's a husband. Nah, no poofter has got that bad a haircut. Definitely a wife."

"What the fuck is wrong with you? Do you want to die?" Otis shouted at him.

"I bet she's pretty. Good-looking bloke like you," he continued.

"Fuck off," I spat at him.

He smiled at me. "I bet she likes to party!"

My blood started to boil as soon as he started his next sentence.

"P-A-R-T-Y," he spelled out every single letter as if he was enjoying it.

He was sitting on the floor propped up against a stack of shelves. He'd tilted his head back and was resting it on a porcelain bread bin, acting as if he owned the place. It didn't matter how helpless he was, he was still laughing and with every breath he was still spelling out the word 'party' over and over again. I continued to stand right in front of him and I couldn't tune out the words from my head.

I'm ashamed to say it, but he baited me and I lost control. The rage coursed through my veins and completely took me over. This was different than with the zombies, that was fuelled by self-preservation and fear. This wasn't anywhere near as noble. There was no righteousness here. This was fuelled by hatred. If I had been asked five minutes before I walked back into that Sainsbury's whether or not I could take the life of another human being, my answer would have been an emphatic 'no'. But hearing that sick bastard's threat against my wife flicked a switch inside me. Let's face it, Bill deserved to die, Pavel wanted him to die and now I wanted him to die.

I stared into his eyes and it didn't take long for my rage to hit fever pitch. With ferocity that I still can't believe I sent my right boot hurtling into his throat. His head cracked back and smashed into the bread bin. He gasped for breath as his head jolted back against his chest. Otis tried to stop my next kick but he wasn't quick enough and I connected with him again, this time in the nose. Now the bastard could barely breathe, but he was still cackling away, still trying to spell the word 'party'. I wanted to kick him again, but I couldn't get close enough as Otis had pulled me away. I wanted to get past him, but I was stopped by the panic in Jeff's voice.

"Dean, we've got to go! The zombies are here!"

As quickly as the rage came, it dissipated as my mind raced back to the two zombies that came into the car park as we entered the store. Two of them wouldn't cause much of a problem. Then I heard their moans. There were far more than two of them. And they were in the bloody store. I heard glass breaking under foot. There must have been scores of them. How much time had we spent in here? 'Too much' was the only answer that came to mind.

"Come on, Dean, just leave them," Otis said motioning at Bill and Lee.

Lee was still out cold and it would have taken three of us just to lift him. I looked down at Bill sitting on the floor, his face and the top of his shirt were covered in his own blood. His hands were still cuffed behind his back; basically he was fucked. He was trying to say something to me, as the blood continued to stream from his nose and down his front. I leant in to hear his words, hoping to hear this scumbag beg for mercy, but he didn't, his final words to me were, "You should have killed me. Cos I'm going to kill you and all of your family."

"Big words for a dead man," I replied as the zombies entered the bottom of the aisle. I ran to the others, following them out of the fire exit.

At least a hundred zombies were between us and the main gate. They paid the X5 no attention as they relentlessly made their way into the front of the store.

"Go out the back way!" Jeff said.

"I'm way ahead of you," I replied.

Selma turned around and looked at the back window. "What are those things?"

"Zombies."

"Zombies! Are you joking?"

"I wish I was."

"You're mad! I knew we shouldn't have come with you."

I shook my head. "Just watch the telly when we get back to the flat. It's all over the news."

That evening I tried to take solace in the fact that I did not personally execute Bill and Lee, I was grateful to Otis for stopping me from going through with it. Technically, I wasn't yet a murderer but what worried me was that I could easily have been and that did not sit too well at that moment. But thinking about it now it was all semantics anyway, by leaving them there I did the next best thing.

Society no longer existed and the only person who could hold me to account is me. As repulsive as my actions were I knew that I had to get past them. I had already managed to compartmentalise the deaths of my brother and my step-dad, what more were the deaths of a couple of degenerate thugs? If I had to do it all over again I would. The world is a better place without them and a guilty conscience was and still is a small price to pay for the safety of my family.

So I decided to learn to live with it.

CHAPTER SEVENTEEN

The next morning I sat on the living room sofa shaking my head at the image of the Prime Minister that was staring back at me from the telly. He no longer looked like the confident statesman that the country had re-elected only two years before. Sullen eyes and sunken cheeks filled the screen. "It is with regret that I am informing you that our nationwide aid operation will not be completed by the end of the day."

"I knew it," I said.

Sweat started to bead on his forehead. "More people have been infected than we originally thought and we need more time to get the situation under control. I have spoken to other world leaders and it seems like we are not the only ones to have underestimated the scale of this problem."

Jeff looked around the room. "Well, how long's it going to take then?"

"Shush!" Emma said. "Give him a chance."

The Prime Minister used his handkerchief to mop his brow. "Our latest estimates show that the situation will be under control within seven to ten days."

"We can manage that," Derek said.

The Prime Minister offered a weak smile to the camera. "So, by next Wednesday everything will be back to normal. I ask you all for your patience in this matter. Please do not leave your homes, and allow us to do our job. With your support we can keep this great country strong."

Sarah squeezed my hand. "What do you think?"

"We need to get everybody here for a meeting as soon as we can."

Less than an hour later everybody was squeezed into my living room. Some sitting but most standing. That was except for Pete, who still hadn't left his flat since we'd got back from Sainsbury's and Julie, who was looking after him and all of the children. I'd really wanted Pete in there with me, but he had flat out refused to come. Troy had taken up a position by

Sarah's feet, he was either guarding her from all of these new people or he thought that she was guarding him.

I took up a position in front of the TV and started to speak, "First things first, I don't want any of you to panic. A few of us guessed that this might happen and we're actually pretty well placed because of it. Thanks to our trip to Sainsbury's we've got at least a month's worth of food. But I think that we need more than just food to make sure that we will be okay."

"Out with it then, Baker," Shane said gruffly. "What do you think is so important?"

"The first thing we need to do is try and strengthen the fences."

Shane shook his head. "Do me a favour!"

"Look, it doesn't mean that we have to go to B&Q or anything. I was just thinking of checking the garages. I've got a few sheets of ply in mine from when we did this place up. Who knows what could be in the others? It might make all the difference if the zombies start banging into it."

"Oh leave off, will ya? They've hardly touched the thing."

Sarah knitted her brow and stared at him. "It doesn't mean they won't though, does it?"

I smiled at her. "Exactly. And anyway what else are we going to do with our time? It's not like we have anything better to do."

Shane looked over to Poppy and winked at her. "I don't know, Baker, I can think of other things."

"Come on, Shane, this is serious."

Shane rolled his bloodshot eyes. "Fine, whatever. Next."

"Okay. My next concern is power. I wouldn't be surprised if it went off at some point."

"Have a day off. This is all meant to be over by next Wednesday. Everything will be fine."

"You're probably right, Shane," Otis said, "but it's just something that we need to be prepared for."

"Didn't you just hear me? This will all be over in ten days. So there's no way that's going to happen."

I ignored him. "If the power goes off we not only lose our lights and heat, we will also lose our fridges and freezers as well as any water out of the tap."

"You don't need electricity for water, genius," Shane retorted.

"Actually you do. Without electricity none of the water-pumping apparatus will work and without that no water will come out of the tap. I think it would be sensible to try and set up some water butts; just so we can keep a fresh water supply. Also, a generator or two wouldn't go amiss. But I doubt we'd find those out in the garages."

Shane stared directly at me and slowly rolled up the sleeves of his plain white shirt, revealing his musclebound heavily tattooed arms.

I think he was trying to intimidate me.

"Next!" he shouted.

Jeff chipped in, obviously he was as annoyed with Shane as I was, "Jesus, Shane, why are you being like this?"

"You lot seem to be enjoying this far too much. Everything will be alright next week."

"Enjoying it, you're out of your mind! I've already lost half my family!" I snapped.

"Stop getting your knickers in a twist, you mug."

"Fuck you, Shane! If you don't want to be part of what we are trying to do here then why don't you just fucking leave?"

Shane stood up (he really was quite intimidating). "You need to watch how you speak to me, Baker. Don't say anything that you'll regret."

Sarah put her hand on my arm.

I took a deep breath. "In fairness, Shane you might be right. I could be making a big deal out of nothing and all of this might well be overkill. But try and remember that there are things outside of those fences who want to eat us and who have already eaten people that we all know."

He scowled at me.

I looked at all of the faces around the room. "I'm not prepared to lose anybody here. If we do what I am suggesting then we stand a better chance of surviving."

Harold cleared his throat and stood up. "I am grateful for all that you have done, Dean, but I agree with Shane. You are asking us to do too much. The Prime Minister said that everything will be okay in ten days. I am happy to do what is needed around here, but I will not go outside of the fence to get generators or some such thing that we do not need."

I could feel the anger bubbling up inside me. "The Prime Minister has already been wrong about this once. Things could be even worse by then."

Harold didn't say anything; he just looked down at the floor.

"Dean just wants us to be prepared," Otis said. "It doesn't matter what tasks people do as long as everyone is contributing in some way. Isn't that right, Dean?"

I nodded and said something to the whole room in a slightly harsher tone than I actually intended. "Yeah, that's right. Either help out or get out."

The room was stunned to silence by my remark.

I glared at Shane, waiting for him to challenge me. And you know what? I think a part of me wanted him to. But he didn't and the meeting was adjourned.

It wasn't an ideal ending, but at least everybody knew where they stood.

⇒╫╪⇐

'Help out or get out' became our motto over the next couple of days. It may sound harsh but it was the reality that we were now living in and those words were born out of necessity. I mean let's face it, the enormity of what we were undertaking was huge. There were over thirty of us spread out over the two blocks and on the surface some people may have appeared to be more capable than others. But it all depended on how you looked at it. Sheila may not have been the right choice for guard duty, but she certainly was the right one for food preparation and kitchen work. It's just horses for courses and in my opinion both jobs were equally valuable to the survival of our little group.

Since this had all started we'd had plenty of luck. The problem was that it was mostly bad. We were due some good luck, and opening up the garages in the communal car park was our chance to see if the tide was going to turn. It never ceases to amaze me quite how much junk people keep. Mr Trotter may well have been the extreme, but even the most 'normal' every-day people are still unable to say goodbye to the most useless and antiquated items. Why did we find a gram-ophone (yes, a gramophone), but no records in one of the garages? And who in their right mind keeps thirty-year-old completed puzzle books? Despite all of the junk we did find some really useful bits and it meant that we probably wouldn't need to venture out quite as soon as I had initially feared.

One of my former neighbours must have been a bit of an outdoorsy type, because thanks to them we now had a couple of camping stoves, enough butane to boil a few hundred tins of beans and an old set of six walkie-talkies. We also found three cricket bats and enough building materials to reinforce the most vulnerable parts of our fences. We were all pretty happy with the haul and even Shane begrudgingly admitted that it wasn't a total waste of time.

Despite the success of the garage raid, it didn't take long for a few people to start complaining, namely about Pete.

The issue finally came to a head whilst we were outside working on the fences.

"He's a fat, lazy bastard," Shane said to his two new best friends, Jon and Harold, as they started packing away their tools. He may have said it to them, but he deliberately said it so that I would hear him. The other two just nodded as he continued, "We're out here doing all this unnecessary work and he's in there living it up, sitting on his massive arse."

I walked over to them. "Why don't you just say it to my face, Shane?"

Shane turned to look at me. "Good idea. Your brother is a waste of fucking space."

"Why's that then?"

"Don't be a mug. We're all out here working our nuts off, doing guard duty and all of that shit and he's in there doing fuck all!"

"Listen, I know it seems like that, but he can't help at the moment. He's not... well."

"What the fuck's wrong with him? Has he got a cold?"

"No, it's not like that," I sighed, "he's not coping mentally with everything. He's finding it really tough; we've lost a lot of family and he blames himself for the death of our step-dad."

"Yeah well, we've all lost people. But we don't have the luxury of crying about it. Why's he so special?"

"In fairness I understand what you're saying. But he can't do anything at the moment. Can you please just give him a break?"

Shane turned to Jon and Harold. "Help out or get out, unless your name is Baker that is, and then you can do what you fucking well like. What a load of bollocks. Fuck this. You and Jeff can pack this gear away, us three are going inside for a drink."

Jon and Harold looked like a couple of deer in the headlights. They didn't know whether to stay or to go, but Shane didn't back down. "Come on, you two, you've done enough for today."

The two of them looked at each other and got to their feet.

"Good lads," Shane said as they followed him into the block.

Jeff stepped beside me. "If Pete doesn't sort himself out, then this could get nasty."

"I know, mate. I know."

Despite everything that was going on, the mood in my flat was good. We had plenty of people over for a Sheila special and Derek was regaling us all with tales from his army career. Everybody adored him and he played up to the new people who hadn't yet heard these stories. It's funny how the most unlikely people can become friends in these situations, but it was heartening to see people still able to be people.

I excused myself from dinner and went across the hall to where Pete and his family were staying. Abby and the two boys were quietly playing in the corner while a haggard Julie watched over them. Everything was really taking its toll on her too. She may have had us, but the rest of her family were a hundred odd miles away somewhere on the coast; Bournemouth, I think. She never got to speak to them after it all happened and she had no way of knowing if they were okay. Like a lot of people she was just constantly filled with worry. It was clear that her state of mind was contributing to Pete's own.

"How are you all doing, Jules?"

She shrugged her large shoulders. "Look at us, we're fine."

My mum came out of her new bedroom and rescued me from the conversation. Despite everything she looked a million times better than Julie. "I saw you all working hard out there today, darling."

"It was good, we got a lot done."

"Trying your best to protect us all."

"Trying, Mum, although it doesn't seem that I've been too successful so far."

"Don't speak like that! You are trying your best."

Mums; you can't beat them. I was kind of semi-responsible for the death of her husband and yet she didn't want me to beat myself up about it. "Well okay, Mum, I will try my best not to. But I don't think that I can promise that."

"Dean, I mean it. It wasn't your fault what happened to Graeme. Just think about all the good that you have done. Without you we wouldn't have got Abby back, now would we?"

She had me there, I suppose. "Alright, Mum. You win."

I looked at Julie. "Do you think that Pete will mind if I go in and see him?"

"Don't force him to do anything, Dean!" she growled. "He nearly died the last time that you did."

"He's a big boy, Julie. He does what he wants. I've never forced him to do anything."

She glowered at me.

"Look, I just want to see how he is."

Mum stepped in between us and ushered me to his door. "I'm sure he would love to see you, Dean. Just don't be too long as he's not feeling himself."

I knocked on the bedroom door and didn't wait to be called in. Pete was lying under the covers of the double bed.

"I was wondering when you'd turn up," he said with half a smile on his unshaven face.

"I can't keep away. Anyway, I'd thought you'd like to know that we shored up most of the fences today."

"That's good. But you didn't come up here to tell me that, did you?"

"You're right, I didn't. I need you out of here and back on your feet."

"Well, I don't feel like it."

"Shane is really starting to kick off about you not helping out and he isn't the only one. He's got Harold, Blessing and all the students with him on this too."

"So?"

"So you're making it really difficult for me. It looks like I'm making other people do stuff and letting you off."

"Difficult for you? How do you think I feel about everything? Steve's dead, Sandra's dead, and Graeme's dead."

"They had other family too. And we're still out there trying to survive."

He turned his back on me and faced the wall.

"Don't be a child, Pete, for God's sake!"

He continued to ignore me.

"I know you're finding it… difficult. But I need you. We all do."

He turned back to me. His eyes had welled up. "I know I'm letting everyone down. But I can't help it. I'm suffocating under it all. I just can't cope."

"You can cope, Pete. I know you can."

He shook his head. "Last week when all this start-ed, I thought that I would be okay with it. But I'm not. I'm just fucking useless. I've lost count of the amount of times that I've nearly died since this started. And each time I've put someone else in danger too. How many times will I need to be bailed out?"

"You're looking at it all wrong."

"No, I'm looking at it the right way!" he said, tears now starting to fall from his eyes. "I don't care what you say. You tried to convince me otherwise but Graeme died because of me. Because I can't take what's going on. He should never have been in that flat. It should have been me. End of."

"Pete—"

"Shut it, Dean! I'm not finished. And even after ev-erything, you persuaded me to help again and I nearly got my throat slit by some crazy bird because of it. Who, I might add, you've ended up bringing back here."

I just stared at him. I had no reply.

After twenty seconds or so, Pete composed himself. "I don't want to be a burden, but I really can't help you at the moment. I can't even leave this bed. You're just going to have to deal with it."

I still didn't have anything to say, so I just left the room. What more could I do?

Mum approached me as I left the flat. "How did it go with him?"

"Not well. He's a shadow of the man I thought I knew."

She hugged me. "Don't give up on him, Dean. He needs your support to get through this."

"I know, and he's got it. I'd never give up on him."

"What are you going to do about Shane and his lot?"

"I'll just have to make them understand."

"Do you think you will be able to?"

"I hope so, Mum. But even if I don't, Pete's my brother and rightly or wrongly I'm always going to take his side."

CHAPTER EIGHTEEN

Despite our early setbacks the group settled into a routine. Basic needs were being met and as long as you didn't mention either Pete or Julie, then for the most part people seemed to be in good spirits. New friendships were formed as we worked side by side and it appeared that we had a group of people who wanted to pull together. However, appearances can be deceptive as the truth was that bubbling beneath the surface was an acrid pot of hate-filled tension, just waiting to explode. We were only a couple of days in really, but there were moments when I didn't know if the true enemy was either in or outside of the walls.

Another crisp November morning saw Jeff and me paired together on guard duty. Despite the big coats and warm clothing, the cold air bit at us as we slowly walked around the grounds. There still wasn't a hint of moisture in the air and if the zombies hadn't taken over the country, everybody would be talking about what a dry month we were having.

The two blocks of flats proudly stood side by side in the middle of the property. We walked around them following the contours of the perimeter fence. Our lap took us along the paved pathway to the gravel car park and past Graeme's white van (the improvised barrier sitting between our sanctuary and the zombies) and into the fenced-off garden area. Days of walking the same beat had worn the grass away to form a neat track. Large trees sat just behind the fence and gave us extra protection all the way around to where Nan and Shane's cars sealed up the second smaller entrance to the street. This was where the worn grass track met the paved pathway and led back to my block's front door and onto another lap of the grounds.

As we passed Graeme's van for what must have been the sixth time of the morning I pointed at the tall wooden fence and then at the block of flats. "They're the only two things that are standing in the way of us and death."

"Bloody hell, Dean! You're in a good mood this morning."

"I'm absolutely fine, mate. I'm just stating a fact, that's all. We've just got some wood and some bricks between us and a hell of a lot of zombies. And the funny thing is that those bloodthirsty animals aren't even our biggest problem at the moment."

Jeff nodded. "Shane's still not happy about Pete, is he?"

"He's not the only one. Harold, Blessing and the three students are all kicking off about him too. Pete's not left that room for three days now and there's nothing that any of us can do about it."

"Did you speak to him yesterday?"

"I tried to, but Julie wouldn't let me in."

"She didn't let you in?"

"Apparently my seeing him makes him feel worse."

"I didn't realise he'd gotten so bad. I mean, I understand what he's going through and everything. We're all going through it... Thinking about it, I suppose the only real surprise is that we all haven't reacted that way."

"I don't agree."

Jeff screwed up his face. "No?"

"No. You and me, we want to live. But not Pete, he just doesn't want to die."

"There's a difference?"

"Of course there is. We know that we have to fight to survive. But Pete thinks that he can survive by doing nothing."

"That's deep. Does Sarah know she's married to a philosopher?"

"No, I'm being serious, Jeff. He doesn't understand that sooner or later his inaction will kill him and the people around him."

"So you're saying he won't leave the room because he thinks that people are dying because of their actions."

"Exactly."

"But doesn't he have a point? I mean Graeme would have been fine if he never went into that flat."

"True. But if we didn't do anything and just stayed where we were, you and Emma would still be in ASDA and the rest of us would all be starving to death because we'd run out of food."

Jeff nodded. "I see what you're saying."

"Pete doesn't though, and that's the problem. Everything is so frustrating… And then there's Shane and his mob. They all think I'm on some kind of power-er trip. That I'm getting off telling everyone what to do. Did you know that Jon and Harold have both flat out refused to do guard duty today? Both of them are blaming Pete, saying why should they do it, if he doesn't have to?"

"I suppose they've got a point."

"Which is half the problem."

"Help out or get out, and all that."

"Yep."

"Do you think Pete will snap out of it anytime soon?"

"I hope so. But I won't be holding my breath."

As I finished my sentence Otis walked up to us in his freshly pressed uniform (good old Sheila). His dark face was etched with concern.

"What's happened?" I asked.

"I'm sorry to have to tell you this, mate, but some other people are now starting to get upset with Pete and Julie."

I threw my hands in the air. "Who now?"

"Natalie, for one. She started mouthing off about them earlier."

"Natalie?" Jeff said. "The ungrateful cow! She'd be dead by now if it wasn't for us."

Otis shrugged his shoulders. "Well, that's what I told her. It calmed her down a bit. But I don't know for how long. She really is on edge."

I blew out a deep breath. "Do you think Shane put it in her head?"

"He's certainly not helping things, but I think she got there on her own."

Jeff shook his head. "Pete and Julie have no idea about the trouble they're causing."

"No, they don't. Resentment can be pretty contagious. We're all going to get the blow-back for sticking up for them."

"Look, Otis," I said. "I'm really grateful for you standing by us on this. I know Pete and Julie look like they're okay, but I need you to understand that they're in the middle of some kind of breakdown. They're not idle. If they were able to help, they would."

"Don't worry, Dean. I get it."

"I thought so, but thank you. I think it will be okay if I can just get the others to understand it too."

Otis put his hand on my shoulder. "I'm sorry to say this, Dean, but even if they understood it, I doubt that some of them would care."

"You might be right. But do me a favour. If anyone has a problem, tell them to come and see me about it next time."

Later that afternoon I met Shane in the hall as he was coming out of his mum and dad's flat. He was wearing a white skin-tight vest, and his muscles and tattoos were bulging out.

"Hi, Shane, I'm glad I caught you," I said.

"Oh yeah?"

"Is it alright to have a chat?"

"What is it, Baker?"

"It would be great if you could start helping out again."

"Fuck off," he said as he rubbed his nose and sniffed.

"Look, I understand that Pete is frustrating you. But he's having a nervous breakdown. He's not in his right mind. Can't we all just work together? So we can get through this?"

"Oh boohoo. Fatty is sad. I don't give a fuck."

I stared at him. I couldn't believe what he was saying. I could feel the anger rising within me, but I managed to gulp it down.

"Oh poor Baker. Have I upset you?"

"Don't worry about me, Shane. I'm a big boy."

He sniffed again. "Listen, Baker, do you want me to give you a little clue?"

"If you want."

"I don't give a fuck about what your brother does or doesn't do."

I slowly started to nod. I finally understood. "It's all an act isn't it? This isn't about Pete, it's about me."

He smiled at me. "You're quick! Don't get me wrong, Baker. I can't stand that fat whiney cunt. But yeah, this is about you. You're a jumped up little wanker and I've hated ya since the first second I saw ya. Which was okay, because I didn't see ya that fucking much. But now you're telling me what to do and I'm not fucking having it."

"Jesus, Shane! I've never liked you too. Big deal. We have a better chance if we all work together."

"Fuck off with your bullshit, Baker."

"If you hate me so much, why did you help when we went to Sainsbury's?"

"I'm not a fucking idiot. I'd just turned up and I had to. Every cunt here likes you! But not everyone likes your brother. Him going crazy is my ticket to fucking you up."

"You do realise that I never wanted to be in charge?"

"Do me a favour! You fucking love it."

"Seriously, Shane. It just happened."

"I don't care, Baker. Now if you don't mind, I've got somewhere to be. So just fucking do one."

I didn't go anywhere. I just stared at him. Our eyes locking in some kind of macho stare out. Eventually he blinked and started to laugh. "You've got a good stare on you, Baker. I'll give ya that."

Unsurprisingly, my chat didn't work and Shane carried on being the architect of the group's discontent. He continued to skilfully manipulate Pete's issues to further his own means and he caused a split within the group. He sufficiently turned the students, Jon, Tara and Poppy, along with Harold and Blessing and to a lesser extent Natalie, against the rest of my family. And the funny thing was not one of them realised it was because he hated me.

Thankfully, even with this conflict things were still getting done and our situation wasn't a total loss. We had food, we had shelter and our household utilities were still working and that is why I think that we managed to keep some level of normality. My worry was that if we lost one of these the group would fall apart and that was the last thing that I wanted to happen.

As the days passed more and more zombies started to drift past our walls; most paid us no attention, but every now and then a few of them would bang against a fence panel. I didn't know if they were trying to gain access or just testing it out. I can't say that either hypothesis particularly filled me with joy. I just hoped that they were more curious than expectant, but either way it didn't bode well. Eventually they would soon grow bored, probably because there must have been far easier pickings than us around.

Call me selfish, but that at least gave me a small degree of comfort.

⇥ ⇤

After a relatively quiet afternoon of guard duty, probably about a week or so after everything had begun, I returned to my flat to be greeted by a steaming hot cup of tea, Sarah's smiling face and a very excitable Troy. I joined Jeff and Otis in the living room and soon discovered that the BBC and every other TV channel had now stopped broadcasting.

"This is really bad, guys," Jeff said looking shocked at the lack of signal.

I ran into the spare room and dug out my old pocket radio from the cupboard. Every channel was filled with static until we came to BBC Radio Four Long Wave. A deep baritone of Received Pronunciation came out of the tinny speakers. It sounded like it was straight out of 1935 and was on constant loop.

"People of Britain. Television broadcasting has now ceased. News updates will be disseminated via this channel."

I looked at the ceiling and shook my head. "We knew this was going to happen. I bet that the electricity won't be too far behind. We can't put off getting a generator for much longer."

Otis got up and looked out the balcony window. "It's getting dark so we will have to see out the night and go first thing."

Jeff scratched his head. "Do you think that we will have any trouble getting a group together?"

"It doesn't matter," I replied. "No doubt me, you, Otis and Pavel can handle it."

"Yeah, I'm sure we can. But this is meant to be a team effort. Whatever we get we end up sharing. How is it fair that we always end up putting our arses on the line?"

"I know. You're right. But what other option do we have?"

Otis sat back down at the table. "We're the only proactive ones here. Nobody will do anything unless they have to. When the heat and lights go off, then they will all be queuing up to help."

Jeff started to nod. "Otis is right, Dean. I know we want to try and be prepared for everything, but we might have to play it that way."

I took a long hard look at the pair of them and I knew they were right. "Okay. Let's at least have a plan for when it happens. In the meantime we better make sure that the radio stays on all day, every day."

They nodded and laughed.

"What's so funny?" I said.

"Just as the TV went off, Jeff bet that you would want to come up with some kind of plan."

They knew me far too well. So I joined in with the laughter and started to drink my tea. Before I'd got halfway through it I heard a commotion in the communal hallway. The three of us went out to investigate and saw Shane having an argument with Bernie outside of Eddie and Iris's flat.

"Do you think you're Sherlock fucking Holmes or something?" Shane shouted, poking Bernie in the chest.

Bernie shrank with every poke and he started leaning on his cane more and more. "I don't know what you mean. The door was unlocked. I didn't know you were in there!"

"You lying old bastard. You've had a problem with me since I turned up."

"What?"

"I don't want your shit anymore. Do yourself a favour and stay out of my business."

"I didn't mean to walk in on you. It was an accident."

"Save it! Now fuck off downstairs and leave us alone!" He shoved Bernie and the old man fell into the wall.

Jeff ran over to help Bernie, whilst Otis and I went up to Shane.

I looked directly into Shane's bloodshot eyes. "What's the problem? Be careful with him, you're twice his size and half his age!"

"It's got nothing to do with you, Baker. I don't want that dirty old codger in my house."

"What do your mum and dad want? It's their house. They all seemed to be getting on well with each other. What happened?"

"I've already said it's nothing to do with you. So fuck off back to your lazy brother and take that old cunt away with you while you're about it."

Jeff stepped in between us. "You need to calm down. The world's gone mental out there; we need to stick together if we are going to get through this. Have you seen what's happened now?"

"What are you going on about?" Shane spat.

"None of the TV channels are broadcasting anymore. Things are going to get even worse. We've got to stick together."

Shane looked at me. "I bet you're fucking loving this, aren't you?"

I just stared at him, my look conveying the contempt that I felt. "I know you've got your issues with me, but why are you acting like such a dick to Bernie?"

Shane's eyes opened wide. "Who the fuck are you calling a dick? You jumped up little cunt!" Every word dripped with venom and every syllable sent spittle hurtling out of his mouth and into my face.

My contempt turned to anger as he continued his barrage of abuse at me, and I wanted to punch him in his big ugly face so much; not only for what he was saying but for everything he had done over the past few days. I could see in his eyes that he wanted to hit me almost as much as I wanted to hit him, but we both managed to hold ourselves back before either one of us raised our fists. I held back because he was a big bloke and could have done me some damage. He probably held back because he would have had Otis and Jeff to contend with too and it was obvious that neither of them were shrinking violets.

Jeff pushed me back towards the stairs. "Leave it, Dean. Come on. Let's go."

Otis tried to calm Shane but he was still hurling all sorts of abuse at me as we ascended the stairs with Bernie following closely behind. The poor bloke was really rattled by the events of the past ten minutes or so. Otis was still with Shane as we got back into the flat.

Jeff sat down on the sofa. "We have to watch him."

Bernie still looked quite confused. "He just turned on me in there. I don't really understand what happened."

"Sorry about that, Bernie, it all got a bit out of control back then. Are you okay? Did he hurt you?" I said.

"I'm fine. I'm just in a bit of shock."

"What happened? Why did he chuck you out?"

"Well, I was just speaking to Eddie and I just wanted to use the toilet. Shane was already in there and I didn't know until I walked in on him. I think that he might have been doing drugs or something. But I'm not really an expert."

I looked at Jeff. "What was he doing exactly?"

"I just saw a bag of white powder and the next thing I knew I'd been chucked out of there."

"That's just brilliant!" Jeff said. "A coke-head is the last thing we need."

Otis walked into the room just as Jeff finished his sentence. "I see you've worked it out then," he said as he sat down.

"We can't take the credit, mate. Bernie was the one who found out and that's why Shane was going mental at him."

"All of his aggression and posturing is pretty typical for someone who is doing a lot of gear."

I nodded. "I first met him a few years ago and he has always given me a bad vibe. Maybe the coke is making him worse? He's acting seriously unhinged now."

"You're not wrong, Dean, I've seen his kind an awful lot over the years. Anyway, I called him on it when you three went back upstairs. I listed it all off, the bloodshot eyes, the sniffing, the mood swings. He tried to deny it; but it's just so obvious."

"What should we do about it?" Jeff said.

"I think we have to try and keep him onside."

"How do we do that?"

"We should try and stay out of his way. I think he's using more to get through the day and that's only going to make him worse."

"Jesus, that complicates things then," I said.

"Yes it does. I've thought it for the last couple of days, but wasn't sure. But it does explain a lot. Everyday he's become more moody and aggressive."

"If he keeps it up he may alienate himself from his gang."

"Sorry to say, but I think they're all in on it."

"Are you sure?" I said. "I can see the students, but the respectable middle-aged African couple? Really?"

"Respectability doesn't mean anything, mate. I've never been surprised about what goes on behind closed doors. And anyway, why do you think they've all been getting on so well?"

I shook my head. "I've got to admit that I never saw this coming. I thought he just hated me, but it's worse than that. The bloke is a complete liability."

All of our utilities went off at approximately four o'clock the following morning, about twelve hours after television had stopped broadcasting and about nine days since it all had started. You can say what you want about the British, but our infrastructure really did hold together for as long as it possibly could. Nine days of power after the apocalypse is nothing short of miraculous. I don't even know if there is a word to describe what ten days of power would have been. I can only think of bloody miraculous, but that's two words.

An hour after the power went out a new message was looped on the radio in the same clipped voice. "People of Britain. Do not despair. All power is being routed to our military personnel in order to help them with their operations. Ration your supplies and do not leave your home. Normality will be resumed on schedule."

CHAPTER NINETEEN

I couldn't get back to sleep. My mind started to work overtime and eventually I gave up and got dressed. I wandered into my lounge with Troy in hot pursuit and the pair of us disturbed Emma and Jeff who were asleep on the sofa.

"Dean?" Emma said.

"Sorry. I'm just getting some air."

"Are you okay?"

"Yeah, don't worry, I'm fine," I said with not nearly enough conviction as I stepped onto the balcony and into the extremely cold night air. I sat on one of the rattan chairs and stroked Troy as he stood next to me. I heard Jeff and Emma talking in the living room.

"Go back to sleep. I'm going outside," she said.

"Just leave him, love. He wants to be by himself."

She ignored him and was outside sitting on the other chair before he could say anything else. The full moon illuminated the night sky. Through the trees I could see scores of zombies shuffling along the road. It didn't look like they were going in any particular direction, they were just milling around.

"Are you sure you're okay?" she asked, rubbing the sleep out of her eyes.

I looked at her. Her usually immaculate hair looked like a bird's nest. "I'm as okay as I can be, all things considered. How are you?"

"I'm worried, that's all. Do you think the radio was right about everything being okay soon?"

"I hope so. But who knows?"

She nodded. "Do you think Pete will be alright?"

"I think he just needs more time to adjust."

"I don't think he will be. He's lost it. Julie wouldn't even let me see him earlier. She only lets Mum and Nan in there because that's where they're sleeping."

"I know. She's been doing the same to me. He'll be okay. Just give him some time."

"And what if he isn't?"

"Then we look after him until he is."

"That could be a long time."

"We will do it for as long as it takes."

"You're right. We will," she said, getting up from her seat, but before she went back into the flat she hesitated at the door. "Do you really think this is the end of the world?"

"Sometimes I do and sometimes I don't. Do you?"

She shrugged her shoulders. "I don't know."

She went back inside and left me to my thoughts. I stroked Troy and watched the zombies pass by. They moaned and groaned as they moved, and my mind flooded with questions. Why all the moaning and groaning? Were they communicating with each other? And if they were, then what were they saying? I closed my eyes and realised the futility of my internal dialogue. I was sure that there were greater minds than mine trying to work that out. And even if there wasn't, what difference was that going to make to the here and now?

⇒⊢⇐

The next morning a group of us were sitting in the now electricity-less living room listening to Derek regale us with stories, primarily about times when he didn't have the luxury of electricity when he was in the army. I think that he was becoming a parody of himself, but I found myself becoming closer to him every day. I can't believe that it took the zombie apocalypse for me to properly bond with him.

It wasn't too long until the room was invaded by people all asking what I was planning to do about the electricity. Yeah that's right, what I was planning to do. I shared more than one look with Jeff and Otis whilst it was all going on. I even had the students in there acting like we were all best friends. Fucking crawlers (sorry, but it needed to be said).

We all played it very cool. Jeff, Otis, Pavel and I had already agreed that we would do what needed to be done. But we weren't letting the rest of them know that. If they wanted electricity then they were going to have to be a part of the solution and volunteer to help. It was all going to plan, with Jon, Tara, Poppy, Harold, Natalie and Gerry all offering their assistance in a generator run. That was until Shane barged into my home.

I saw him out of the corner of my eye, but ignored him. I carried on speaking to Derek and didn't say anything until he interrupted me. "Oi, Baker. What are you doing about the power?"

"What are you asking me for?"

"Cos you've set yourself up as the boss, ain't ya!"

"I think you were right the other day. The Prime Minister did say it would all be okay soon. I'm sure we can handle not having any power until this is over."

"Don't fuck with me. There's no way that you wouldn't want to do something about this."

I sighed. "Well, lots of people are keen to try and find a couple of generators. But to be honest, I'm not sure if it's worth the risk."

"Don't give me any of that shit! That's not what you were saying the other day."

"I know that. But things change. There seems to be more zombies than ever out there now."

Shane looked around the room. I could see the cogs turning behind his eyes. "What about if we all went?"

"Who's we?"

"All of us, Baker."

I saw Jeff trying to supress a grin. Shane was walking into our little trap.

I slowly nodded. "I suppose that could work. I mean we did all work well together when we went to—"

He cut me off. "Hold on, Baker, my old son. Not so fast." As he spoke a broad smile crossed his face. "All of us means all of us. So, I'll make a deal with ya. If you can get that fat brother of yours off his arse, then I will get off mine too. Let us know if the lazy so and so is up for it."

He left the flat as soon as he finished his sentence.

Jon looked at me nervously and pushed his glasses up his nose. "I think Shane is right. It's only fair that Pete gets involved too."

Shane's sentiments were echoed by everybody else and they all trudged out of my flat. Shane hadn't walked into my trap; instead I had walked into his one.

"We were so bloody close!" Jeff said.

Otis put his hand on Jeff's shoulder. "Let's not panic. We've got enough blankets and candles between us. We'll be okay without electricity for a day or two."

"I hope Shane isn't."

"Me too. Hopefully, a couple of cold nights might make him reconsider."

I nodded. "I think you're right, mate. But I'm worried that there won't be anything left by the time we get back out there."

"I'm not. Most people will be petrified to even leave their house. But in any case that's a chance that I'm willing to take. I've said it before and I'll say it again, everybody here needs to learn that we've got to work together."

"Yeah," Jeff said. "We can't keep on risking our lives for people who wouldn't do the same for us."

"I see what you're saying," I said. "But I don't want to wait that long. I'm going to have another word with Shane tonight. I know he doesn't like me, but I think it's worth a go. Who knows, just a day in the cold might make him have a rethink?"

"It's worth a go, I suppose. Me and Otis can come too if you want."

"Thanks, Jeff. But it might be best if I go by myself. He might take it the wrong way if all three of us paid him a visit."

⇒⊦⊣⇐

I waited until seven pm before I went to his door. I felt sufficiently cold and I hoped that he did too. I admit that I had to steel myself before I knocked on it. As the door opened I winced slightly at the thought of him launching into a full on tirade at me for the disturbance, but instead I was met by Iris's friendly smile and her wild white hair.

"Hi, Iris, sorry to bother you this evening. Can I come in and speak to Shane please?"

"Sorry, Dean love, he isn't in. I think he is at his new friend Jon's house."

"Is that Dean?" I could hear Eddie say from inside the flat as he approached the door. "I just wanted to say that I'm sorry about Shane. I know he can be a bit of a handful... and he hasn't been making it too easy for you."

"I understand, Eddie, that's why I wanted to speak to him. I just want us to be able to work together a bit more."

"Well, it should all be over in a few days anyway."

"With any luck."

"You mustn't pay any attention to him," said Iris, "He likes to show off a bit sometimes. We know that you only want the best for everybody."

I ran down the stairs into the other block, passing Selma and Semra, who were doing a stint of guard duty on the way. They both looked identical in their big grey coats and headscarves. The feeling of trepidation hit me again as soon as I walked into the other block and knocked on Jon's front door. I had to keep on reminding myself not to get too angry with Shane and be as calm as possible. I could hear laughter coming from inside the flat and I hoped that it was a good sign. A smiling Poppy opened the door but her expression changed as soon as she saw it was me.

"What are you doing here?" she asked.

"Yeah, sorry to bother you. I just wanted to speak to Shane for five minutes."

"Well, we are kind of busy," she said, making her best effort to avoid eye contact with me.

"That's fine," I replied as I gently pushed past her small body and into the flat.

"Well come in then," she said.

I rose above her remark. I could well have got annoyed by it, I mean, there's me trying to keep everyone alive and stuff and she's giving me attitude. But I reminded myself to stay calm. There would be nothing to gain from getting into an argument with her.

I walked straight into the living room and the whole gang was there; Shane, Jon, Tara, Harold and Blessing, living it large. The room was quite sparsely furnished with a sofa and a couple of kitchen chairs arranged in a circle around a wooden coffee table. Two bottles of half empty Jack Daniels stood proudly on the table along with a mirror, a razor blade, a couple of ten pound notes and a mountain of cocaine. I have no idea how much there was, but it looked like they had enough to get by for quite a while. I tried not to stare at it, but I couldn't help it. I'd only ever seen something like that on TV before.

"Sorry to interrupt," I said confidently. "Shane, do you have five minutes?"

"Can't you see I'm busy? This stuff doesn't snort it-self you know." They all broke out into fits of hysterical laughter. I showed no emotion as I stood there star-ing at him. Eventually the laughter died down and he continued, "Oi, misery guts, I'm only playing in' I? So I'm assuming you're 'ere to tell me that your brother is coming out of his cave and you want me to as well?"

"Not exactly. Pete isn't going anywhere. And we both know that the whole Pete thing is a load of bol-locks anyway. I was hoping that you'd have the sense to change your mind and help out."

He smiled at me. "I don't know what you're talking about."

"For God's sake... Don't think about what I want. Think about what the group needs, and the group needs you to get on board and cooperate."

"I think that my friends here would disagree with you, Baker. And anyway I already told you. No Pete, no me."

I took my time as I composed my response. I kept on telling myself not to get angry. "You've only got a couple of candles in here," I said gesturing around the room. "Have you even got enough blankets? It's getting colder and colder."

"Don't bring that up. You said it yourself, that the Prime Minister said it will all be okay soon. So what if we don't have power for a couple of days?"

"I just want to be prepared."

"Fuck your preparations, Baker." He then pointed at the mound of coke sitting on the coffee table. "And anyway, that shit will keep me warmer than any blankets." His words were followed by another bout of hysterical laughter.

I clenched my jaw. I was frustrated and again I told myself not to get angry; after a few seconds the laughter died down. I didn't say anything and that seemed to annoy him. "Well if there is nothing else, Baker... Why don't you just fuck off?" More laughter came out of the mouths of his coked-up friends.

"What about your mum and dad? They're getting on a bit. You wouldn't want them feeling the cold?"

Shane gave me his trademark scowl. "Don't bring my parents into this; it's got nothing to do with them."

"I didn't mean any offence. It's just that I know it will be tough on Nan, but luckily I've got enough stuff knocking about the flat for her to be okay. I've known your mum and dad for years now and I would hate for them to suffer."

Shane's scowl turned to daggers as his face reddened; he wasn't finding my presence amusing anymore. I knew I'd pushed him about as far as I could. Maybe a night thinking about his parents struggling might be enough for him to help out. Before I could turn to leave, Poppy opened her mouth and unwittingly set the touch paper that would irrevocably change all of our fates; "He's kind of got a point, and you wouldn't want them to get ill or anything, would you?"

She meant it innocently enough. She didn't know that her new 'drug buddy' was a bit of a wrong 'un. It took less than a second for Shane to process what Poppy had said. He rose to his feet and backhanded her full on across her face. Her red hair whipped the air as her head jerked back. She fell back into Jon's lap and started to howl with a mixture of shock, pain and fear. Everybody in the room was stunned, apart from me, I was more surprised. I can't say that I thought that he would hit her, but I did see the rage building in his eyes as I spoke. Poppy may have been his first victim but she wasn't the one that he wanted. She wasn't Mrs Right, she was Mrs Right Now. And you guessed it, yours truly was the one that he really wanted.

And you know what? I really didn't care! I'd been trying really hard not to rise to his baiting for days now. He'd taken the opportunity to dig out Pete, criticise me and generally bad-mouth the rest of my family at every chance that he got. Despite trying to remind myself not to get angry when I knocked on the door, I think that I actually wanted this. I wanted to teach him a lesson; I wanted to bring him into line but most of all I wanted to kick his fucking head in.

I had an inch or two height advantage on him and maybe a little more speed, but he more than made up for it in weight, strength, experience and just sheer nastiness. It was pretty obvious that he'd been in more than one brawl and that I was the underdog. I suppose you would have thought that I would have been scared, but I wasn't. I'd spent the week facing down zombies, for God's sake!

"Jesus, Shane! You've really fucking hurt her!" Jon shouted.

"Shut the fuck up. She should have kept her mouth shut!" he replied as he walked towards me. "Have you got anything else to say about my mum and dad, you cunt? Have ya?"

To say that Shane was angry would be putting it mildly. He had full-on cocaine-fuelled turbo rage. He was pissed and he wanted blood. My blood.

I didn't have anything to say and that seemed to annoy him even more, I swear that he got bigger with every syllable. Fuck! Maybe I did care. Maybe his scheming wasn't so bad after all. But it was just a fleeting thought; I wasn't going to back down. This was it.

I stayed perfectly still and waited. The tension was building. Who was going to make the first move? It was him; it was always going to be him. Eventually he just exploded at me. Just launched himself forward with his right arm flying at me, I swear that it was the size of a giant ham. I managed to sidestep his fist and thankfully he connected with thin air. The only problem was that I was now backed up against the wall. He spun around and got me back into his sights. I think he was surprised that I'd got out of the way, but the truth was that he was about as fast as a pedalo and I saw him coming from about a mile off. He also turned like one too, so I was easily able to sidestep him again. He just managed to stop his fist short of the wall. If it had connected he would have been in all sorts of trouble. I was now one hundred and eighty degrees from where I'd started with my back to all of his friends.

Shane was breathing hard. He obviously wasn't that fit. Maybe I could wear him out before he did me any damage. All the ladies were screaming at him to stop, with Blessing the most vocal. I have no idea what Jon and Harold were up to. But their pleas didn't work; in fact I think that it revved him up more. He charged me again, no qualms at all. The geezer backed himself big time. He threw the same ham-sized fist at me, but this time I was ready for it. I took one step back and threw a right jab into the side of his body. His body was like a rock and his muscles took the blow with ease.

He was panting and I wasn't. He was like one of those body builders that looked great, but couldn't even run up the stairs. I was in with a shout here. Maybe he wasn't such a great fighter after all. I bet he was used to landing with his first punch and taking victory. He'd already thrown three at me and not got anywhere. Yes, I was in with more than a shout.

This time he changed it up a bit and lunged at me with his left. It was quicker than his right and seemed to be just as big. I thought that I'd dodged it and I countered with my own left. But I hadn't. I hadn't dodged anything and I ended up kissing his fist as I walked straight into it. I was hurled into the seated Harold and we both hit the deck as the chair split in two. Thankfully he broke my fall. But come on, was he for real? The bloke was just sitting there watching it all unfold. There was chaos all around, his wife was going mental and he was just enjoying the show. Not anymore he wasn't.

I had the metallic taste of blood in my mouth as I untangled myself from Harold and got to my feet. And thank fuck that I did. Shane tried to wipe me out with a huge kick. His Dr Martens missed my head by no more than a centimetre. Lucky for me. Unlucky for Harold. The big boot clattered into his head and drilled it into the floor. The poor bloke was out for the count and Shane had probably just lost another couple of friends. As Shane's body passed me by, I took my opportunity. I slammed my elbow into the back of his skull, throwing all of my weight into the manoeuvre.

I literally gave it everything that I had. He staggered forward and smashed into the coffee table. The table broke under his weight. The ten pound notes went into the air. The razor blades went into the air. The cocaine went into the air. A white cloud settled over his head. I took a step back.

"Shane, that's enough. This is getting out of hand."

He picked himself up from the ground and stared at me. All I could see were his bloodshot red eyes staring at me from behind the Class A substance that covered his face, and a trickle of blood coming out of a small cut on his cheek. He looked like an albino devil ghost or something. He hadn't had enough. He might have been panting, but he wasn't hurt. I'd just smashed the back of his head with my elbow and he was fine.

Oh fuck.

I think that he read my mind, because he smiled at me and said, "Is that all you've got, Baker?"

I really wasn't in with a shout, was I? I felt like the plucky non-league side in the FA Cup tie that has just conceded the late equaliser against the Premier League giants. The game was going into extra time and we didn't have a prayer.

He rushed toward me and I feigned to the right. But he had anticipated it and he landed his big right into my rib cage. He hit me in exactly the same place as Steve had with his metal bar a few days earlier and this time I'm sure that a few of my ribs exploded into a million pieces. I didn't just feel the pain; I saw it and smelt it too. I couldn't take in any breath. I felt like I was going to die. I saw white light and everything. Sensory overload.

He took his time coming back at me and thankfully it started to pass. I was still standing, propped up against the sofa. I stumbled to the side and he laughed. He was enjoying this. How much did this bloke hate me? *Not as much as I hate him*, I thought. And my own hatred kept me in the fight. My ribs made breathing difficult and I no longer had the edge with my speed. He threw off a couple of punches that I somehow dodged and I managed to hit him with a few gut shots of my own. By rights he should have been winded. But his iron abs lapped it up.

I took a few steps back to try and increase the distance between us, but it wasn't enough as I was nowhere near escaping his next blow. A massive right hook clocked me on the side of my head, right on my ear. I'm sure the drum exploded on impact. The pain was phenomenal and my brain felt like it was flying around my skull like a pinball. This time I hit the deck. I rolled away just in time as Shane's Dr Marten tried to squash my face. His boot slammed into the floor and I somehow managed to get back up on spaghetti legs. I felt sick. I was dizzy. I had a ringing in my ear and every breath hurt more than the previous one. I was there for the taking.

I looked around the room, hoping that one of the others would help me; I could see Harold stirring in the corner of the room, but no one else. It was just me and Shane.

"You're tougher than I thought, Baker," he said with a smile on his face. "Just not tough enough."

He charged me again and landed another big right; this time on my left arm. The blow threw me onto the sofa and my arm went dead. How much more punishment was I going to be able to take? He lunged at me and I felt the breeze on my cheek as I got out of the way of another one of his punches. His right fist connected with the padded cushion, but as he turned to throw another one his foot got caught on something and he missed again. He tried to right himself and I saw my chance. I jumped on to his back and tackled him to the floor; he let out a muffled cry as the weight of my body drove his forehead into the ground. He was groggy, but he was still conscious. I somehow managed to straddle his back, despite the protestations of my screaming ribs. I knew that this would all be over with one more blow. But before I could raise my arm I felt two pairs of hands lift me off his body and put me back onto my feet.

"Dean! It's alright, we're here," said Jeff. "Are you okay?"

My head was still ringing and I was unable to formulate any words. It took everything I had just to nod.

"Jesus, Dean! You looked wrecked. Let me get you back home."

"Okay," I gasped.

Jeff led me towards the door past the now conscious Harold. I didn't know how badly he was hurt. I didn't care, and Blessing was now tending to him anyway.

"Jeff, hold on," I said.

I looked around the room; we had pretty much destroyed it. The only thing still in one piece was the sofa. I then looked at Shane, who was now propped up against the wall in a sitting position. His eyes were still red and most of his face was still covered in coke, the only difference now was that blood was leaking from his nose as well as his cheek. He looked shell-shocked. Neither one of us had really expected me to come out on top.

"Shane, we've got to get past this."

He stared at me for a good ten seconds. "You're a dead man," he grunted.

"Oh my God! What has happened to you?" Sarah said when I hobbled through the door and into the living room.

"I'm fine. Just a little sore. It could have been a lot worse," I said as I gently lowered myself onto the sofa.

She held a candle up to my face and gasped. "I thought that you were just going to talk to him?"

"I did... I mean... I was. He just lost it."

"Why?"

"I was trying to reason with him and I kind of touched a nerve. Then Poppy said something to him and he went mad. He smacked her and then he came for me. I swear he nearly killed me." I winced as I said those words. My ear was still ringing and my ribs were heavily bruised. They were definitely cracked. Breathing was becoming easier, but every breath was still laced with pain.

"He's an animal," Derek said, disgust contorting his face as he paced around the room.

"True," Jeff said. "But what are we going to do with him? He just threatened to kill Dean."

"It was pride talking," Otis replied. "I'm sure he didn't mean it. I think we should just give him the night to cool off. And tomorrow we go back and try to sort everything out when he's calmed down. Who knows, maybe Dean has knocked some sense into him?"

"I don't think we should give him the time of day," Derek said.

"In an ideal world I'd agree with you. But it's not like we can ignore him. We're all living under each other's feet."

"In my day we used to deal with his sort by throwing them in the brig! A couple of nights behind bars would straighten him out."

"We don't have a brig and even if we did we can't just lock him up."

"I think it's a cracking idea," Jeff said.

"Oh come on, Jeff."

"We have to consider it, Otis. He's dangerous."

"Maybe he is, but we don't have the right to lock him up."

"We need to do something. He tried to kill Dean, for God's sake."

"I know it looked like that, but Dean was more than handling himself when we got there."

I stirred in my seat. "I got lucky, Otis. I really did. He's not all there and he hates me. I'm telling you that he would have killed me if he had the chance."

"That wasn't him, Dean. That was the coke. I will make him see sense tomorrow."

Derek cleared his throat. "And if you don't?"

Otis shook his head. "We can't lock him up, okay? It would probably only make him worse. It just wouldn't be right. Especially if everything gets sorted out in the next few days."

"It's not right what he did to Dean and that young girl."

"I know it's not, Derek, but we're not savages."

"But he is a savage and that's the problem. We have to do something that he understands. Fight fire with fire."

"Like I said, we're not the savages. I will speak to him tomorrow morning and straighten all of this out."

"Fine, but if you can't get through to him then I think that we may need do something a bit more drastic."

"Don't worry, Derek. It will be okay."

"Famous last words, Otis," Derek scoffed. "Famous last words."

CHAPTER TWENTY

The next morning Sarah and I were awoken by the sound of Troy's barking. He was hopping on the spot by the bedroom window. Hop, bark, hop, bark, hop, bark.

"Be quiet, Troy," I commanded.

He ignored me and continued. Hop, bark, hop, bark, hop, bark.

"Troy!"

He ignored me again. Hop, bark, hop, bark, hop, bark.

I tried to lift myself from my bed. "Ow, my ribs!"

"Stay there. Can you just try and rest for one minute, please?" Sarah said.

"Only if you can get him to be quiet!" I replied, smiling at her.

"What's wrong, Troy?" she called to him.

He ignored her too! Hop, bark, hop, bark, hop, bark.

"Babe, my ears have only just stopped ringing," I whined.

Sarah got out of the bed and walked over to the window. She gently stroked Troy and opened up the blinds. "Troy, what's .... Oh my God! Oh my God!"

"What is it?" I said, getting off the bed.

"They're everywhere!"

I joined her at the window. Dawn was only just breaking through, but there was enough light to see into the communal garden and there were zombies everywhere. I could see at least fifty from my window and I just knew that there was going to be far more of them.

"Oh shit!" I cursed.

"How did they get in?"

"I don't know. They must have broken the fences down somehow. But I can't see where."

I ran out of my bedroom. "Jeff! Emma! Otis! Wake up!" I cried.

"First the dog, now you. What's going on?" Jeff said.

"Look," I said as I pulled open the blinds.

"Oh fuck! But how—"

I cut him off before he could finish his question. Now at the balcony, I had a proper view of the garden.

I knew exactly how they had got in. "He's moved his fucking car!"

At some point in the night Shane had left the block, taking his car and part of our makeshift barrier in the process and in doing so he had left a massive gap in the fence ready for every zombie in Eltham to come through.

"But why?" Emma asked.

"Payback, for his fight with Dean," Otis said.

"We don't know that," I said. "It doesn't matter anyway. We need to get out there and plug that gap before it's too late."

"It already looks like it is too late," Derek said as he entered the room. "I knew we should have locked him up."

"Dad!" Sarah snapped as she followed in behind him. "That's not going to help anything."

"Look, let's just get dressed and get down there," I said with as much confidence as I could.

Otis, Jeff, Derek and I were dressed in record time and we rushed outside of the front door. I froze in my tracks as I took my first step into the communal hallway. The words 'Get ready to die, Baker' were emblazoned in black marker pen on the magnolia wall opposite the flat. Otis was right. This was payback. But now wasn't the time to beat myself up about everything that I should have done differently.

"You three get Pavel and make sure that you're ready for this. See if you can radio anybody in the other block to help out. Whatever you do, do not leave the block without me. I'm getting Pete."

I banged on his door. "Pete! Let me in!" I banged again. "Pete!"

When the door opened it wasn't Pete. It was my mum. "Dean, what's wrong?"

"Zombies are all over the grounds. We need to get out there and stop them."

"But how?"

"It doesn't matter!" I said as I walked past her. "Pete!" I yelled again as I barged into his bedroom.

Pete, Julie and the two boys were all in the bed together.

"Calm down, Dean!" Julie shouted. "You're scaring the boys!"

I ignored her and spoke directly to my brother. "You need to snap out of it and help me right now!"

"Don't speak to him like that! He doesn't have to do anything!"

"I can say anything I fucking well like! Pete, get dressed!"

Pete was the proverbial rabbit in the headlights. "What's going—"

His question was interrupted by frenzied shouting and bloodcurdling screams coming from outside.

"Daddy, what's that noise?" PJ cried.

My mum was already at the window. "Oh my God!"

"What's wrong, Mum?" Pete asked.

"That young boy and his mum... both dead."

Pete got out of the bed and joined Mum at the window. "Tammy and Theo," he whimpered.

"Well, it won't just be them if we don't get out there now," I shouted.

Pete was dumbstruck. "I can't leave them," he said, gesturing at his family.

"Get real, Pete! For fuck's sake! If we don't get out there now you won't even have a family left. You need to man the fuck up!"

He just stood there in silence, looking at me.

"I said you need to man the fuck up!"

He opened his mouth, but no words were coming out.

"Do you want all of your family to be zombie food? Is that what you want? Is that what you fucking well want?"

There must have been silence for a good ten seconds or so.

"You're a coward. You're a fucking coward, Pete!" I seethed.

Still nothing from Pete, but this time I got a response from Julie. She open-palm slapped me right across the face.

"Don't you ever speak to him like that again!"

I was not expecting that at all. It really fucking stung.

I looked at Julie then back at Pete. "This is how it is then?" I said.

Still nothing from Pete.

So I left the room.

I slammed the front door behind me and ran down the stairs. I was stopped by Eddie's voice, "Shane!" he shouted.

I ran to his front door and I saw him staggering out, clutching his face. He hadn't noticed me. "Shane!"

"Not Shane, Eddie. It's Dean."

He looked up at me, but kept his hand in front of his face. "Where's Shane?"

"He's trying to kill us!"

Eddie removed his hand from his face and looked up at me. His eyes opened wide. Well, only one eye opened wide. The other was closed. It was blue and purple. "What?"

"He's fucked off and left us, Eddie. What's happened to you?"

"He didn't mean it."

"He didn't mean what?"

"He came back from Jon's last night. He was so angry. Iris and me, we tried to calm him down. But he wouldn't have it. He was really angry."

I started to shake my head back and forth. "We don't have much time. Eddie, what did he do?"

"He's a good boy really. He didn't mean it."

"Eddie!"

"He wanted to leave. But we told him not to. He said we were taking your side. He picked up his keys to go. So I put my hand on his shoulder, I just wanted to stop him. He turned around and hit me."

"He hit you?"

"It was my fault. I shouldn't have got in his way. And neither should Iris."

"What did he do to Iris?"

"I fell on the floor and she went up to him to try and calm him. But he started to shake her. I couldn't stop him. I banged my head on the floor when I fell."

"Where is she?"

He turned and pointed to the master bedroom. I walked into the hallway and I could see blood. It was on the floral rug and it was all over the sky blue wallpaper. I approached the door and I could see more blood on the handle.

"What's happened, Eddie?"

I opened the door, being careful not to touch the blood. Iris was lying in the double bed. She had the pink duvet pulled up to her neck and a flannel on her forehead. I took a step closer and I could see that her face was bruised.

I turned around and looked at Eddie. "What has he done?"

"He didn't mean it. He's a good boy really. He just gets carried away."

I kept staring at her. Her face was white. I realised she wasn't breathing. "She's dead. She's fucking dead, Eddie! He's killed her."

"No, he didn't. She's just sleeping."

"He's killed his own mum!"

"He didn't mean it! He's a good boy. It was my fault, I shouldn't have touched him."

To be honest I didn't know what to think. I was frozen in the room, staring at the body. Shock doesn't even begin to describe it.

I heard Jeff's voice from the hallway. "Dean, we're nearly ready."

I couldn't be in there any longer. I had to go. I shook my head and muttered, "I'm sorry, Eddie. Your son is a fucking animal."

I joined Otis, Jeff, Pavel and Derek by the exit.

"No, Pete," Jeff said. It was certainly more of a statement than a question.

"No."

"Was it that bad? You look terrible."

"Iris is dead."

"What?"

"I think Shane killed her last night after the fight."

"Bloody hell!"

"Three people are dead now because of him. We can't lose anyone else. Okay?"

Everybody nodded.

"What are we waiting for?"

Otis raised the walkie-talkie. "Gerry, how long?"

Gerry's voice came out over the radio. "Two minutes, Otis. We're nearly ready."

"Who was on guard duty?" Jeff asked.

"It was Pavel and I until four, when Jon and Poppy relieved us. Why?" Derek replied.

"Well, why didn't they raise the alarm? Shane might have killed them too. Just to shut them up."

"Surely he wouldn't have done anything to them. They're his friends. Maybe they all went off together?"

Otis shook his head. "Maybe, but I doubt it. They volunteered to help because—"

"We're helping," Sarah said, interrupting Otis. I turned to see her, Emma and Magda all coming down the stairs holding small weapons.

Jeff, Derek, Pavel and I all shouted 'No' at the same time.

"No way. No fucking way! You lot are not to leave this building until we are done," I said.

"But—" Emma tried to interject.

"No buts!"

Otis cut in, looking to placate the situation. "You three stay here and make sure that none of them get in the block. Okay?"

"Agreed?" I said, looking at the three of them.

"Agreed," Sarah, said nodding at me.

"God knows how many of them are coming in. We can't wait for Gerry, we've got to go now," I said.

Otis spoke into the radio. "Gerry, we're going out now. Get out there as soon as you can."

My anxiety levels reached new highs as I stepped through the door and was confronted by I don't know how many zombies. They were streaming down the paved pathway from where Shane had moved his car and they were filling up all of the available space as they headed towards the car park. If we didn't act fast we were going to be penned in and we wouldn't be able to go anywhere.

"We've got to get to the campervan and use it to plug the gap!" I shouted over the zombies' groans.

The five of us charged into what was to become a massacre. Thankfully we were pretty quickly joined by Gerry, Selma, Natalie and Harold.

"Where's Jon?" I shouted.

"Don't worry about him," Pete's voice boomed behind me, "I'm here now."

I turned to see my big brother with his trusty machete by his side. As soon as I saw him, all was forgiven. My brother was here and at that point I knew that we could do this. I was sure that the ten of us were going to save the day.

We headed for the car park and immediately engaged the enemy. Ten zombies went down within a second and that was the perfect start. As we got onto the main pathway I saw what was left of Tammy and Theo. I'd heard their first screams no more than five minutes earlier and now only their bones remained.

We made slow progress as we slashed and bludgeoned our way to the car park. Only sixty seconds in and my ribs were screaming at me and I was gasping for breath. I caught a glimpse of Derek and Pavel fighting side by side in my peripheral vision. They were bringing up the rear, despatching the zombies with ease. Pavel with a piece of lead piping and Derek with an old cricket bat. They looked like a formidable duo and despite the age gap you could see that they moved in a similar way. It was clear that Pavel was ex-military too.

Derek was strong and fit, but he wasn't as fast as he used to be. For the most part this didn't matter as Pavel more than made up for it. That was until Pavel got caught out of position and Derek slightly lost his balance. As a pair of zombies approached, Derek took a step forward and threw all of his weight into a thunderous blow. He didn't expect the zombie's head to give way quite so easily and his forward momentum sent him into the path of the second zombie.

Pavel tried to get to the zombie first, but he was too far away. Derek fell onto the zombie and they both crashed to the ground.

"Get up!" I screamed at him.

My father-in-law tried in vain to pick himself up, but he was unable to and within the blink of an eye the zombie that he fell on top of was able to bite into his face. The zombie's incisors ripped into Derek's cheek and seconds later others were on top of him. We'd barely even made it ten metres.

Pavel started hitting the zombies that lay on top of Derek, but it was an exercise in futility. To my eternal shame I screamed at him, "Leave him. It's too late! We've got to get to the camper."

Pavel stepped away and those things devoured him. Derek was the first of our number to fall and I could only hope that he would be the last.

The bodies were piling up around us as we made slow but steady progress. I nearly lost my footing a few times as I tried to step over the rotting corpses that only seconds earlier had been trying to kill me. By the time we had made it to the communal car park we must have killed sixty of them, but there must have been that many again between us and the campervan and more were still coming in from the gap. I swung my crowbar, killing them indiscriminately. I was covered in the blood and guts of the dead. The smell was indescribable. But we fought on.

For such a slight woman, Selma was fighting remarkably well. Though she was armed with just a meat cleaver, every one of her strokes was measured to devastating effect. But as good as she was doing, she was now starting to tire. Two of them approached her as we closed in on the camper. She drove the heavy blade into the top of the first one's head and it collapsed to the ground. She bent over and used all of her strength to try and retrieve the cleaver, but it was stuck. She screamed as she fought against her tired limbs and eventually the heavy blade came free. But the extra half second that it took for her to remove it was the difference between life and death. She was powerless to stop the inevitable and her cry for help was the last sound that she made. Her death thinned the zombie numbers between us and the campervan as others bundled on top of her dying body and there were now less than twenty of them between us and our prize. But we were being pursued by many more of them. It still seemed like they were everywhere. The exertion was incredible. My heart was pounding and I was panting hard. Adrenaline was the only thing keeping me from passing out from the pain in my ribs.

Jeff was battling away by my side and he was clearly even more exhausted than I was. He was slowing down. One particularly rotten bastard dived at him and all Jeff could manage was a glancing blow with his mallet that only momentarily deterred it. The problem was that upon connection the mallet spilled from his grip and he was left defenceless.

The mallet landed inches away from me, but too far away from him. I'd already lost my father-in-law and there was no way that I was going to lose my brother-in-law too. I threw my crowbar to Jeff who caught and then swung it in the same motion, clobbering it into his advancing foe. That was great for Jeff but it left me dangerously exposed.

My next opponent was only a couple of metres away from me and it was coming in quickly. I feinted to the left and picked the mallet up in my right hand. It was now too close for me to take a head shot so I struck the heavy tool into its trailing knee with all of my power.

I felt its kneecap shatter and a split second later it fell to the ground, where Pete slammed his machete into its waiting skull. The path was now clear and we ran the final five metres or so. Pavel jumped into the driver's seat and Jeff opened the side door. I was lucky enough to be the first of us to get to relative safety as I leapt into the cabin. Thank God one of them hadn't got in there before us! I turned to see Jeff, Natalie and Pete make it inside as well. Otis and Gerry were still outside battling against our pursuers. Pavel started the engine and we were ready to move.

"Hurry up!" I shouted at them.

Otis managed to floor his one and turned towards us. Gerry had only managed to push his away but he appeared to be free of it. Otis climbed into the back and Gerry was now only feet away himself but his attacker was still on his tail. He couldn't help but check to see how far away his pursuer was. The split second it took him gave the zombie the advantage. It jumped onto his back and brought him to the ground. As he fell he banged his head on the campervan steps. He was that close to safety. I saw his eyes roll into the back of his head as he lost consciousness. He really should have made it.

Jeff slammed the door shut. "Pavel, drive!"

The old campervan did a wheel spin as it accelerated off. We ploughed into the backs of a couple of unsuspecting zombies. Their heads slammed into the gravel as the classic Volkswagen struggled to mount their bodies.

"Don't get stuck, Pavel!" I screamed, hoping that he wouldn't run down any more of them. We would be well and truly screwed if we couldn't move the vehicle into place.

"Is obvious, Dean," Pavel said right back at me as we finally got clear of the bodies.

There were even more zombies milling around on our communal grounds and Pavel did well not to hit them head on, although quite a few got sideswiped as the camper rumbled on. He couldn't go any faster than about two miles per hour and after what felt like an eternity Pavel finally got sight of the hole left by Shane's car. Zombies were still coming through it.

"Hold on!" he screamed as he slammed his foot down on the accelerator.

I braced myself as we pounded into the latest pair of zombies that were coming through. The old vehicle violently crashed into place between a large elm tree and Nan's old car. I didn't know what was worse, the scream of metal on metal or the sound of the bodies breaking beneath us. With the campervan finally in place I turned to see scores of zombies behind us in the communal gardens, some minding their own business but most fixated on the contents of the surf mobile that we sat in. If that wasn't enough, the ones outside the grounds started banging on the windscreen and this prompted Pavel to climb into the back with us. We had already lost three people just getting this far. I had no idea how many more we would lose in just trying to get back inside the block, let alone making our grounds safe again.

Scores of zombies were heading towards us. They could smell blood.

"We must go now," Pavel said.

"He's right," I said. "If we don't get out there now, we will never be able to."

"Okay, on three," Jeff shouted.

Jeff and I swapped our weapons back and I was united with my trustee crowbar. He then positioned himself by the door and started the count. "One, two... Three!"

Jeff opened the door and we all sprang out. Reinvigorated by our two minute break we set about maiming and killing our way back to the safety of the block. My ribs were aching with an intensity that I had never felt before. But I didn't let it bother me. Achy ribs or zombie food? That is a very easy answer. The closer that we got to the block the more their numbers started to thin, but it still wasn't enough and it didn't take long for us to suffer another casualty. The worst thing about it was that I didn't even see what happened. I just heard a muffled scream from behind me and I turned to see Natalie's flesh being hoovered up from her body. It was too late to do anything for her so we had to carry on going forward.

"There's too many of them," Pete shouted, "We'll never be able to get through them all and back inside the block!"

He was right. There were at least fifty of them on the paved pathway between us and the front door and I was now bordering on exhaustion. They all headed toward us, hoping to get a good feed. My ribs burned more and more and every swing of my crowbar became more laboured and less effective.

"Dean!"

That was Sarah's voice. I looked around trying to see her, but there was still a sea of bodies between us and the block.

"Head for Trotter's," I heard her shout.

Of course! His French doors were much closer to us than the block's front door.

The others must have heard her too as we collectively changed our direction and headed for his flat. I must have killed another couple of them before I could actually see the doors. And what a sight it was!

Standing there in Trotter's lounge were Sarah, Emma and Magda. They were shouting and waving at us trying to get our attention. Thankfully the zombies were so preoccupied with us, they didn't even notice them.

Seeing my wife and sister that close to these monsters risking themselves for us spurred me on, and I wielded the crowbar even more ferociously than before. Their presence spurred on my companions too as we somehow managed to reduce their numbers enough for us to try and make a break for it into Trotter's.

"Run for it!" I screamed at the top of my lungs.

The six of us sprinted as fast as we could and within a few seconds we were standing in Trotter's lounge with the French doors locked behind us. We'd cleaned it up a lot but it was still horrible. The walls were beyond dirty and the awful smell was still in there. But we still weren't safe as the zombies saw where we went and they knew exactly where we were.

No sooner was the door closed than scores of fists started pounding against the glass door. Bang! Bang! Bang! It wasn't going to hold them forever. Although, we'd really tidied up Trotter's, it was still full of stuff and we put it all to use as quickly as we could.

"We've got to set up a barricade!" I said as I started to push Trotter's old sofa towards the doors.

"What are you doing? My dad's still out there!" Sarah screamed.

She didn't know. I looked her in the eyes and I could barely make any sound. "He didn't make it," I managed to mumble.

She looked at me, shock and horror in her eyes. "No! No! No! He's still out there, you've got to go and get him."

"I'm sorry," I whispered as I took her in my arms. I just wanted to comfort her. She pressed her face into my chest and burst into tears.

"Why didn't you save him?" she sobbed.

"I wish I could have. But there was just too many of them." I was crying now too.

It broke my heart to see her in so much pain. Her body shook as she cried and all I could offer her was a 'sorry'. Magda and my sister were now crying too, we had lost somebody else so close to us. Derek was a good man and loved by everybody. It was another devastating setback.

When you throw in the losses of Tammy, Theo, Natalie, Selma and Gerry, it was easily our group's worst day so far and it was only going to get worse, due to the numerous zombies that were still on the grounds and now trying to get into the block. The glass doors were now barricaded, but they wouldn't hold forever.

"Take Sarah upstairs to her mum," Jeff said to Emma.

I desperately wanted to comfort Sarah, but now was not the time. I passed her off to my sister and they left the room.

"Any idea how many of them are still out there?" Otis asked.

"There's got to be around fifty of them," Pete replied.

"Well the sooner we get out there the better," I said, pulling myself together.

I looked around the group. I saw steely determination in everyone's eyes. We could do this. We could finish this job. We left Trotter's flat and went back into the communal hallway.

"Right then," I said. "There are six of us and around fifty to sixty of them. We go out fast and hit them hard. We won't stand a chance if we try and take them all on at once. We need to lure them to us and pick them off in smaller groups. We don't want to get too far away from the door."

There was a group of ten or so of them ambling around on the pathway pretty much just outside the communal door. They shuffled in pairs and there were a few feet between each of them. They were close to us; but they weren't that easy to reach as the floor was littered with bodies. There were so many of them that you couldn't even see any of the paving slabs.

We charged at them. Well, charged is a bit of an overstatement. The truth was that we gingerly traversed the sea of dead bodies. We may have found it difficult going but it was even more so for the zombies. Their lack of coordination and dexterity meant that they struggled to get anywhere near us and that gave us a massive advantage. They tried to walk on and around their dead comrades but they had little success and they became easy pickings. They were all dispatched into the next life with little fanfare.

The noise of our attack drew more to us and none of them fared any better in trying to complete the dead body assault course. They would trip and fall, try and pick themselves up and then trip and fall all over again. It was like taking candy from a baby. There was so many of them all in varying states of decay. Some were missing limbs, others faces, but some looked perfectly normal apart from a wild look in their eyes. It was a truly horrendous scene. The blood, the guts, the brain matter, the smell. Yes the smell. That was easily the worst part of it. It was atrocious. It was obscene. The rancid smell of death will be with us all forever.

The six of us only had one thing on our minds and that was to make the grounds safe again. The ground was covered in zombie bodies. We were literally all standing on them. We stood back to back in a circle and cut and flayed at anything and everything that came near us. We were tired, but we were focussed. This was not only life and death for ourselves but if we didn't succeed it was life and death for the people that we loved most in the world. And we never stopped until the job was done. When the last zombie went down, we looked at each other like we couldn't believe that it was over. There were piles of bodies all around us. We were all covered in blood and guts. It was truly disgusting, but it didn't matter.

"We've done it!" Pete croaked. "We've only fucking done it!"

I looked at my feet and I saw that I was standing on a torso, like it was some kind of surfboard. All of us were standing on something grim. Eventually, relieved smiles started to appear on everyone's faces and then after a few seconds Pete started to laugh. A hysterical, uncontrollable belly laugh.

"Why are you laughing?" Jeff said.

"I have no idea!" Pete replied as he continued to laugh. "I just can't help it."

He started to do a jig on a pile of bodies. A jig of unbridled joy. He was throwing all kinds of shapes and we all started to clap him. And we were all laughing too. It was absolutely mental. Here was us standing in a pile of human detritus and we're having a party. He jumped up and down and his feet squished the rotten bodies that were beneath him. He eventually stopped knee-deep in what was left of someone's intestines.

"Fuck me. I don't know what came over—"

Before Pete could finish his sentence he started to scream and he fell to the ground. Well, not really on the ground. Just kind of on a pile of freshly killed zombies.

"What's wrong?" Jeff said as we both ran towards him.

"Fucking bastard! Fucking dirty bastard!" Pete shouted as he clutched the back of his calf.

My eyes went from Pete's bleeding calf directly to the mouth of a zombie who was lying underneath a pile of bodies. Its eyes were fixated on Pete's leg although it still had a large chunk of his flesh in its mouth.

"No!" I screamed. It paid me no attention and just carried on chewing.

"You fucking bastard!" I shouted as I slammed my boot onto the side of its face. Pete's flesh flew from its mouth as all of my weight bore down upon its skull. I kept on stamping, each time filling the air with a new obscenity. I don't know how long I stamped for, but by the time I finished there was nothing of its skull left. Nobody stopped me. Jeff and Otis pulled Pete away and into the hallway, whilst Pavel and Harold started hitting anything that looked like it still might be alive.

When there was nothing left to stamp on, I walked into the hallway and sat next to Pete. He had been silent for some time and was sitting up straight, his bleeding leg bandaged with a shirt.

"Worn yourself out now?" he said.

I couldn't speak. I was trying to hold back the tears.

"It's okay, Dean. It's okay."

"It's not okay," I whispered.

He pulled me over into a hug and said, "It is. It's my time to go."

I lost all composure when he said those words and my body started to shake.

"It's okay, Dean. Let it out."

So I did.

He let me cry for a good couple of minutes and then he took charge. Just like he had always done.

"Right, Dean. I've only got an hour or two left. Get me inside that flat and get me cleaned up, so I can say goodbye to everybody. I'm not having them come out here to see me like this, covered in all of... this."

To be honest I was a bit of a passenger over the next hour or so. We took him into Bernie's downstairs flat, cleaned him up and brought everyone down to him. The adults knew what had happened, but nobody had told the boys.

Pete dosed up on all sorts of painkillers was still in control, despite the fever starting to set in. "Come up here, you two," he said to PJ and Justin.

"Dad, why are you down here?" PJ said.

"I didn't fancy the stairs, son," he said, smiling.

"Why are you shivering, Dad?" Justin asked.

"I'm just a little under the weather. Now I need you two to promise me something. Can you do that?"

"Yes, Dad," they both said.

"Good boys. Now I need you to promise me that you will be good for your mother."

"We already are, Dad," Justin said.

"I know you are. I just want you to promise that you always will be."

Julie's eyes were watering. In fact, I think that everybody's were.

"We promise."

"Good boys. And now I need you to promise that you will always listen to your Uncle Dean."

"Okay, Dad we promise."

He pulled them both into a giant hug. "I love you," he said as he kissed both their foreheads and ruffled their scruffy black hair. "Why don't you both go back upstairs and play with your cousin?"

The boys went off happily, leaving Julie, Mum, Nan, Emma, Sarah and me in the room. His fever was getting worse and his shivering was becoming more violent. I left the room with Sarah as people started to say their goodbyes to him. It was surreal. Everybody was very restrained. Mum and Nan were amazing. So stoic. They comforted everybody else, when they were clearly in such pain themselves.

Sarah and I walked into the hallway to be alone.

"I'm sorry," I managed to say to her.

"So am I."

As soon as she finished her sentence I started to cry. My tears were for her, for Derek, for Pete, for my mum, for Sheila, for Julie, for the boys, for Emma, for Steve, for Abby, for myself. My tears were for everybody. At that moment I had never felt more beaten in my life.

Soon people started to leave the flat and return upstairs. Julie then came out of it and glared at me. "He wants you in there with him."

"Okay."

"I don't know why, because this is all your fault!" she spat.

I had no reply to her.

"Julie!" Sarah said. "That is not true!"

I never said anything. I just looked at Sarah with such heartfelt gratitude and went back into the flat to be with Pete.

I stared at my big brother and looked around the sparse room. I couldn't believe that this was it. He was no longer sitting up on the old sofa. He was lying down and he was covered up with a thick white duvet. He was now shivering very violently and his face was turning grey. I could tell that he didn't have long left. He tried to raise his large frame, but he couldn't. The exertion was too much.

"Look after my boys," he said.

I nodded at him. "You know I will."

"Yeah, I know. I just wanted to double check," he said as a small laugh escaped his lips. "I'm glad it was me and not you, Dean. You're the only one the family stands a chance with."

"Fat lot of good I've done so far."

"We'd have been dead days ago if it wasn't for you."

I shrugged my shoulders.

"Don't argue with a dying man," he laughed.

Pete's eyes started to glaze over. "Just sit here with me. I don't have long left."

I took his hand and he closed his eyes.

"I'm going to miss you so much, Pete. You've always been my hero," I said as I wept.

He started to convulse and I knew that this was the end. I closed my eyes and bowed my head, waiting for him to stop breathing.

"I've just seen Steve, Graeme and Dad," he whispered, "And we are all so proud."

His chest stopped moving after his last word. I put my hand to his nose and I could feel no breath. He was dead. I was never going to wait for him to turn.

So I made sure that he didn't.

CHAPTER TWENTY-ONE

I stood outside of my front door, but I couldn't bring myself to go inside. I must have been out there for a good ten minutes or so.

I heard Jeff inside the flat walking to the front door. "I'll go and see how he is," I heard him say.

He opened it up and saw me standing there. He looked at me and slowly shut the door behind him. "Are you okay?"

I shrugged my shoulders. What could I say? I just had to stab my brother in the brain before he turned into a zombie.

"Sorry, mate. Stupid question."

I sat on the floor and leant back on the wall. "Did you think that the end of the world would be so bloody?"

He knelt down next to me. "Come on, Dean, don't speak like that. It's not been confirmed that it's the end of the world just yet. And even if it is, it's not like we're just going to give up. You said that yourself."

I ignored him and continued. "I mean, I'd have laid money on World War Three; you know whole cities being wiped out by nukes or even a meteor hurtling into the earth." I then looked him in the eye. "Seeing people eating each other was never on the cards. Was it, Jeff?"

"No I don't suppose it was, mate… We've just got to get through to Wednesday."

"Yeah. Wednesday."

I walked back into my flat and went into the living room. It was full of people comforting each other. Everybody had lost someone.

I found Sarah and Sheila in the spare room. They were sitting on the bed talking. I hesitated in the doorway and Sarah looked up and waved me in. She'd obviously been crying again.

Sheila turned to me. Her eyes were red and puffy, but there was a resolve behind them.

"Sheila, I'm so sorry."

"It wasn't your fault. You did what you had to do and that's exactly what Derek would have wanted."

Words escaped me.

"I've been an army wife for over thirty years and even after he retired I knew that he still had one more fight left in him. He died defending his family and it's how he would have wanted to go. As painful as it is, it is something that I will always take comfort in."

Sarah's eyes started to well up. She smiled and nodded. "Me too."

Derek was a hero.

I hoped that one day Julie would understand that Pete's death wasn't my fault. He died for her and their children. He was a hero too.

—✦—✦—

I could go on for hours about how bad it was after that morning, but I'm sure that you can easily imagine it. We worked non-stop for two whole days to purge the grounds of the battle and restore some level of normality to our group. I was on auto-pilot throughout it. I don't want to say that I was numb to the carnage, but I was something close to it. I mean how much death can you see before you're immune?

After the second day of back-breaking toil, Sarah and I sat on the rug in our lounge under our duvet, both stroking Troy. It was dark out and the cold night air chilled the room. A solitary candle on the coffee table provided a small flicker of light. I pulled her into my arms and kissed her. We were disturbed by a knock on the door.

"Who's that?" Sarah said. "Everybody knows they can just come in."

"I'll get it," I said as I gingerly picked myself up from the floor, my ribs still aching.

I opened the door to Eddie. He hadn't left his flat since Iris died. Never mind let anyone else into it. It was just him and Iris's lifeless body in there. I think that he was in denial. His white hair was unkempt and he was wearing the same blood-stained cardigan from the other day. He was a state.

I didn't know how to feel towards him. Of course I felt sympathy, but another part of me felt that what had happened was his own fault. Maybe if he was a better parent, his wife wouldn't be dead and neither would my brother or father-in-law. Maybe I was being too harsh.

"Hello, Dean," Eddie said from behind his bruised eye. It was a much deeper purple now. But it had opened up a little.

"Eddie."

"I just wanted to ask for your help with Iris."

I shuffled uncomfortably. "Yeah. Of course."

"He didn't mean it, you know? He isn't a bad boy."

"Save it, Eddie!" I snapped. "Shane is responsible for all those people's deaths. There is something wrong with him. He's deranged. He was probably born like it."

Eddie started to sob. Seeing an eighty-year-old man cry is a truly heart-wrenching experience.

"Anyway, Eddie, this isn't the time for this conversation. Do you want me to come and help you now?"

"No, no. Not now, Dean. I want to be with her for one more night."

"Yeah what's one more night with a dead body?" I said under my breath as he walked away.

Later that evening Jeff and I were back on guard duty walking around the perimeter of the grounds. Winter was fast approaching. It was seriously cold and the freezing air assaulted my body. I wore my big heavy coat but it wasn't doing much for me and every time I shivered it sent a wave of pain through my ribs. It was bad, but it was the least of my troubles.

We might have spent two days purging the grounds of the battle, but its scars remained. The sickening stench of death was everywhere. The residual smell of burnt bodies and petrol had somehow clung to everything around us, whether it was natural or manmade. It was all over the trees and the bushes and it was even radiating off brick walls. If something didn't stink of death, it was stained with it. The once grey paving slabs were now a bloody black red. Half of the gravel car park was covered in a dark ash and the red garage doors were now black with soot. But the worst thing was the garden area. The once lush grass was now just mud. There had been no rain; the ground was saturated with blood and other bodily fluids.

Oh yeah, and on top of all of that the soundtrack of the evening wasn't much better too. For some reason the tortured moans of the zombies were even louder than ever. The pitch of their desperate cries pierced my ears. Funnily enough, I wasn't making for good company.

"Cheer up, Dean," Jeff said. "With any luck this should all be over tomorrow."

"I think we'll need more than luck."

"If it does take longer, how long do you think we can survive here for?"

"For as long as we have to."

"So what's next then?"

"We need to focus on something other than death."

"Like what?"

"Nan is really struggling with the cold. Maybe now's the time to get a generator."

Jeff looked unsure. "But we won't need to if everything is okay tomorrow."

"It will still take a while for everything to get back to normal. The power will still be off for ages."

"I never thought of that. Will doing that make you feel any better?"

"Who knows, but it can't make me feel any worse."

"Unless we get killed out there trying to do it."

"If my brother hadn't just died, I might have laughed at that," I said trying to suppress a small grin.

"And there was me thinking we could have a rest tomorrow."

"You can rest when you're dead, mate."

"I'll hold you to that."

"I guarantee it."

"Well, that's something to look forward to then."

The next morning a group of us met in the car park ready to get the generator. The car park looked even more grim in the daylight. Ash had covered the floor and soot had covered everything else, including the cars.

"Right, lads, let's go over it one more time," I said, looking at everybody. "Bernie, you start."

"I'm in the van and will be responsible for quickly opening the entrance whilst you all come in and out. You will each call me on the walkie-talkie to let me know you're coming back."

"Excellent. Remember, do not leave the car park. You have to be ready when we all return, as we don't know the range on these things," I said as I waved the walkie-talkie around.

"Of course. You can all count on me."

Jon interrupted. "We better be able to, Bernie, you've got the easiest and the safest job."

"Don't be so fucking rude," I shot back at him. "Maybe you'd be in the van if your mate Shane hadn't fucking killed everybody else."

"That wasn't my fault," he protested. "He hit me."

"Yeah, that's right. He hit you and knocked you out cold for all of six hours and you only woke up after five people had lost their lives defending this place. Very convenient."

"If you don't trust me then why are you making me help now?"

"Because there isn't anyone else."

That shut the prick up.

After a few seconds I continued, "Anyway, what happens next?"

"I'm the diversion," Harold said, "So I will be the first one out. I'm going to drive my car out and try and get them to follow me down Court Road and away from here."

Otis was next to speak. "When Harold's lured them away, Dean, Jeff and I will go to B&Q and try and find a generator."

It was now Pavel's turn. "I take Jon to petrol station. We get diesel and petrol."

"Excellent," I said. "Just remember, nobody is dying today."

"You can say that again," Otis replied.

I smiled. "Is everybody ready?"

Everybody nodded.

"Let's get this show on the road then," Jeff said.

People started to move off into their positions, but I wanted to speak to Pavel before he left, so I quickly pulled him to the side. "Are you sure you're going to be alright with Jon?"

"If he gives problem, I kill him."

The words should have chilled me, but they didn't. Pavel could do whatever he wanted to him as far as I was concerned.

I walked over to my mum's car, but stopped before I got in as I couldn't help but take a look at my one. I smiled at it; it had been over a week since I was last in it and boy, had it done me proud. Whether Derek was still here or not, that car helped give Sarah more time with him. I touched the bonnet with the palm of my hand and looked at the head-sized hole in the windscreen. How was it still in one piece? There were still bits of brain and scalp on the dashboard and a pool of blood had congealed on the grey leather seat. It didn't matter how bad it looked, I knew with absolute certainty that it would get me from A to B.

"Lads, I'm going in mine."

"Fair enough. More space for supplies," Jeff said.

I opened up the car and was met by the stench of death. The hole in the windscreen had given the aroma of the zombie bonfire free rein to take over the interior, but I didn't care. I think I was used to it. I sat in the driver's seat and tried to get comfortable, but was unable to. The warmth of my backside seemed to heat up the congealed blood and I swear I could feel it seep through my jeans. I just about resisted the urge to gag.

The windscreen wipers took ages to clear enough of the soot for me to be able to see out. In fairness everyone had the same problem, but no one else had the soot come into their car. A fair amount of it fell through the hole and landed in a pile on the dash. I really had to accept that the car probably wouldn't be able to regain its former beauty.

We were all now in position. Each car sat behind another down the thirty metre long driveway. Harold was at the front in his very old tank-like tan Mercedes, perhaps ten metres away from the gate (Graeme's van). It may not have been particularly fast but it would absolutely dominate any zombie that was unfortunate enough to be in its path. It was the kind of old Merc that any Middle Eastern or African dictator would be proud to drive around the desert. Otis and Jeff were in my mum's Corolla, then it was me in the Celica, and Pavel and Jon were in the X5.

After a few minutes Bernie's tinny voice came out of the walkie-talkie, "Get ready, Harold. I'm moving now."

Bernie slowly pulled the white Transit forward to reveal two zombies standing on the dropped kerb with their backs to us. They noticed the van moving and turned around to investigate what was going on. Before they could work it out they were met by Harold's tank of a car. The old Merc was probably only travelling at about fifteen miles an hour, but it sent them flying across the road. I couldn't see anything else as Bernie dutifully reversed the van back into position.

After thirty seconds or so Bernie's voice came back over the airwaves. "It's working. They're following him down the road... Otis, Dean, get ready to go in five, four, three, two, one."

As Bernie said 'one' he pulled the van forward again and we both shot out of the car park. Harold had done a good job in luring the zombies away and even the two that he'd hit with the car were crawling in his direction.

I hadn't been off the property in ten days and I couldn't believe the changes that I saw. Most of the big homes had been broken into. Doors were smashed in and windows were now missing. I could clearly see zombies shuffling around inside them. I didn't know if they were trespassers or the former occupants, but it didn't really matter, whoever they had been before were gone.

I have to say that it wouldn't be right to just blame the zombies for the intrusions. The tell-tale signs of looters were there too. One large double-fronted de-tached home had clearly been ram-raided. A gaping van-sized hole was where the front door used to be. The paved driveway of another home was covered in electrical goods and bones. Whoever had been stupid enough to try and steal the widescreen TV hadn't counted on being attacked in the process.

The homes were bad, but the pavement was worse. The brown autumn leaves tried in vain to hide the devastation. They valiantly tried to cover the human detritus that littered the street, but a stray leg here and an upper torso there gave the game away. It was like someone had taken scores of bodies and put them in a giant blender without the lid on. But despite the desolation in the streets that surrounded my home there was an eerie stillness.

I heard Bernie's voice come out of the receiver as I reached the end of the road. "Good luck, everyone. Hope to see you back here soon."

"Me too, Bernie," I said out loud.

The local B&Q was only a mile or so away and I was there before I knew it. I'd spent so much time looking at what was left of my home town, that I didn't notice Jeff and Otis stop at the entryway to the giant warehouse. Our view of the car park was obscured by a tall red brick wall.

"Go in slowly, guys," I said over the walkie-talkie. "We have no idea what's around that corner."

We both drove into the large car park. It must have been the size of two or three football pitches. At first glance it all looked rather orderly as all of the cars were prudently parked between the lines in their allotted bays and it must have been at least fifty percent full. The second glance was when you could tell that things just weren't quite right. Unlike the neighbouring streets there were no leaves trying to hide the carnage. Dead bodies, both human and zombies were dotted around. A lot of people had been caught short whilst trying to get some home improvements done.

Both of us drove very slowly. I looked at the large brick building and could see that the glass entrance had been barricaded from the inside. Sheets of plaster board covered the door and goodness knows what had been put behind them. *More survivors*, I thought to myself.

A red Royal Mail van was parked at the fire exit at the far side of the building. "Let's pull up by that red van over there. We could get even more gear in that," I said over the radio.

We parked side by side about ten metres away from the van and walked over to it.

"At last some good luck," Jeff said, looking at the van. "The perfect vehicle; now if we can find the keys."

"Big if, mate," I said placing my hand on the bonnet of the van. "Anyway, it's still warm."

"Bloody hell! You're right. Someone's got the same idea as us," Jeff said as he put his hand on the bonnet too.

I walked around to the back of the van and pulled the door handle. It wasn't locked and the door popped open. Inside it was the mother lode. There was all sorts in there. Timber, nails, hammers, extension leads. But the best things in there were the two large generators.

"Lads, we should just help ourselves," Jeff said.

"We can't do that!" Otis replied.

"Yes we can. We can just load up our cars and go. It will be easy."

"I can't believe you sometimes, Jeff! They could be just like us; just trying to survive. We wouldn't want it done to us."

"Listen, Otis, I've got to agree with Jeff on this one," I said. "It's every man for himself now. But my problem is that we don't know how many of them there are in there. It will seriously kick off if they come out and catch us in the act."

Before Otis could reply, I heard a noise. "What was that?"

"I didn't hear anything," Otis said.

I looked around and noticed that the blue fire exit door had been prised open. It was slightly ajar. "It must have come from in there. You two wait here. I'm going to take a quick look."

Jeff shook his head. "Don't be silly, Dean. You can't go in there by yourself."

"I'll be fine. I'm just going to poke my head in and see what's what. I'll be back in two minutes."

〰〰

I opened the door and slowly walked into the dark corridor. I gripped my crowbar. The metal felt good in my hands. It had become an extension of me since this had started and I have no idea how many times it had saved my life. In other words it had got to the point where I had no idea how many zombies I had killed with it.

Soft white light lit up the doorway that was at the end of the corridor. It must have been about a hundred metres away. It felt a little damp in there and my nostrils were filled with the pungent smell of stagnant water. I followed the sound of a gurgling overhead pipe, being careful not to make any noise myself.

I got to the end of the corridor after what felt like an eternity. A fire extinguisher had been used to prop the door open. I poked my head through and looked up and down the aisle. Light was streaming in through the giant glass ceiling and I could see to the other end of the superstore. I was in the paint department and I saw hundreds of tins carefully stacked on the shelves. Brand names were aligned with OCD precision. Everything was untouched and it looked like the store was ready for business.

I took a step in and I could hear moaning... but not of the zombie variety. It sounded more like high-pitched cries. I crept through the door and took a few steps into the store.

"Shut your whining," a deep Scottish voice said.

"Please just take what you want and leave us alone," another man said. Whoever he was, he was definitely a local.

My breath quickened when I heard the tell-tale sound of a squeaky trolley being pushed towards me. I got back into the corridor before whoever it was came past. I needed Jeff and Otis, so I made my way back towards the fire exit, again being very careful not to make any noise.

I was about to push the blue doors open when I heard an angry voice coming from outside. I didn't know whose it was. I only knew that it wasn't Jeff or Otis's. "Answer the man's question for fuck's sake!"

I peered through the crack and I saw two men with their backs to me. One was tall and the other was quite a bit shorter than him. I couldn't see past the tall one, but I could just make out Jeff in front of the smaller one. He was being held in place by a lanky, buck-toothed grease ball. It's not that I want to be nasty, but this guy was one of the ugliest people that I had ever seen, and I'm including some pretty far gone zombies in that too.

"I already did. It's just us two," Jeff said.

"Bollocks! You two wouldn't be here by yourselves," the shorter man replied.

I knew that voice. Every muscle in my body tensed up simultaneously when I realised who it was. It was Shane.

"Have a look around, Shane. Can you see anyone else?"

"Don't be cheeky with me, you cunt," Shane said taking a step forward to Jeff and punching him in the gut. It was a total mismatch. Jeff was being held in place and couldn't protect himself. Shane was wearing a skin tight red top. The bloke was solid muscle.

I heard the air explode from Jeff's lungs as he doubled over in pain and gasped.

"I've wanted to do that for the last couple of weeks," Shane cackled.

I couldn't see Otis, but I could hear him. "Get off of me! Jeff, are you okay?"

I was already angry at seeing Shane, but hearing my brother-in-law struggle to breathe made my blood start to boil.

Shane then turned his attention to Otis. "Where's Baker?"

"He's dead," Otis said. "He died on Sunday."

"Are you winding me up?"

"Pete too."

He laughed. "This day keeps on getting better and better."

"And your mum."

"What did you say?"

Jeff started to cough as he tried to speak. "He said your mum's dead, you deaf bastard. You killed her."

"Shut your mouth," Shane said as he punched him again. This time in his face. I heard a sickening crunch, but he remained upright. It was a big punch and no disrespect to Jeff, but he was probably only standing because of Ugly Bloke holding him up.

Jeff spat blood out of his mouth and started to stammer, "I helped bury her myself."

"I told you to shut your mouth!" Shane let fly with a combination of punches. Two rights to the body and one huge left to his head. This time Jeff fell to the floor. "Do not speak about my mother!"

Otis started to struggle again. "Jeff! Jeff! Are you okay?"

Jeff never said anything. He was out cold.

My blood wasn't just boiling now. Pure unadulterated rage started to course through my veins. I wanted to burst through the doors and smash him with my crowbar, but I had to wait for the right moment.

"You bastard, Shane," Otis spat. "What is your problem? We only ever tried to help you!"

"I wasn't going to swing by yours today, but I think that's probably where we're going to be heading to next. I've got to check on me mum and dad now. Haven't I?"

"You're mental. You know you killed her. Just admit it to yourself."

Shane ignored him and looked at the taller man to his side. "Do you want to shut this copper up or should I?"

"Don't mind if I do," the tall man said as pulled out a small knife.

He took a step towards Otis.

"What the hell are you going to do with that?" he said nervously.

"Oh come on, copper. Isn't it obvious?"

It might not have been to Otis, but it was to me.

Now was the moment. Consumed by rage, I raised my crowbar and kicked the fire door open with the sole of my boot. It cannoned into the brick wall and the loud bang rattled my eardrums. I ignored the noise and instantly accessed the scene. There were four of them; Shane, the man with the knife, the one holding Otis and Ugly Bloke holding Jeff.

Everybody instinctively looked to where the noise had come from. "Fucking hell, Jock!" the man with the knife said as he spun around. The crowbar was already sailing through the air, from high above my right shoulder, before he realised that I wasn't Jock. He turned his face in a desperate attempt to get away, but it was no use. The middle of the crowbar connected with his jaw, instantly obliterating it and knocking him out cold in the process. Which was obviously very bad for him. What was worse though, was that the tip of the crowbar pierced his cheek and went inside his mouth. The impact sent him hurtling to the left and the crowbar's follow-through with a little help from gravity and his own body weight tore through the rest of his cheek and came out of his gaping mouth. He dropped the knife at the same time as the blood started to piss out of the wound. His cheek flapped in the wind as his unconscious body hit the deck.

As I turned to face Shane I saw Otis use my diversion to break free of the man who had been holding him. Still with his back to him, he delivered a devastating elbow into the man's face. His nose literally exploded and blood poured out of it soaking the front of his white sweatshirt in the process. His eyes watered so badly that he couldn't see a thing and it only took one more punch to the face from Otis to put him out of the fight.

Only ten seconds before it had been four against one. Now it was two against two.

"What the fuck?" Shane said as his eyes bulged out of their sockets. He couldn't believe what he was seeing.

Neither could Ugly Bloke. He tried to make a run for it, but Otis was having none of it. He skilfully jumped over Jeff's unconscious body and rugby-tackled him onto the bonnet of a car. I lost sight of him as they rolled off it and fell onto the tarmac floor.

Shane and I were only about five metres apart. He quickly recovered his composure and cracked his knuckles. "Well here we are again, Baker."

I was too angry to speak. I just stared at him.

"Not exactly a fair fight now, is it? You with the crowbar and little old me with nothing."

He was right, it wasn't a fair fight, but I didn't care.

He started to say something again, but I have no idea what it was. Adrenaline was surging through me and I could only hear my beating heart. His big shoulders went up and down as he started to laugh; like he didn't have a care in the world. And this made me even angrier. So I charged him.

I covered the five metres before he'd even finished laughing. I aimed low and swung the crowbar with every ounce of my very being. Shane tried to back away but he couldn't. The metal bar struck him on the shin just below his left knee. He screamed. I couldn't blame him. I heard the bone crack. It was a truly savage blow. His foot went from under him and both of his knees slammed into the ground.

"That was for Pete!" I screamed.

I have to give him his due, most people would have been on the floor at this point. Not Shane though. He was on his knees. He looked at me defiantly. If he wanted to live this really wasn't the right way to go about it.

I was growling and snarling like a wild animal. Fuelled by my mania, I threw the crowbar to the ground. I didn't need it. I wanted to kill him with my bare hands. Before it had stopped clanging, I was already half way through throwing the biggest punch of my life. It was as if the planets had aligned for this moment. I pulled my right hand back and let it rip with everything that I had. My fist was turbo charged with vengeance and it couldn't have connected with Shane's left eye socket any better. I heard multiple cracks. His neck snapped back violently and then his whole body seemed to fall in slow motion. The force of the blow had not only broken his face, but it had also broken some of my fingers too. My hand felt like it was on fire. But I didn't care.

"That was for Derek!"

Shane had a pretty deep gash above his left eye and it had already closed up. He lifted his head up and glared at me. "I'm glad that old cunt is dead," he spat.

I pulled my leg back and took aim at his head. I was about to let a giant kick go when I was interrupted by Jeff's croaky voice. "Dean, watch out!"

I looked up just in time to see an aluminium baseball bat hurtling towards my body. I took a step back and somehow managed to evade it. "Come on, have some of this, ya English bastard!" the ginger Scot screamed.

So I did. I hurdled Shane's body and jumped on top of the skinny ginger fucker. I was on him so quickly that he hadn't been able to raise the bat in defence and we both fell to the ground. The weight of my body pounded him into tarmac and I felt all of the air leave his body. I straddled his stomach and just started punching his face. Right, left, right, left. Over and over again. My already broken fingers screaming in agony as they turned his face into pulp.

When I finally stopped it wasn't because I wanted to. Someone had kicked me in my already tender ribs. I instinctively held them and turned to face my attacker. I wore a huge punch in the face for my trouble. I caught a glimpse of the person before the blow hit, but I had no idea who he was. As I fell backwards off the Scot my only thought was, how many more of them were there? I braced myself for a follow-up blow, but nothing came. I looked up to see Otis grappling with him. He really saved my bacon.

I grimaced as I picked myself up. My body was awash with pain. My ribs were aching, my fingers were screaming and my nose was bleeding. But it kind of didn't matter. My righteous anger was sustaining me. I spied the knife that the tall bloke from earlier was going to use on Otis, picked it up and crouched over Shane, who was still lying on the floor.

"What are you going to do with that?" Shane asked.

"Isn't it obvious?" I said back at him.

He tried to sit up and grab at me. But I saw it coming from a mile off and I struck my right elbow into his temple, just above his already bleeding eye. His head slammed back into the ground and bounced back up at me.

I have no idea how he was still conscious. He looked up at me defiantly. "You don't have the balls."

"Don't I?" I said as I plunged the knife into the side of his throat. The four inch blade tore through his flesh and cut into his carotid artery.

"That was for my nephews," I whispered into his ear.

I smiled in his face and twisted the knife in the wound. He was too dazed to do anything about it.

I then picked my crowbar back up and swung it at the side of his head. I swung it with every fibre of my being and the cold hard steel tore through his ear, cut into his scalp and did irreparable damage to his skull.

He was close to the end, but I was only getting started.

I caught a glimpse of Otis in my peripheral vision, still struggling with the man. The pair of them fell into the fire exit. I should have gone to help him, but I couldn't tear myself away from Shane.

Shane was in a semi-conscious state lying in between his dead comrades. Some may say that he had no idea what was happening. That he could no longer process what was going on around him, but I knew that he could. I knew that he felt everything that had happened and that he was going to feel everything that would happen. I smashed the crowbar into his body, not once, not twice but three times and I felt his ribs splinter and then break under the repeated blows.

"That was for my family!" I screamed, tears now flooding my eyes.

I wiped the tears away and looked him in his eyes. They were still open although he was fading fast. I threw my crowbar to the ground and crouched over his face.

"And this one, Shane. This one's for me."

I spat in his face.

I stood over his body and waited for him to die. I wasn't going to speed it up for him. I don't know how long I stared at him for. I watched as he lost control of his bladder. I watched as he emptied his bowels. I watched as every breath became shallower than the last. I watched as his life force left his body. And I watched as his soul went down to hell.

I turned to see Otis picking Jeff up from the ground. Otis's uniform didn't look too clever, but he looked like he didn't have a scratch on him. Jeff, on the other hand; was ruined. His eye was split and he had blood all over his face and top. I mustn't have looked that much better myself.

I looked around and surveyed the scene. Six bodies. All were either dead or close to it. I heard the tall bloke start to moan. He was lying face down on the ground and blood was still pouring out of his face. I walked over to him and he tried to make eye contact with me. I could see the fear in his eyes. He knew he was dying. I couldn't have done anything for him even if I had wanted to.

I turned him over him and started to root through his pockets, looking for the van keys. I couldn't help but stare at his cheek. The bottom half of it hung down over his face. It was covered in dirt and grime. It looked like a rancid piece of meat. Luckily, I found the keys in his front pocket. I didn't fancy doing this all over again to another five bodies. I fished them out and left him to die. Call me heartless if you want. Call me a bastard. But this was about me and mine.

Otis and I took Jeff over to the Corolla and laid him on the back seat. "Wait here," I said to him. "We've got to go back inside."

Jeff nodded. He was too broken to speak.

Otis put his hand on my shoulder. "Dean, we don't need anything else. Let's just take the van and go."

I shook my head. "There's some more people tied up inside. I came out to get you both and that's when I saw what was happening."

"Thank God you came out when you did, then. He was going to stab me. You saved my life. Again."

"Don't mention it," I said, pointing at the man who had kicked me in the ribs. "You saved mine back there too."

Both of us walked back into the corridor and we could hear whispering as we came out into the giant DIY warehouse. They stopped when they heard our footsteps. We walked down the middle of the store and passed aisles containing all sorts of things. Bathroom suites, tiles, kitchen units. It was B&Q, after all. We finally got to the power tool aisle and that's when we saw four people all tied up back to back right in the middle of it. Two men and two woman. They quite literally shit themselves when they saw us.

"Please don't hurt us," a large lady in a bright purple blouse cried.

I smiled at her and shook my head. "It's okay, love. We're the good guys."

I'd always wanted to say that.

⇒╍╍╍⇒

I drove the van back and left my car at B&Q. Maybe one day I'd go and get it back. The large lady and her overweight teenage son were with me in the van. I didn't say anything to them. I was consumed by my own thoughts. I was thinking about what had just happened with Shane. I'd killed him; I'd killed a human being. In that moment I accepted that things would never be the same again; that I would never be the same again. And I was okay with that, because I knew that if we were going to survive then I was probably going to have to do worse. A lot worse.

"We're here," I said to them both as Bernie moved the van.

I felt a sense of relief as I pulled into the communal car park and saw Pavel standing by the X5. Everybody I cared about was back.

As I parked up, Sarah, Emma and Mum walked towards us from the block.

I pointed at them all and looked at my two new passengers. "We are all good people. You'll be safe with us until this is over."

I climbed out the van and walked over to everybody. "Well, the good news is that we are going to have some heat tonight."

There was only a light murmur of approval from everyone.

I scanned their faces and saw red eyes, tears and frowns. There was an aura of despair. "What's wrong? Has someone else died?"

Sarah stepped towards me and shook her head and gently touched my face. "No, no. We're fine. Everyone's fine. What happened to you?"

"It's nothing. It looks worse than it is."

She started to cry.

I put my arms around her and she buried her face in my neck and really started to sob.

"I'm fine. I promise," I said.

After a few seconds she composed herself. "I know. It's just…"

"What's wrong?"

"It's the radio. There's a new message."

I paused for a few seconds. "They've set a new date, haven't they? How long do we have to wait now?"

She shook her head. "There's nothing they can do."

"What?"

"We're on our own."

ABOUT THE AUTHOR

David Brinson is a novelist from south-east London. *Dead South* is his first novel. When he's not writing, he's most likely spending time with his wife, Leyla, and his greyhound, Troy, or playing squash.

Visit his blog: davidbrinson.blogspot.co.uk
Like his Facebook Page: David Brinson Author
Follow him on twitter @dbrinsonauthor

Printed in Great Britain
by Amazon.co.uk, Ltd.,
Marston Gate.